D1520101

Prayers for Evil

A NOVEL

P. G. Smith

FORBUSH MEMORIAL LIBRARY
PO BOX 468
118 MAIN ST
WESTMINSTER MA 01473

This book is a work of fiction. The characters, incidents, and dialogue are drawn from the author's imagination and are not to be construed as real. Any resemblance to actual events or persons, living or dead, is entirely coincidental.

Copyright © 2017 P. G. Smith

All rights reserved. In accordance with U.S. Copyright Act of 1976, the scanning, uploading, and electronic sharing of any part of this book without the permission of the author constitute unlawful piracy and theft of the author's intellectual property. If you wish to use material from the book for purposes other than review, prior written permission must be obtained from the author.

Published by:
Mill Cove Press
10 Holden Street
Ashburnham, Massachusetts 01430

ISBN 13: 9781542547239
ISBN 10: 1542547237

Cover art by Lawrence Szalay

"Beware that, when fighting monsters, you yourself do not become a monster ... for when you gaze long into the abyss. The abyss gazes also into you."

—*Friedrich Nietzsche*

Chapter 1

THE RUMBLE OF the locomotive shook the night, and the blast of its horn pierced the stillness. The train screeched to a halt in front of the dark station. The New Englander Line made its stop at the little station every night except Saturday. The train's engine continued to growl and chug as if eager to be on its way. The conductor stepped onto the deserted platform, but there was no one waiting to get off the train into the darkness and there was no one waiting to board. Although it was already spring, he shivered in the late evening chill.

There was only one unseen figure at the station, hunched down into a black overcoat. The figure watched the train from a rickety wooden bench in the shadows at the far corner of the platform. The conductor took one more look up and down the platform as he fidgeted with his ticket punch. Then he hopped onto the nearest car, eager to return to the warmth and light of the familiar passenger car. The train chugged and squealed on its southerly journey, and the dark figure's gaze followed the last car until its lights disappeared around a curve on its way to Boston and New York. A half mile from the station, the headlights of a truck pierced the darkness with two beams like searchlights, otherwise there was nothing but the silence of a sleeping Maine mill town that had seen better days.

The figure shouldered its worn leather bag and stepped carefully down the dark stairs of the railway station. As it passed by the underpass of the railroad bridge, an old man huddling under the bridge felt a cold breeze chill his bones. He took the last burning swallow from a bottle of cheap whiskey, tugged his tattered Army jacket up around his throat, squeezed his eyes closed tight, and tried to retreat into dreams of better times, warmer times, softer times.

The dark figure made its way through a silent side street where two startled raccoons scampered away into the woods, disappointed that their feast of moldy pizza crusts had been interrupted. The figure warily stepped down the quiet streets past peeling three-decker houses and through a haphazard trailer park until it came to the banks of a river. Beer cans and plastic shopping bags littered the muddy ground, and a solid row of dented pickup trucks lined each side of the roadway. The figure stepped in and out of the shadows as it made its way toward the glare of a flashing pink-and-blue neon sign.

The neon sign spelled out "Ambassadors Lounge" during the day, but at night the flashing tubes could only muster up a half dozen letters. A wrinkled vinyl banner rustled in the cool breeze under it. Next to an icy beer bottle the block letters read "Amateur Night Tonight—Great Prizes!"

The figure watched from under the trees just across from the doorway to the club. It turned its collar up against the chill and clutched the leather shoulder bag tightly. A flash of light spilled out onto the street as the bouncer, a burly man dressed in black with a shaved head, dragged a drunken teenager out into the roadway. The teen retched when he tumbled to the pavement. As the door swung open, the hidden dark figure glimpsed a slender young girl wearing nothing but silver high heels and a thin chain belt. She clutched a chrome pole with one hand and reached between her legs with the other. The dancer swayed her hips in time to the thumping music, but her gaze was up over the heads of the customers as if she wanted to be somewhere else, far away from the leering eyes, catcalls, and groping hands. The door slammed shut, cutting off the figure's view, but leaving behind a whiff of stale beer, cigarette smoke, and vomit. A growl, slow and barely perceptible, rose in the figure's throat as it turned away from the river.

Suddenly the thump of dance music gave way to shrieks and shouting. Smoke filled the air as a wall of flame tore through the interior of the building. The patrons pushed, shoved, and trampled one another as they squeezed through the narrow doorway and sprawled on the pavement outside the club, coughing and gasping. Soon sirens split the stillness of the night air, and firefighters quickly aimed the torrents of their hoses on the structure, which was now fully engulfed by the fire.

The dark figure smiled as it made its way through the town center. It glanced at a spotted, flaking sign on the town common that read "Welcome to Ashton Falls—The Friendliest Village in Maine." The only sounds that could be heard were the faraway wail of ambulances, the echo of dogs barking, and a low mutter that said, "We'll see ... we'll see."

The first time Chris Murphy saw Ashton Falls, Maine, was in late March after most of the winter snow had melted and before the warmth of spring brought out the buds on the trees—what New Englanders call "mud season." It reminded him of the set of a B-grade 1950s black-and-white movie. Shuttered store fronts, spiderwebs of power lines, and nothing but three-decker houses as far as the eye could see. The entire town seemed to be either black, dirty white, or gray. Adding to the general gloom was the stench of the Micmac River that flowed, or rather oozed, through town and emitted a low, sulfurous odor caused by low tide and failed septic systems. But in some odd way, on that damp, foggy March morning, this down-on-its-luck New England town had a sort of attraction for a thirty-something engineer who was stuck in a stalled career while his marriage was gradually falling apart.

"Armpit of New England" was how Chris described Ashton Falls to his New York friends at the local bar after he and his colleague, Tom, returned from their visit to the power plant in Maine. "It was so dead at night, Tom and I had to choose between the baked bean supper at the Methodist church, bingo at the high school, or drinking lukewarm light beer cans staring at the fisherwomen doing the bump and grind at the strip joint."

"Which one did you two city slickers choose?" asked one of the guys.

"Tom, tell them how much money you made on that winning bingo card," Chris replied.

The guys all laughed, and Tom added, "I hope we don't have to go back anytime soon, because I heard that strip joint went up in flames the week after we visited."

Chris couldn't resist coming back with, "Maybe they actually found a smokin' hot dancer from New Hampshire who lit up the place." Then he ordered another round.

He continued to make them laugh as he mimicked a Maine drawl and gave vivid descriptions of the tourist attractions of Ashton Falls, from the ancient candlepin bowling lanes, which served as the town's unofficial youth center, to last year's first-run movies playing at the drive-in theater. Somehow, though, as he exaggerated the town's peculiarities, he realized that he had spent a lot of time thinking about it. Perhaps it reminded him a little bit of the small town in the Berkshires where he went to visit his grandparents when he was a kid. Life was simpler away from the big city, and he always remembered being happy there. He recalled the good times when he went for long walks in the pine forests while his grandfather told him stories about Indians and the first settlers. Then they would come home to the smell of fresh-baked Toll House cookies as his grandmother offered him the first one from the oven, still warm and soft and gooey.

Maybe that's why, when his boss called him to the corner office on the Friday before the Fourth of July weekend, he had a sense of what was about to be discussed.

Elliott Jackson, his boss, had never been particularly cordial to Chris in the past. Now Elliott invited him into the corner office with a broad smile and motioned for him to sit in the soft upholstered chair next to the couch. As Chris settled into the chair, he noticed that it placed him a few inches lower than anyone seated on the couch. Elliott offered Chris a drink and, before Chris could state his preference, Elliott poured two meager shots of scotch into elegant cut-glass tumblers, explaining that the whiskey was a twenty-year single malt that he had acquired on his last golf trip to Scotland. Chris realized that the drink was not so much meant for his enjoyment as it was an effort to cultivate his host's image of himself as a gentleman of refinement and good taste.

Elliott eased himself onto the couch and, draping his arm casually over the back, struck a pose of exaggerated nonchalance. After making small talk about their respective plans for the Fourth of July weekend, Elliott tugged his pants up over his considerable paunch and leaned forward.

"So, Murphy, what did you think about the operation up in Maine?" Elliott asked.

"Well, obviously the place has a lot of problems, Elliott. The infrastructure is badly aged, and some of the equipment is definitely in need of replacement. There are also a few issues that could become environmental hazards if we're not careful." Chris shifted uncomfortably in the overstuffed chair. "The workforce seems hardworking and committed, but they need a good deal of professional development to update their skills. But, I guess it has the potential to be a profitable power plant with a few changes and some hard work. It's all in the report we filed in April."

"Do you think you have what it takes to turn it around?" Elliott's hawk-like stare locked onto Chris's eyes. Chris's suspicion about the purpose of the meeting was confirmed, and he was prepared for battle.

"I'm sure I could," Chris responded carefully, "but you're asking an awful lot." He took a sip of his whiskey and concluded that it tasted like cough syrup. "You're asking me to relocate my family to a shit-hole town in Maine, and you're asking me to invest a hell of a lot of time and effort in a turnaround plan." Chris wanted to be sure that Elliott knew that this would be a sacrifice, and to be prepared to bargain accordingly.

Elliott smiled as his eyes narrowed. "Yup. That's what I'm asking." He paused and sipped his whiskey. "But what I'm prepared to offer is a ten-percent raise and an opportunity to prove yourself as a manager."

Chris leaned back and looked at Elliott hard. "Make it twenty-five percent, complete autonomy up there to hire and fire, full payment of relocation expenses, and a reasonable profit-sharing offer. Maybe then I'll consider it."

Elliott chuckled. "You really are a prick, Murphy." He shook his head, massaged his chin, and stared intently at Chris. "Okay, you got it. But I need an answer this afternoon."

Chris was stunned. Elliott must have been desperate to get the Ashton Falls plant back in the black to go for a raise of twenty-five percent. Chris disregarded the voice in the back of his head that warned him to go slow. He stood up, thrust his hand toward Elliott, and said, "Let's work out the details next week."

Chris's friends celebrated his promotion at their usual Friday after-work watering hole. Despite their cheery intentions, the evening felt more like an Irish wake than a party. They toasted him with round after round of trendy microbrews and shots of vodka while wishing him luck, but there was a subtle sadness in the air. As one by one they congratulated him, his friend

Tom's last words stuck in his mind: "One year in Ashton Falls, Maine—it's kind of like a criminal sentence, but there isn't any chance of time off for good behavior." Tom chuckled at his own wit. Chris laughed too, but he didn't really find it all that funny.

He wasn't quite sure how his wife would deal with the news of his new assignment. His marriage to Mimi had never been what he hoped it would be. She was still the most beautiful woman in the world to him, but, to be honest, he didn't really know how much longer she'd be his wife.

Chris would always remember the night they first met at an upscale cocktail party at someone's apartment in downtown Manhattan. He didn't know how he managed to be invited. It was a very chic loft with very chic modern art on the wall and a very chic three-piece jazz combo playing softly in a corner of the main room. Servers in black and white floated silently by offering colorful cocktails and unidentifiable little tidbits on paper doilies. Chris was immediately aware of a beautiful young woman who was surrounded by two adoring older men in expensive suits. She was wearing a tight little sleeveless black dress that hugged the gentle curves of her athletic body. Her blond hair fell to her shoulders, and her deep blue eyes sparkled when she laughed. Chris watched her for at least an hour before he had the courage to talk to her.

"I thought you'd never make it over here," she said as she sipped her martini. "You've been making me a little nervous the way you've been watching me. Are you a cop or a private investigator or something?"

After she had nearly convinced him that she was a princess from Malta, she confessed that she was really an aspiring actress from Vermont who had a weekend job with an improv group over in Soho. Chris admitted that he really wasn't a CIA operative as he had claimed, but a junior civil engineer with a big power company who came from a working-class South Boston neighborhood.

She took his arm and confided, "I'm starving. There's a wonderful all-night diner about five blocks from here. This place isn't exactly my style. Let's get out of here."

They spent the rest of the night talking, laughing, and drinking cup after cup of coffee until the waitstaff at the diner made it clear that they were sick of them. Chris's heart pounded and his mouth dried up as he thought about asking Mimi if she wanted to come over to his apartment. It wasn't as if he hadn't been on plenty of dates in college, but he had never met a woman before who was so beautiful, so witty, so wonderful.

He blurted out the invitation. She smiled, squeezed his hand, and said, "That sounds like fun."

Chris didn't know what to say or where to put his hands on the long cab ride to his place. Fortunately Mimi cut the tension by continuing to make small talk, just like she did at the diner. He fumbled with the key to the door, turned on the lights, and wondered what he'd do next.

Mimi made it easy for him. She told him she was exhausted and asked where his bedroom was. After he opened the bedroom door, she kicked off her high heels, unzipped her dress, and wriggled out of it. Wearing nothing but a black lace bra and panties, she looked over her shoulder and said teasingly, "Do they mail out invitations in South Boston?"

He had never seen such an amazing woman—from her full, round breasts to her washboard tummy to the sculpted tuft of hair between her legs, she was absolutely perfect. No, more than perfect—she was simply the most beautiful being in the universe.

Chris took her in his arms and they made love with an intensity he had never experienced before. As he watched the first rays of sun peek through the window, he knew he never wanted to let her go.

After that first night together, they were never apart for more than a few days at a time. Mimi brought out a crazy, creative side to him that was too often bottled up by the logical thought processes of his civil-engineering career. He loved the fact that he could never predict what life with Mimi would hold—running through Central Park to catch the sunrise, grabbing the train to Newport for dinner by the sea, or driving for hours upstate to sample the best Niagara vintage right at the vineyard. Life with Mimi was rich and exciting and always surprising. He would do anything to hear her giggle, to see the light that radiated through her luminous blue eyes, and feel the warmth of her hand as she squeezed his. Sometimes, when she wasn't looking, he watched the breeze ruffle her long honey-colored hair and wondered what a gorgeous woman like her was doing with an ordinary slob like him.

Making love with Mimi was absolutely amazing. She was always curious about trying things she'd read about, usually in

Cosmopolitan or some novel, and he was only too willing to oblige her. When Chris had a few too many beers, he liked to brag to his buddies that they had never had sex the same way twice that he could remember. Sometimes in the middle of his work day she'd call the office just to describe, in fine detail, what she had planned for later that night. The office staff would tease him about his bright red cheeks after one of Mimi's calls, but they could never imagine what delights lay ahead in Chris's future.

Chris and Mimi spent so much time together that it only made sense for her to move into his place. One night he came home from work late and found her sobbing at the kitchen table. Mimi was embarrassed that he caught her crying. At first she wouldn't talk about it, but after he pressed her gently, she opened up.

"Chris, I'm pregnant," she blurted out and instantly melted in tears.

Although he was startled, he said unconvincingly, "That's great, honey." He reached over and hugged her hard.

"No, it isn't," she sobbed. "It ruins everything." Then she added, "But it's okay, because I have an appointment at Planned Parenthood on Monday. They'll let me know how soon I can schedule an … a time to get things taken care of."

He made her a cup of tea and tried to comfort her, but she wouldn't stop crying. They lay together in bed entwined in each other's arms, not saying much at all. Mimi drifted off to sleep, but Chris lay awake most of the night.

They were quiet in the morning until Chris broke the silence. "Mimi, I've thought about this a lot. I know that it's your body and your decision, but I want to marry you. I want to raise this baby together. I want to spend the rest of my life with you." He continued, kneeling down in front of her on one knee as he grasped her hand, "I guess this is the stupidest marriage proposal in the world, but I love you and want you to be my wife."

Mimi's tearstained face broke into a half smile. "I love you, too, Chris, and I want to be your wife some day. But I'm not sure I want this to be the way we begin our marriage. I need some time to think."

It wasn't exactly what he wanted to hear. All day long at work, he was preoccupied. So much so that he left work right after lunch claiming that he was sick. He decided to walk home instead of taking a cab, even though it was a gray, drizzly September afternoon.

When he walked into the apartment, he was surprised to see Mimi still sitting at the kitchen table. He sat down next to her and asked, "How was your day?"

Without looking at him, she replied, "I talked to my mother for the longest time this morning, and I made up my mind." Turning toward Chris, she grasped his face between both hands and said, "I love you and I will marry you. We'll have this baby together, and we'll start a family."

He grabbed her in his arms and kissed her face again and again. The tears rolled down her cheeks, and he hoped they were tears of joy.

Christopher Edward Murphy was married to Marie Elizabeth Sunshine Julien in a park overlooking Lake Champlain in the bride's hometown of Burlington, Vermont. Immediate family and a few friends attended the ceremony on an unusually warm afternoon for late October. The red and orange maple leaves glowed and the sunshine sparkled on the water as the couple vowed to "love, honor, and cherish 'til death do us part." Chris wore a new black suit and a pair of stiff shoes that gave him blisters. Mimi was radiant in a full-length white gown with a wreath of white roses in her hair. The gentle breeze off the lake ruffled her hair, and her blue eyes glistened as Chris bent his head to kiss the bride at the end of the ceremony.

Chris assumed that Mimi would learn to become a wife and mother and settle down a little bit while she continued with her unpredictable creative side, but that just wasn't the case. Time after time, Chris had to remind her that she needed to ease up on her gym workouts, get to bed instead of staying up all night watching movies, and that it wasn't good for the baby when she cheated with a glass of wine or a joint every now and then. As her pregnancy advanced, they both agreed that having a child might be good for their relationship and maybe help them both grow up a little.

In late April, Mimi gave birth to a baby girl. At the moment the doctor held her up in the delivery room, all pink and slimy, and squealing at the top of her lungs, Chris felt a powerful sensation rip through him like an electric shock. Tears rolled down his cheeks as he laughed in embarrassment and grasped Mimi's hand tightly. He couldn't explain what he felt, but he knew his life was changed forever. He only hoped that Mimi felt the same powerful emotions.

They decided to name her Veronique Marie, after Mimi's grandmother. The first few weeks were difficult for Mimi. Thankfully her mother came down from Vermont to help out with the baby. Mimi tried to nurse the baby for a while, but she said she couldn't deal with feeling like a cow, so they quickly shifted to baby formula. More often than not, Chris found the baby in his arms the moment he came home from work as Mimi complained that she just needed a few hours away from the baby or else she'd lose her mind.

Perhaps the mixture of infatuation and lust soured a bit when blended with obligation and commitment, but a few years after they had their daughter, their relationship began to change. Mimi often talked about how she felt like a caged bird. Chris found himself caring for little Ronnie, as they called her, many nights while Mimi went uptown to the theater, or for a walk, or only God knows where. After five years he thought she might work through it or at least get used to it. Sometimes Mimi was loving and told him that she was going to try to make their marriage work. Sometimes when she crept into their apartment in the dark hours of the morning and slipped into bed beside him, he could faintly smell the unmistakable scent of marijuana smoke, or tequila, or another man's aftershave. Still, he was thankful that Mimi was a good mother to Ronnie, at least while the sun was up.

When Chris told Mimi about his transfer to Ashton Falls, she took in the news with little comment, and said flatly, "A change of scene might do us all some good." Ronnie was full of questions about lobsters and lighthouses and their new house.

Chris answered every question and surprised even himself with his upbeat, enthusiastic answers. Maybe this will be just what we need, he thought to himself.

Just after dinner that night, Chris heard the front door click shut as Mimi slipped out. Maybe this will be her last fling, he thought as he dried off the dinner dishes and put them away.

Chris bundled Ronnie into his arms, scooped her up off her feet, and plopped her down on her bed as he growled like a bear and nuzzled her neck. She shrieked and giggled until he tucked her under the covers all warm and safe and protected from life's disappointments. Chris squeezed onto the side of Ronnie's little bed and read her favorite story, *The Runaway Bunny*. By the time he read the last page Ronnie was already sound asleep, clutching her own little pink bunny with the well-loved, ragged ears.

Chris looked down at her sweet face. Gently he reached out and stroked her golden hair, just like her mother's, barely touching her silky head so as not to wake her. He thought with a smile, I wonder if Mimi knows what she's missing?

He woke to the sound of the front door opening a few hours after midnight and heard a table bump into the wall as Mimi stumbled into their bedroom. He could see the outline of her slender body in the dim light as she pulled her sweater over her head and wiggled out of her blue jeans. Even in the semi-darkness Chris was aroused by the sight of her round breasts, taut tummy, and firm ass. She shook out her hair and moved gracefully, almost gliding to her side of the bed despite the fact that his nose told him that she had obviously had plenty to drink.

Mimi stood over Chris with her hands on her hips. He could see her beautiful body in the half light as she peeled off her thong. With a quick swoosh, she threw the covers back and reached into his pajama pants, grasping his erect penis. She chuckled in a low, seductive way and said, "Pretending to be asleep? We'll see about that."

Then she straddled his legs and, leaning down low, licked his erect member starting at the base and slowly working her way up to the tip. She wrapped her warm mouth around the head and swirled her tongue around it until he thought he'd explode. She crawled forward until her thighs cradled his hips. Grabbing his penis, she gently eased him inside her and began to slowly rock forward and backward. Gaining momentum, she bucked and rotated and dug her nails into his chest. Chris reached up and squeezed her breasts as she arched her back. When he could stand it no longer, he picked her up and rolled her onto her back, entering her with a force beyond his control. As he increased the power and pace of his thrusts, they both moaned, grunted, and finally shrieked as they climaxed together.

They lay side by side, panting, both staring up at nothing, trying to catch their breath. Chris wondered for a moment if Mimi was really making love to him or just getting off on the most convenient penis she could find. After all, she didn't even kiss him. He quickly banished the crude thought—of course she still loved him.

Chris squeezed her hand, but she quickly pulled it away. He could sense that something wasn't quite right. After five minutes or so, Mimi broke the silence. "I really need to talk with you," she blurted out, her breath sour with stale smoke and wine.

He knew what was coming and resigned himself to it. "Okay," he whispered.

"I can't go to Maine with you, or Australia, or Paris, or Africa, or anywhere," she said, beginning to sob. "I love you, Chris, and God knows I love Ronnie more than you'll ever know, but the two of you are like two chains holding me down, keeping me from doing what I want to do, flying away to where I want to go. I just can't live this lie anymore." She rolled over and buried her face in his chest as she began to weep.

He knew this had been coming for some time, but that didn't make it hurt any less. Still, he stroked her hair and gently rubbed her back. "Is it another man?" he asked softly, although he feared the answer.

She stopped crying, propped herself up on her elbows, and looked intently into his eyes. "No ... and yes, it's a thousand other men. You're the sexiest, kindest, most gentle man I've ever known, but I can't be faithful to you, Chris. You can make me crazy and satisfy me physically, but you can't satisfy my soul. I need to explore, to search, to create, to spread my wings."

Her eyes searched his face for understanding, and he thought that she hadn't looked so beautiful in years. She gently kissed his cheek, and he realized that this was the first time they had kissed in a long time. He wrapped his arms around her and they drifted off to sleep, her warm tears dripping onto his chest.

Chris woke up alone to the pale gray light of dawn. He heard the front door gently shut and then noticed the soft whimper of a little girl crying in the next room.

Chapter 2

THE OLD MAN ducked behind a lilac bush in the far corner of the backyard as he took the final puffs from his cigarette. He carefully pinched out the butt and buried it in the trash barrel near the back steps. He climbed the stairs to his study, turned on the television, and stared intently as the Boston Red Sox were getting their butts soundly kicked by the Toronto Blue Jays.

"When are those damn Sox going to get their act together?" he muttered as he turned toward the window. The far-off rumble of thunder caused his frown to become even darker. He uttered a curse, then quickly made the sign of the cross and raised his eyes to heaven.

It was a beastly hot, humid afternoon, so all the windows in the house were open in the futile effort to find a cooling breeze. Suddenly the skies grew dark and the rain cascaded down, like someone had just turned on a shower. Lightning crackled across the sky, and thunder shook the house. The old man quickly slammed the windows shut to keep out the rain as he made his way through the large, empty house. When he entered the bedroom of another resident, he closed the windows, but he was fascinated by what he spotted on top of the desk.

It was an old satchel with a long shoulder strap that had been crudely mended at some point. At one time it must have been highly shined black leather, but now it was scuffed and scratched. The old man examined the center of the outer flap and traced the outline of a Nazi swastika that someone had tried carefully to obscure. He knew he probably shouldn't look inside it, but he couldn't resist the urge to just take a peek under the flap. Inside the satchel was a lock of blond hair, an Iron Cross war medal, a worn set of black rosary beads, and several old notebooks with yellowed pages. On top of the desk was a scuffed leather-bound journal with loose papers sticking out here and there.

Yes, he realized that this was someone else's room. He understood that these were probably very personal items. But curiosity overcame him. Besides, the Sox were losing and he was certain that the room's occupant wouldn't be back for at least two hours. So, despite the faint voice of caution from his conscience, he opened up the leather-bound journal. It took a few moments before he recognized that the elegant handwriting was written in classic Latin, which he remembered well from his studies in the seminary. He began reading the first page:

"My name is Siegfried Benedict Von Halstead. I am a monk of the congregation of the Order of Brothers of the Germanic House of Saint Mary in Jerusalem. Our community was founded during the Crusades, and we carry on the legacy of the Teutonic Knights, which is to protect the adoration of our Lord from those heathens and blasphemers who would harm His followers.

My arrival in this world was a complicated and tragic event that resulted in the death of my poor mother, whom I never knew. My father's sorrow at the loss of his beloved wife was somewhat tempered by the news that his tiny son had survived the arduous birth process. But any joy he might have felt soon faded when he learned that my twisted spine would never allow me to walk fully upright.

My father was Count Otto Von Halstead, commander of the 3rd Bavarian Cavalry Regiment, a highly decorated hero of the war with France. As a serving army officer, he could not care for a small boy, so I was sent to live with my aunt, Gertrude, who raised me as if I were one of her own children. I grew to be a scholarly boy who was more interested in the campaigns of Napoleon than the study of Latin and Greek. Although my heart longed to follow in my father's footsteps, my body was not suited to the life of a soldier. I rarely saw him, but I adored my father, and I was devastated when he was killed in a hunting accident. I was thirteen years old, and I was an orphan.

I sought comfort in prayer and the gospel of our Lord. Kindly priests in our parish took me under their wing and helped me realize that I had a true vocation to serve God as a priest. Because of the physical deformity that the Lord chose to give me, worship and study in a monastic community was considered the best path for me, and, indeed it has proven to be so. I chose the Brothers of Saint Mary in Jerusalem because I have always admired the medieval knights of Germanic history, and I dreamed that one day I could serve them with prayer to protect our land and defeat our enemies, despite my bodily limitations.

But this journal is not about me. I write this so that my spiritual son will understand his origin and how he came to be the man he is today. More importantly, he will understand why he has been entrusted with the sacred mission of defending our Lord and Savior from those who have turned against Him and chosen a life of sin. He will know why he has been selected to avenge the suffering and crucifixion of our Redeemer.

My spiritual son was born on Christmas Day 1941 to Major Gerhard Friedrich Bachman and Marte Mary Koenig in Colmar, Alsace, France. His father came from Munich, where he was a brilliant, if penniless, student of the classics. When Adolf Hitler rose up to restore the dignity of the German people in the late 1930s, Gerhard was inspired by the Führer's message. The dream of regaining the ancient glories of the fatherland enflamed his soul. When a Nazi party recruiter visited Ludwig Maximilian University, where Gerhard was enrolled, he was an eager volunteer.

Gerhard's scholarship was recognized by SS chief Heinrich Himmler, who assigned him to the newly formed branch of the SS tasked with studying the early foundations of the German people and defining their racial superiority. The Ahnenerbe, as this special branch was named, sent teams of scholars worldwide to research the roots of the Aryan race and their early history.

The young scholar gained Adolph Hitler's favor when, along with other members of his team, he presented conclusive information that linked the legacy of the Olympic flame to ancient Aryan tradition. The Führer was delighted with the findings, and the Olympic flame became a centerpiece of the 1936 Berlin games. As a reward for his scholarship, Gerhard was promoted to major and placed in charge of a group of scholars investigating the occult practices of the early Middle Ages, or Dark Ages, as they are sometimes called.

After the fall of France in 1940, Major Bachman joined the victorious German forces in Alsace as they regained possession of the region for the fatherland. Alsace is a unique territory that has been passed between Germany and France following the outcomes of many wars throughout the ages. The population of the region is made up of towns and villages that are either ethnically French or ethnically German. Depending on which nation was in control at the time, the ethnic population of the other nation often suffered neglect, prejudice, and sometimes outright persecution.

So, when the armored columns of the victorious Wehrmacht rolled into Alsace, they were greeted with either flowers and kisses or locked doors and tears.

Although he rode atop a Panzer tank like the other victorious German knights, Major Bachman's secret mission there was to investigate religious practices in medieval France and explore powerful forms of prayer and worship that had been obscured by the dust of time.

Shortly after he arrived in Colmar, Gerhard's attention was drawn to a beautiful young girl at the market. She was blond, blue-eyed, pink-cheeked, and well formed. He couldn't help but notice that she wore the full dress and tight bodice of the dirndl, the native German dress for women. He also noted that she wore a small gold cross around her slender, graceful neck. In short, she was the ideal Aryan bride and future mother of the Third Reich, and I must guess that she made the major's heart beat a little faster. He found himself searching the market whenever he could get away from his duties, just to catch a glimpse of her. For nearly two weeks he wore his best uniform and ensured that his orderly shined his boots to a mirror-like glow as he hoped for a chance encounter with this young Germanic goddess in the market.

Finally, one rainy Friday, he found her carefully inspecting apples at a fruit vendor's stall. His confidence was a little shaken by her fresh beauty, but after a few moments of small talk, he summoned the courage to ask if he could accompany her to the cinema on the following evening. She could hardly speak as she blushed and accepted his invitation. Marte almost ran the entire way home so she could tell her sister about the tall, handsome soldier in the spotless black uniform who had invited her to see a film with him.

When Gerhard came to escort Marte to the cinema, her father carefully inspected and interviewed the young major. He was impressed by Gerhard's intelligence, fine manners, and Germanic patriotism. Herr Koenig was even more delighted when Gerhard asked where he might hear a mass in German, explaining that he was a Bavarian Catholic and hadn't been to church in nearly two weeks. Herr Koenig invited the young major to join the family at mass on Sunday and to honor them with his presence at dinner afterwards. Gerhard gratefully accepted. The entire Koenig family was almost as infatuated with the dashing major as their daughter was. Gerhard was handsome, intelligent, and heroic. And even more important, he was a devout fellow Catholic who was madly in love with Marte.

Gerhard and Marte were married in the chapel of Our Lady of the Valley in March 1941, just as spring arrived that year. The couple moved into a sturdy brick house in the center of town that had recently been vacated by a Jewish jeweler. On Christmas Day they were blessed with a son, who was as blond and blue-eyed as his parents. Although Gerhard's duties required him to travel extensively as he conducted his research, he was thankful that he was able to spend more time than most soldiers with his beautiful wife and baby son. When she casually asked about his duties in the army, Gerhard told Marte that he was a railway transport officer because his true mission in the Ahnenerbe was too confidential even to share with his wife."

The old man was startled by a sound coming from the kitchen downstairs. Was it the sound of footsteps? He quickly closed the journal and carefully placed the satchel where he had found it. Moving swiftly for a man of his age, he shuffled to the study and sank into the easy chair in time to catch the final out of the last inning. The Red Sox lost to Toronto by a score of ten to two.

-->⬤ ⬤<--

She just disappeared. At first, Chris thought Mimi would be back in a few days after she got it all out of her system, but he was wrong. The phone rang twice late at night, but whomever it was on the other end hung up a few seconds after Chris answered. He called Mimi's cell phone and texted her, but there was no reply.

Initially he was depressed and heartsick because he realized that he loved her much more than he thought. Then his depression turned to panic as the complexities of life as a single parent sunk in. Surprisingly, Elliott agreed to let Chris make his own work schedule so Chris could adjust to the demands of caring for Ronnie—that is, provided Chris still agreed to take over the Ashton Falls project. And so, Chris worked out a schedule that enabled him to get Ronnie over to daycare, attend midday meetings at work, and pick her up on time in the afternoon.

With the wonderful resilience of childhood, Ronnie adjusted to life without a mother, and there were fewer and fewer nights when Chris had to cuddle her and dry her tears in the darkness. Apparently Mimi had told Ronnie on the morning she left that she was going on a long trip for a wonderful acting job, and that she would be so busy that it would be hard to call or write. And so Chris played along with the fantasy and found that Ronnie asked fewer and fewer questions. Life went on, and the two of them managed to adapt to their new circumstances a little bit better each day.

One night as Chris was getting Ronnie ready for bed, she asked to write a letter to Mimi. Chris copied down her words faithfully:

"Dear Mommy,

I miss you a lot. I hope your new acting job is good. Daddy is taking good care of me. His macaroni doesn't taste as good as yours. I hope you can come home again soon. I love you.

Hugs and Kisses.

Ronnie"

Chris helped Ronnie seal the envelope, draw a daisy on the outside with a red crayon, and put a stamp on it. After the little girl was asleep, he took the letter from the shelf over the sink, tore it into little pieces, and flushed it down the toilet.

In those first two weeks without Mimi, Chris drew even closer to his daughter and actually began to enjoy the new little tasks that he took on, like playing on the swings in the park, or helping Ronnie get Barbie into her new outfit, or setting up the kitchen floor for the teddy bear's tea party. There wasn't any time to get together with the guys at the bar after work, but he really didn't miss it that much. Still, the more time he spent with Ronnie, the more he saw Mimi in the child's radiant complexion, sparkling blue eyes, and golden hair. And when he remembered Mimi, he was filled with longing that was soon replaced by a sense of guilt, then anger and resentment, which gradually grew into smoldering rage.

His friend Tom asked him how he was doing one day over lunch. Chris opened up and shared how angry he had become.

"You sound really pissed off, man, and you have a right to be," his friend said after listening without comment. "I'm no shrink, but I know this—if you don't find someone to talk to soon, your anger is going to eat you up and you'll do something really stupid."

Tom gave him the phone number of his therapist, and Chris agreed to call her. He visited the therapist for three or four sessions, and maybe it helped to talk about the way he felt. But, more often than not, he left the therapist's office wondering if she really cared what happened to him or if he was just another billable hour. He decided not to go back.

The long, hot days of summer grew shorter. During his final week at the New York office, Chris's cell phone buzzed from a private number one afternoon. When he answered, he heard Mimi's voice.

"Where are you?"

"It doesn't really matter." Her voice sounded faint and detached.

"How are you?"

"I guess that doesn't really matter, either." She paused and added, "I just really need some space to think things through and figure out what comes next."

"Did you ever stop to think about what this is doing to Ronnie?"

"Don't go there, Chris. You know that's dirty fighting." Her voice rose, and he could hear her choking back the tears. "If you think for one second that this has been easy for me, then …" He could hear the bitter sobbing now.

"Well, our lives haven't exactly been fucking paradise since you walked out, or should I say 'ran away.'" The rising anger made his voice thick and low.

"I didn't call to fight with you, Chris. I just needed to say that I'm going to the apartment today to get the rest of my things. If I leave anything behind, just give it to the Salvation Army or something … I'll leave my key on the coffee table." Although she held her hand over the receiver, he could still hear her crying.

"Mimi … Mimi," he gently whispered, regretting his angry outburst. He wanted to beg her to come back, but somehow he couldn't find the words.

"I'll stay out of your life, Chris … I guess this is good-bye," she said with resolve. Then she added, "Please give my love to my baby."

"Mimi … I love you," he added, but he didn't really know why. It didn't matter because she had already hung up.

The late August weekend was hot and humid in New York as Chris loaded the last of Ronnie's dolls into his old green Volvo station wagon. His office buddies always laughed at the boxy station wagon with the roof racks and the hubcaps that didn't quite match. It had over 200,000 miles on it, but Chris loved it like an old friend.

Fortunately the company paid for movers, who had already loaded up the furniture and boxes. Chris and Ronnie had made the journey up to Ashton Falls one weekend in late July to find a place to live and had settled for the first place they'd been shown—a second-floor apartment in a two-family house on a quiet side street that was lined with maple trees. It was clean and quaint and smelled of Pine-Sol and fresh scrubbing. Every house on the street looked like it had been built before World War II, but the homes were all well cared for and tidy. The neighborhood was about as different from New York City as it could be, but it was uncomplicated and safe.

Chris noticed the extra attention that he received from the real estate agent once he told her that Ronnie's mother wouldn't be moving in with them. She was in her forties with unnaturally red hair, altogether too much makeup, and a cloud of sickly sweet perfume that smelled like a car air freshener and made him cough. Her five-inch heels clicked on the kitchen floor tiles, her red leather skirt was way too tight, and she placed her hand on his arm far too often for someone he had just met. But he was actually kind of flattered when she leaned up close and looked into his eyes over her half glasses as she handed him her business card.

"Please give me a call when you move into town and get unpacked," she said with a flirtatious grin. "I'd like to show you around and help you get comfortable with our little town. I promise you'll find that Ashton Falls can be a really friendly place. So, call me when you're settled in, huh?"

He noticed that her cell phone and home phone numbers were written on the back of the card. Clearly she wasn't taking any chances that she would be misunderstood.

Later that night, Chris took a good look at himself in the bedroom mirror. He wasn't half bad-looking for a guy of thirty-three. At just over six feet, one might say he was lean, although the slight roll above the waistband of his jeans made him wish that he could get to a gym more often. His thick brown hair, which he knew was too long for the corporate jungle, was only showing a few gray hairs, and Mimi had always said that his penetrating brown eyes and firm jawline had first made her fall for him. Perhaps he really was the kind of guy that women might find attractive, although he knew too well that the real estate agent looked like the kind of woman who would have found any guy under seventy-five to be attractive.

He almost laughed when he thought about his new job as a power plant manager for a small city. He had always thought of himself as more of a dreamer, an artist, a lover than a businessman—more comfortable in old jeans and a flannel shirt than a Brooks Brothers suit. Perhaps Ashton Falls, Maine, would be a good fit for him after all. The pace of life would be slower, a small community would allow him to be his own man, and he could start a new life with Ronnie after this nightmare that had shattered their world.

The journey from the city to their new apartment in Maine was hot and tiring. They sang "This Old Man" and "The Itsy Bitsy Spider" a hundred times as they rumbled along the north-bound highways. With each passing mile, Chris sensed that he was leaving his old life behind and entering a new world. Ronnie dozed off just before they hit a passing thunderstorm in Connecticut that turned the roadway into a blur as the wip-ers swished the rain off the windshield. Chris had a passing thought that the showers were washing away his past life with all its mistakes and disappointments. The sky cleared, and the sunshine raised trails of mist from the highway as they passed over the massive Piscataqua River Bridge in New Hampshire and crossed the state line into Maine. He passed the sign that read "Welcome to Vacationland" and thought that things just had to get better—didn't they?

After the movers were gone and Chris began unpacking the stacks of boxes scattered about the hollow rooms, he stopped to hear Ronnie singing quietly to herself as she played with her dolls on the shiny wood floor. He tiptoed over to the open door of her bedroom and smiled as she whispered to a well-loved Raggedy Ann with too few pieces of red yarn hair remaining, "Don't be scared, Annie. Daddy will make this house a happy place where nothing bad can happen to us. You'll see, everything will be fine."

Just then there was a knock on the door, and a voice echoed through the empty rooms, "Hullo, ho! Is anybody home up here?"

Standing in the front hall was an older woman in a bright green polyester pantsuit holding a steaming earthenware pot in two oven mitts. Her hair was a solid silver-white helmet that matched the silver chain attached to the silver-rimmed glasses perched on the end of her angular nose.

Chris said, "Come in. Please excuse our mess."

"I thought you could use something special for your first night in your new home," the old woman said as she bustled through the apartment to the kitchen. "So I made you a pot of my special baked beans, with molasses, and pork, and maple sugar, and even a little beer." She gave Chris a nudge and a wink as she set the steaming pot on the stove.

"Thank you so much, Mrs. ..." Chris said.

"Oh, ho, ho, ho," the old woman chuckled. "You don't even know who I am, ha, ha." She laughed again and shook her head. "I'm Jeanine Brisebois, your landlady," she said as she laughed once more for good measure.

"Pleased to meet you, Mrs. Brisebois," Chris said as he shook her hand. "I'm Chris Murphy. I just moved in with my daughter, Ronnie."

"Yes, yes, from New York they tell me," she said, "and here to take charge of our power plant, I hear. Well, it's about time, because the rates have gone up and up, and we've had more power outages than I can ever remember. I was just telling my friend, Louise, that the power plant needs new management to straighten it out. Oh, but listen to me going on like this!" She laughed again.

Stepping gingerly over to Ronnie's bedroom, Mrs. Brisebois poked her head in and asked, "Now where did you get all these pretty dolls?" The old woman set herself on the bed and began to chitchat with Ronnie about each of the dolls. Ronnie just continued to comb their hair and change their clothing as she conversed easily with Mrs. Brisebois. Chris left them to their play, the old woman now cradling each doll as Ronnie told her about them in detail. He returned to the task of unpacking all those boxes.

After an hour or so, Ronnie and Mrs. Brisebois came out of the little girl's bedroom hand in hand. "I can see that we're going to be great friends, Ronnie," said the old woman, "but now it's time for me to go downstairs to my house. From now on, you must call me Grand-mère. You see, that's French for 'Grandma.'"

"All right, Grand-mère," said Ronnie. "Will you come to see us tomorrow?"

"If your daddy says that I can, then I would be delighted, but remember, he's the boss," the old lady said with a wink.

Much to Chris's surprise, Ronnie reached up and kissed the old woman, saying, "Good night, Grand-mère." Mrs. Brisebois returned the kiss and quickly rubbed her eyes. Chris was amazed that Ronnie was so comfortable with their new landlady.

As they walked to the door, Chris said, "I can't tell you how welcome I feel here, Mrs. Brisebois. Thank you for the beans, and thank you especially for taking the time to play with Ronnie."

"First, you must call me Jeanine," said the old woman, grasping Chris's arm. "And second, I understand the challenges of raising a child by yourself. My husband passed away when he was only thirty-six. I remember those hard years when my boys were little. You must call on me whenever I can help you, Mr. Murphy."

"Please call me Chris," he said. "And thank you again, Jeanine," he called after her as she carefully stepped down the stairs.

Chris managed to locate their sheets and pillows. He found their toothbrushes and clothes for the next day. The other unpacking could wait until tomorrow. Ronnie was singing to herself in her new bedroom as the daylight faded into twilight. Chris stepped out onto the screen porch with a warm bowl of Jeanine's beans and an ice-cold bottle of beer and sat down on a folding metal chair. The evening breeze was cool and smelled faintly of balsam. He remembered that Maine was called the Pine Tree State, and he felt a little guilty about that "Armpit of New England" comment back in the city. Maybe things really are going to be just fine, he thought as he washed a mouthful of beans down with beer.

Just then he heard a sharp thwack that made him jump. He flicked on the light switch and spotted a small mousetrap in the corner of the porch. The mouse caught under the bale wire had been almost cut in two so that all Chris could see were pieces of fur and bright red pulp. He moved toward the trap, but decided that the cleanup could wait until tomorrow. Suddenly he wasn't very hungry anymore and he said aloud, "Well, I guess nothing's perfect."

Chapter 3

CHRIS GRIPPED THE steering wheel until his knuckles were white and he raced the old station wagon through the darkening streets, scattering green and gold leaves as he went. It had been a rough day at work—frustrating negotiations with the workers' union, cash flow lower than expected, and a troubling meeting with an inquisitive local environmental group.

"Late to pick up Ronnie again because I have to put this fucked-up power plant back together," he muttered as he increased the pressure on the gas pedal. "And stuck here in this shit hole raising a kid all by myself because that bitch walked out on me," he spit out through clenched teeth as he gripped the wheel a little tighter.

He came to the end of a country road and flirted with the idea of running the stop sign, thinking that no one would be crossing at that hour. Just as he decided to accelerate, a teenager on a mountain bike caught his eye, and the car screeched to a halt at the stop sign. The biker swerved around the front of the Volvo, just skimming the front license plate, and the teenager reached back to raise a middle finger to Chris for his troubles.

"Wow, I could have killed that kid if …" The thought trailed away, and he gradually got a hold of his galloping thoughts and pounding heart.

He took a deep breath and tried to remember what the therapist had told him during the sessions that he had managed to arrange before they left New York. With her crisp business suit, black-rimmed half glasses, and slow, mellow way of talking, the therapist had been full of reason and detachment. While he knew that she was offering basically sound advice, Chris never really connected with her.

As he slowly pulled away from the stop sign, he began to breathe deeply and repeat the "new self-talk" that the therapist had recommended. Maybe Mimi wasn't meant to be a mother. Maybe I pushed her to start a family before she was ready. Maybe I could have made our marriage more exciting for her. Maybe it wasn't all her fault.

There, now he was driving calmly and slowly down a beautiful residential street of brick homes. A hint of barbecued steak scented the air. Two little girls giggled as they walked hand in hand with their mother down the street.

"Bullshit," he barked out loud. Maybe it's a good thing that I don't know where she is because I'd probably fucking kill her, and maybe it's a good thing that I care enough to be pissed off, but I'll never forgive her for breaking my sweet angel's heart … and my own, he thought. And maybe I'm crazy, but that therapist was an asshole.

Oddly enough, he felt better as he turned down a street lined with stately oak trees and came to a stop in front of a three-story rectangular brick building. Orange paper pumpkins and cardboard skeletons smirked down at him from the darkened windows as he walked up the front stairs. He almost needed two hands to pull open the massive oak door and, as he stepped into the entryway, he glanced up at the ancient marble plaque that was engraved "Ecole du Saint-Rosaire—1877." Appreciatively he drank in the absolute peace and quiet.

Thank God for this place, he thought.

When he had asked Jeanine about the nearest school for Ronnie, she had warned him about the Ashton Falls public schools. "Too much trouble in those schools. Not enough discipline. They don't even teach reading, writing, and 'rithmetic these days. I hear they teach sex education in the second grade and have third graders bringing marijuana to school." She then recommended Holy Rosary School over on the next street, which, she claimed, had straightened out her sons and made them into fine upstanding men.

Chris and Ronnie had visited the school the next day. Ronnie made an instant connection with Mrs. Jefferson, the first-grade teacher, who recommended that Ronnie start school right away. As Mrs. Jefferson and Ronnie chatted, Chris noticed a priest in the schoolyard playing kickball with the children there. He looked a bit comical as he ran the bases in his long black cassock, but he laughed and clapped with the children when he crossed home plate. Chris smiled as he remembered his own school days.

He was concerned about an after-school program, but Mrs. Jefferson assured him that Brother Adelard, who was playing kickball in the schoolyard, provided a pleasant, comfortable homework and play group in the afternoon for a very modest fee. Chris was sold.

Oddly enough, Holy Rosary was very much like St. Patrick's Elementary back in South Boston. Chris remembered the square brick building and the spic-and-span classrooms, and he could never forget the clean smell of starch as the nuns passed by in their black-and-white habits. It wasn't always a pleasant place to be, but Chris figured that he grew up to know right from wrong largely because of what he had learned at St. Patrick's Elementary.

Chris had grown apart from the Catholic Church with all the scandals about priests molesting children, homophobia, and the refusal to allow equality for women. When his mother died three years ago, he stopped going to church completely. And he had his own, very personal, reason for leaving the church.

Chris would never forget the last time he went to confession to gain forgiveness for his sins. He was twelve years old and had just had his first sexual experience. Some would call it a wet dream, but it had a lot more to do with a glimpse of Tara Mulcahy's little white breasts than it did with any liquid imagination. One day at recess in the schoolyard, Tara was wearing a loose-fitting red sweatshirt. As she leaned over to tie her sneakers, her shirt drooped down to reveal her newly sprouted mounds topped with pointy pink nipples like little cherries on an ice-cream sundae. She took plenty of time making sure each bow was tied just so and positioned herself so that Chris Murphy had a good long look. She straightened up and gave him a teasing glance before running off to join the other girls.

Chris was startled by the stiffness in his pants, and he couldn't get the sight of Tara's breasts out of his mind for days. Finally, in the predawn darkness of Friday morning, he woke up with wet, sticky pajama bottoms after thinking most of the night about what Tara's naked body must look like. He was startled, repulsed, and guilt-ridden. Somehow he knew he must have done something wrong. He was fairly certain his mother and father would punish him, so he carefully washed out his pajamas in the bathroom sink before anyone was up and hung them in the back of the closet where he hoped they'd dry enough so he could slip them into the laundry basket.

At recess that day he avoided looking at Tara, somehow fearing that she'd sense the shameful thoughts he had about her. Chris found his best friend Steve and told him what happened.

"Oh yeah," Steve confided, "that happened to me last month after I found my older brother's *Playboy* magazines. What a mess, huh?"

Chris was relieved that he wasn't the only one in the world who experienced this disgusting phenomenon.

"My parents found my pajamas, but they were actually pretty cool about it," Steve continued. "They didn't really yell or anything, but they made me go to confession. I guess it's a pretty big sin—one of those that can get you into hell if you don't confess it."

With that admonition from his wise best friend, Chris decided he had better get to confession as soon as possible and get rid of this sentence to eternal damnation.

Chris was the first one waiting on Saturday afternoon at Sacred Heart Church. As he knelt in the gloom of the confessional, the screen that sealed off the priest flew open with a snap.

"Bless me, Father, for I have sinned. It has been one month since my last confession," Chris muttered.

"Yes, my son. Tell me your sins." Chris didn't recognize the priest's voice. Maybe that was a good thing.

Chris started slowly. "I didn't tell the truth three times, I didn't pay attention in mass twice last week, and I swore four times."

"Is that all?" The priest's voice was low and soft.

"No, Father, there's more," Chris blurted out. "I looked at a girl's breasts, and I couldn't get it off my mind until I woke up with a mess in my pajamas."

Chris could hear the priest's breathing quicken, which confirmed Chris's fear that he was in deep spiritual trouble. "This is a terrible sin, my boy. You must tell me all about it before I can grant absolution. I can only judge the seriousness of your transgression if you truthfully tell me every detail. Begin by describing the girl's breasts."

Chris told the priest what he saw as Tara bent over.

"This is indeed a grievous matter," the priest said, his voice becoming thicker. "Now explain how you touched yourself. Describe it very carefully to me."

With growing suspicion, Chris explained as quickly as he could what he remembered of the wet dream.

The priest's voice was just a whisper now. "For your penance, say ten Hail Marys and five Our Fathers. Most importantly, return to this confessional at four o'clock sharp next Saturday so we can continue to discuss this serious sin and save your soul from the fires of hell. Now go and sin no more."

Chris stormed out of the confessional and ran from the church. Even at the age of twelve, he knew that what had just happened was wrong, very wrong.

Before she died, Chris's mother often told him about the night he was born. She had been looking out at the clear, white full moon in the October night sky when she first felt the contractions. Chris burst into the world so fast there was hardly time to get an ambulance, let alone retrieve Chris's father from the Plough and the Stars down the street. According to his mother, Chris came roaring into this world kicking and screaming. He often thought that was why he had no younger siblings. But his lack of brothers and sisters may have been more due to his father's frequent absences, bouts of drunkenness, and eventual disappearance than Chris's abrupt arrival in the world.

His mother once told him about his christening. When Monsignor Daley, an old family friend, dribbled the baptismal water over Chris's head, the baby screamed and flailed about with such energy that it was a struggle to hold him. The old priest stroked Chris's head gently and cooed to him softly. Soon the baby was drifting into sleep. Monsignor Daley looked into his mother's eyes intently and said, "Anne, this one's a fighter. One day he'll face evil in this world. Let's hope he has the strength to win the fight." His mother found the priest's words troubling as she mulled them over again and again. In the end, she dismissed the comments as the usual kind of thing a priest says at a baptism.

Chris's mother often visited Monsignor Daley, particularly after he went into retirement and moved into an assisted living center in Harvard Square. Sometimes Chris accompanied his mother on her visits. Despite his declining health and the creeping onset of blindness, the old priest always had a joke to tell or a funny story to remember, although they were often repeated as he grew more feeble. At the end of the visit, he always placed his wrinkled hand on Chris's head, whispered a blessing, and handed him a Tootsie Pop.

Maybe that's why, after his disturbing confession, Chris made his way through the subway system to Monsignor Daley's retirement home. It had been more than a year since he had seen the old priest, and he was startled to find him confined to his bed, but wearing his full black cassock. He looked grayer and balder and more wrinkled than Chris remembered, but a smile came across the old man's face when he heard Chris's footsteps. As Chris drew nearer to the priest's bed, he could tell from the cloudy light-blue eyes that Monsignor Daley was now completely blind.

"Who has come to see me now?" the old man croaked, although Chris was sure the receptionist had called ahead.

"It's me, Monsignor, Chris Murphy."

"Well, what a pleasant surprise." The priest smiled. "Please forgive me for not rising to receive you, Mr. Murphy." Then he added, "I don't even think I have any Tootsie Pops left."

"I didn't come for a Tootsie Pop, Monsignor," Chris stammered. "I need your advice."

"Well, this sounds serious. I can't do many useful things anymore, but I can still do my best at giving advice. Come over here, Chris, sit down next to me and take my hand," the priest said gently, turning his head toward Chris. "I have no place to go, and I'm a pretty good listener."

Chris grasped the soft, wrinkled hand and told the old priest everything, from Tara's white breasts, to his soiled pajamas, to the inquisitive priest in the confessional. Monsignor Daley listened carefully, nodding his head and offering an encouraging word here and there.

"Well, it looks like you learned quite a bit about life this week," the old priest began with a reassuring smile. "First of all, while it may be difficult for most of us, a gentleman would be advised to turn his eyes away from Miss Tara's breasts, or anyone else's for that matter, the next time she chooses to show them to you," he said with a chuckle. Then his voice became low and serious. "Sexual feelings are a gift from God, but one that must be used privately and with discretion. The good Lord doesn't always tell me what he's thinking, but I'm fairly certain that the loving God I know wouldn't condemn a young man to the fiery depths of hell because of his natural urges. So let's dismiss this foolish notion of hell and damnation, shall we?"

The old priest continued, "What happened to you is natural, and something that's going to happen again and again. Someday you'll fall in love, and that's when it will all begin to make sense. Sex with a person you love is the closest thing we'll ever experience to the ecstasy of heavenly grace." He paused. "But there's a lot to know and a lot to understand about sex, Chris. I urge you to talk with your father about the new feelings you're experiencing. He may not be eager to talk about it, but he'll give you the information you need. It's a father's right and responsibility to explain these things, not really something an old, blind priest should try to do."

Monsignor Daley cleared his throat, and he gripped Chris's hand tighter. "Now, the matter of your confession—that is an old priest's responsibility to discuss. You must understand that evil wears many masks in this world. It might be a beautiful woman, it might be an elderly person … it might even hide behind a priest's collar. You must always be on guard, always be watchful for evil in the world around you. Last week you heard the voice of evil in the confessional, and I think you realized it. As I said the day you were baptized—you were born to fight against evil, Christopher Murphy, which is both your gift from God and a heavy burden to bear. Now here is what you must do …"

The next Saturday, Chris waited outside the confessional at exactly five minutes before four o'clock. His heart pounded. He looked intently at the anguished face of Jesus on the cross over the altar and prayed that he had the strength to do the right thing.

At four o'clock sharp he knelt down inside the dark confessional box. It smelled of dust and furniture polish. His knees hurt as he shifted on the kneeler and waited. His mouth felt like sandpaper. He heard the screen slide open with a thud. He said nothing.

The voice on the other side was the same as last week. "Ah, good, it's you again, my son. Let us begin where we left off from last week's confession."

Chris cleared his throat. His trembling voice was barely a whisper. "I have to confess that I didn't recognize the voice of evil until it was too late—and it was your voice, Father. You had no right to shame me and ask me to tell you stories that are a disgrace to this church. You had no right to use my embarrassment for your own pleasure."

"Stop right there. How dare you …" The voice was shrill and frightened.

Chris's voice grew louder and stronger until he was almost shouting. "I told another priest, a good priest, about your perverted questions and I hope he calls the bishop, but you better not ever treat anyone the way you treated me ever again or I swear to God …"

"Help, help, this boy is threatening me!" the priest screamed as he bolted from the confessional and ran from the church.

The other parishioners awaiting confession glared at him, but Chris walked slowly out of the church. He was still trembling, but he was intensely proud.

Now, however, his life felt like a bit of a confusing mess. He needed both an anchor and a lighthouse. Chris wished he could seek out Monsignor Daley's wisdom again, but the old priest had passed away many years ago. Maybe the church was worth another try. Many things had changed since his boyhood days. Church leaders seemed to be much more watchful for those who would victimize children. And when he thought about the good things he learned from Monsignor Daley and the nuns at St. Patrick's, he was willing to return to the church. Perhaps Holy Rosary might provide the stability and support that Ronnie needed at this difficult point in her young life, in both of their lives.

After almost three full weeks, Ronnie seemed very happy at the school. Although Chris was concerned about all the time she spent alone with Brother Adelard after school, his fears soon evaporated when he heard her talk about how much she enjoyed her time with the old priest. In fact he was almost ashamed of himself for harboring doubts about Brother Adelard. Chris was pleased with everything he saw at Holy Rosary—provided they didn't expel her from the after-school program because her father was late almost every afternoon.

Now as he walked past the deserted classrooms and inhaled the aroma of crayons and chalk dust, a flood of memories came back to him: Sister Dolorosa's round, smiling face wreathed by the white veil of her habit, thick squares of chewy pizza in the cafeteria, Nora Dougherty in her plaid jumper sneaking a kiss in the coatroom.

"Daddy, Daddy!" The giggle of a little girl jolted him back to the present, and he just had time to bend down and catch Ronnie in his arms before she barreled into him. In her little white sweater, plaid skirt, and sturdy black shoes, she was the picture of a Catholic schoolgirl, and when she looked up at him, the radiance of her smiling pink cheeks and the sparkle of her deep blue eyes melted his heart.

"I'm so happy to see you, angel. It's been a really, really long day," he said as he scooped her up into his arms.

"I'm glad to see you, too, Daddy," Ronnie whispered as she gave him an extra firm hug.

For an instant, Chris savored the sweet fragrance of her hair and the light puff of her breath on his cheek. He didn't notice the presence of another person until the soft rattle of rosary beads drew his attention.

"Oh, good afternoon, Brother Adelard," Chris said with a tinge of embarrassment. "I didn't even see you standing there."

"I quite understand, Christopher," the tall, thin man replied. He seemed to belong to a bygone time in his full black cassock and white clerical collar. His thin gray hair was meticulously combed back, revealing a high patrician forehead that sloped into an angular, distinguished nose, giving him an almost exaggerated air of dignity befitting a professor or a diplomat.

"If God had blessed me with a daughter as delightful as Veronique, I should have difficulty taking my eyes off her for a second." Brother Adelard's words were crafted slowly with elegance. His voice had the trace of an accent, which Chris could not quite place. "As it is, I am thankful that I am able to spend a few moments with her each afternoon. Today she was my companion for a stroll in the courtyard and collected a beautiful bouquet of the last daisies of summer for me. Would you like to come see my bouquet?" The long, black rosary beads around his waist rattled again as he gestured down the hallway.

Before Chris could reply, the brother gestured with up-turned hands, "Ah, silly old fool that I am, of course you are eager to get home." Chris noticed that his deep-set blue eyes sparkled in the late afternoon sunshine.

"Yes, Brother, it's late and I want you to know how deeply I appreciate your willingness to stay after school and watch Ronnie. As soon as I get better settled at the power plant—" But Chris's words were cut short.

"I'm sure I can't begin to imagine the cross you bear as a working man and a single father," Brother Adelard interrupted, holding up a thin white hand. "Veronique brings sunshine into my day, and I rejoice that I am able to do the Lord's work in a small way by helping to ease your burden." He then turned away with a wave of his hand. "Enough of this talk. Go home and enjoy this lovely evening."

The brother's long cassock nearly reached the floor, and it occurred to Chris that he almost floated, rather than walked, into the darkness at the other end of the hallway.

"How about pizza tonight?" he asked after he gave Ronnie a quick peck on the cheek.

"That sounds great, Daddy."

Later that week, after Chris had finished washing the dishes and Ronnie was getting ready for bed, his cell phone buzzed and an unfamiliar number came up on his screen. He answered out of curiosity with the faint hope that it was Mimi.

"Well, hello, sweetie," a cheerful woman's voice said. "I've been waiting to hear from you, and I just got tired of waiting."

"Uh, who is this?" Chris replied, quite prepared to hang up in an instant.

"This is Monique Gallagher. You know, that hot little real estate agent who showed you the apartment. I'm sure you remember, honey," she insisted with a giggle.

"Oh, of course, how are you?" he asked, but he wasn't sure he really cared.

"Well, I'm just great, thanks for asking," she purred. "I was just checking in on one of my favorite clients to see how you're settling in."

"Things are just great," Chris replied curtly, eager to get on with the bedtime routine. "Thanks for calling."

"I'm also calling to invite you over to the annual Chamber of Commerce Casino Night at the American Legion on Friday," Monique blurted out before he could hang up, like she had experience with people hanging up on her. "Remember I promised to introduce you to folks in town, and I'm a gal who always keeps her promises."

Before Chris could think of a way to politely refuse, she quickly continued.

"It will be a great way for you to network with the Ashton Falls business community," she continued in a softer voice, "and I know you're a single dad who needs to arrange childcare for that sweet little daughter of yours. I'm a single mom and have been for years, so I know these things. Well, I arranged for my aunt, your landlady, Jeanine Brisebois, to take care of little Sunny—isn't that her name?—so you can come have fun with me on Friday night."

All Chris could say was, "Ronnie, her name is Ronnie."

"Oh yeah, Ronnie," Monique continued. "Well, then it's settled. I'll see you at the American Legion on Friday at eight-ish." Then she added in a throaty whisper, "And I promise you'll have a real good time. Remember, I'm a girl who always keeps her promises. See you on Friday, sweetie."

When Jeanine came up with some freshly baked muffins the following night, Chris tried to politely refuse her Friday night babysitting services, but the old woman would hear none of it.

"Goodness, Mr. Murphy, I've been looking for a chance to spend some time with just us girls. You men get in the way sometimes." Jeanine's smile faded and she looked at him over her reading glasses. "Besides, you're a young man who needs to get out with other adults socially every now and then, or you'll become a hermit."

Chris started to protest, but the old woman dismissed him with a wave of her hand. "I raised two boys by myself, and I know how lonely it can get without adult company. Now, Monique may not be your ideal date, and you'd be wise not to let her get her claws into you. But, for goodness sake, just go out on Friday night, meet some young people like yourself, have a few drinks, and enjoy yourself."

There was no way Chris could argue.

Chapter 4

FRIDAY AFTERNOON MARKED the end of a very long workweek. As Chris was packing up his laptop for the weekend, Peggy, his secretary, came into his office to review Monday's appointments. Once they had gone over the calendar, Peggy glanced at him a bit sheepishly and asked, "Do you have anything special planned for the weekend?"

Chris looked at her suspiciously and said with a sigh, "As a matter of fact, I'm going to Casino Night at the American Legion tonight. Why do you ask?"

Peggy couldn't hold it in any longer and giggled as she asked, "Is it true that you're taking Monique Gallagher?"

"I might be meeting her there," Chris replied cautiously. "All right, Peggy, what's up?"

"Okay," she replied quickly. "Unique Monique has been telling everybody all over town that she's dating the new power plant manager. Now, I don't know much about your taste in women, but she isn't exactly the kind of girl you take home to meet mother. One might say she ... gets around."

Chris smiled. "Thanks for your dating advice and concern, Peggy, but I can assure you I'm a big boy and I can take care of myself. Besides, I don't have time for a passionate love affair this weekend—I have to do the laundry and go grocery shopping. Now, you have a great weekend yourself, and don't worry about me."

Once Peggy was out of earshot, he looked out the window and muttered, "Shit, what have I gotten myself into?"

The parking lot in front of the Ashton Falls American Legion was full by the time Chris arrived on Friday night. He somehow managed to find parking on a side street and hiked a block or two over to the one-story brick building.

The sound system was blaring full blast and smoke hung thick in the air, because, as a private club, this was one of the few drinking establishments in which you could still light up in the state of Maine. As he stepped into the hall, Monique clattered across the floor on her high heels and threw her arms around him. "Oh, Christopher, I'm so glad you're here," she gushed. "Come on, there are so many people I want to introduce you to."

The mingled scent of stale cigarette smoke, alcohol, and too much perfume hit him as his eyes adjusted to the dim light and he took a long look at Monique. She was wearing a fitted green satin blouse unbuttoned to reveal the cleft where her breasts were squeezed and lifted by unseen forces clearly designed to achieve exactly that effect. Somehow she had been poured into the tightest white pants he had ever seen, and he wondered how long the process must have taken. The hand that grasped his arm so tightly was tipped with five long, shiny green nails, one of which had a false diamond set into it. He looked up into her smiling face and noticed her deep red, shimmering lips and heavy green eye shadow offset by an orangish, twinkling complexion that must have been sprayed on and dusted with glitter.

Monique led him to the bar so he could get a cold beer and one more appletini for her. The fact that the bartender didn't even ask him what Monique was drinking before he served it up wasn't a particularly reassuring sign.

Monique then led Chris over to the roulette table where she proudly presented him to her friends. First there was Alfred Thompson, of the Thompson Insurance Agency, whose wrinkled face looked much older than his jet-black, swept-back hair and pencil mustache. Then Chris met Emily and Peter Sullivan, the owners of Sully's Tavern. Peter, a good-natured, balding fellow in his early sixties was pleasant enough, but Emily, who was sheathed in a silver cocktail dress that matched her hairdo, looked like she wanted to devour Chris. And then there was Fred "Last Chance" Lachance of Fred's Buick-Oldsmobile who immediately cut to the chase and tried to sell him a new Sebring convertible. She introduced him to everyone as "Christopher Murphy, from New York City, the principal engineer at the power plant," as if she had carefully rehearsed it and despite Chris's repeated requests that she just refer to him as "Chris."

They made the rounds of the gaming tables and played for a few dollars here and there, meeting business owners and public officials as they went. When Chris won, Monique hooted and hollered like a high-school cheerleader. All the while, she clung to his arm or draped herself on his shoulder as if she were afraid he might escape. At one point, Chris firmly removed her hand from his ass, which, thankfully, wasn't repeated. At first he found this unsolicited female affection kind of ego-affirming, but it soon became annoying, and eventually it was downright disturbing.

"Oh, look, there's our town manager," Monique gushed. "You have to meet him." She grabbed Chris's arm and tugged him over to the blackjack table, where she tapped a burly middle-aged man on the shoulder. The man looked up with what Chris thought was a sneer, clearly unhappy with his hand of cards, or the interruption, or both.

"Big Bill, this is Christopher Murphy from New York, the new principal engineer at the power plant," Monique said. "Christopher, this is our town manager and local legend Bill Benson."

Big Bill stood and took the cigar out of his mouth, exhaling in Chris's direction. As he stood up, Chris realized how the town manager earned his nickname. He was over six feet tall and, although he was probably in his fifties, he projected strength, power, and intimidation. Big Bill sported a flattop, and Chris thought he detected a bit of hair dye. Big Bill quickly sized him up from head to toe without changing his expression. Then he squeezed Chris's hand in a viselike grip and forced a smile.

"Ah, yes, I've been waiting to meet you," Big Bill bellowed over the noise in the hall. "I have a business proposal for you. I think you'll be interested. Call me some time and we'll set up a golf afternoon before it gets too cold," he said in a manner that seemed more like an order than an invitation. "Now, if you'll excuse me, I need to get back to breaking the bank." Big Bill jammed the cigar back into his mouth and picked up his cards, in effect dismissing Chris and Monique.

Chris was somewhat relieved when Monique recommended that they take a break from the gaming tables and the social introductions. When they were far enough away from the sound system, which was blaring "God Bless the U.S.A." for at least the third time, she stopped and faced him.

"I hope you're having a good time, sugar."

Chris assured her that he was. He was a pretty good liar when he needed to be.

"Well, you know, this is the biggest gathering of the best people in Ashton Falls that you'll see this season," she informed him.

Chris nodded but wondered if he might enjoy a gathering of the worst people in Ashton Falls a little bit more.

Monique's tone shifted as she fiddled with a button on his shirt. "Just remember, we can have an even better time later on if you're a good boy … or maybe even if you're a bad boy. Now, why don't you get me another drink while I freshen up?" He watched as she strutted unsteadily toward the ladies' room and clearly knew that her exaggerated swaying hips were for his benefit.

Chris waved to the bartender, and silently another appletini and bottle of beer appeared on the counter as Chris laid down a twenty-dollar bill. He looked around the bar area. It was lit from a dozen or so sooty bar lights that proclaimed the wonders of Budweiser, Miller, and even Schlitz, which hadn't made a local appearance in years. Here and there the dark paneled walls were dotted with yellowed newspaper clippings and plaques that announced homecomings, medal presentations, or funerals.

He didn't really notice an older man in an olive drab Army jacket at the other end of the bar until the old man began to cough convulsively as he staggered off his bar stool and sagged onto the floor. Chris raced over and helped the man to his feet. He could feel his bones through the worn material of the Army jacket.

Placing him securely on the bar stool, Chris said reassuringly, "There you go, sir. Can I get you anything?"

The man took a swig of his beer, looked at Chris directly with surprisingly clear eyes, and said, "Sir? It's been a long time since anybody called me that. Are you a veteran?"

"No," Chris stated. "Are you sure you're okay?"

The old man smiled, revealing a missing front tooth. He thrust his shaky right hand toward Chris. "Pardon my manners. Thank you, friend, for coming to my assistance. I'm not as healthy as I once was." Then he straightened up and added with an air of formality, "Truman Stiles, and to whom might I be speaking?"

Chris shook the frail hand, careful not to squeeze too tightly. "Chris Murphy. Pleased to meet you, Mr. Stiles."

"Well, Mr. Murphy, pardon my appearance, but I am a one-hundred-percent, Purple Heart-wearing, disabled Vietnam veteran." The old man announced as if launching into a prepared speech. "Believe it or not, I am a proud graduate of the United

States Military Academy at West Point and a former captain in the United States Army airborne infantry," he said with a touch of irony as he patted two small rusty bars on the shoulder of his jacket. "Then one day I found myself up in the central highlands of Vietnam, where a Viet Cong mortar round found me."

"That must have been awful for you and your family," Chris replied awkwardly.

"I guess shit happens for a reason," the old man said as he took another gulp from his beer. "When they finished putting all the pieces of me back together as best they could at Walter Reed, they sent me back home to Ashton Falls." He looked up at Chris. "You're new in town?"

Chris nodded.

"It's a good place as small towns go. I hope you like it here." Then the old man's voice lowered. "The funny thing is that when I got home after 'Nam, I realized that I saw things, and heard things, and felt things differently from other people. Sometimes I could see what was coming." He grasped Chris's arm. "I know that sounds crazy, but I knew the Red Sox would win the Series in 2002. I told everybody the Patriots had the Super Bowl at least three months ahead of time in 2016, in spite of the Brady suspension. And I had a real funny feeling, almost panic, on the morning of September 11, 2001."

Chris felt sorry for this poor, old veteran, but he wasn't really buying his claim of special sight, so he replied as sincerely as possible, "What a special gift."

"Sometimes it's not such a gift." The old man gulped his beer and wiped his mouth. "I've lived here most of my life.

It's a good place. It's my home. But I can tell you there's been something bad, something nasty, hanging like a shroud over this town for the past few months."

The old man continued, "Sometimes I can't sleep inside. The walls and ceiling close in like a coffin, and I can hear the whine of that mortar round just before it detonated. Then I go down to the train station and watch the train go by. I like the rumbling and the thought that it's taking people far away to places they dream of. I like to lie down under the Maine Street bridge and doze off to sleep as I think of the places that train could take me." The old man coughed hard into his sleeve. "But lately I feel something dark and dangerous down there, almost like the feeling I got that day before I got blown to pieces. As sure as I'm here talking to you, I know there's something wicked hovering around that train station."

He took another gulp from his beer. "Unless that train takes the evil with it someday, or somebody finds it and stamps it out, I can feel bad things coming."

Chris thought he felt the room grow colder as he stammered, "I'm sorry you feel that way. I hope things change soon for you."

The old man grasped his arm with a surprisingly firm grip, looked him in the eye, and said, "I didn't tell you this to scare you away from town. I can see you're a good man and a good father who's trying to do his best for his daughter. Just be careful is all I'm saying."

"Hey, where's my appletini and my handsome date?" Monique's shrill voice distracted the old veteran momentarily.

For the first time that evening, Chris was actually glad to see her. He said good-bye to the old man, shook his hand once more, and quickly crossed the room to where Monique stood with her hands on her hips. He scooped up her drink from the bar and handed it to her. He couldn't help but notice that her eyelids were a little brighter green, her lips were considerably shinier, and her skin was a deeper shade of orange.

"I hope you weren't hitting on any other girls out here while I was gone," she said as she carefully sipped her drink, ensuring that her lipstick wasn't smeared.

"No, I was talking with my new friend Truman over there," Chris replied, thinking that if there were any other eligible ladies in the bar, he would have been gone by now.

"You mean that old drunk at the end of the bar?" she blurted out, loud enough for anyone in the bar to hear. The appletinis were clearly taking their toll on Monique's powers of discretion. "He hasn't had a sensible conversation with anyone in the past ten years."

"That's a pretty rotten thing to say. That guy nearly gave his life for this country and you make fun of him?" This was the final straw. Chris could feel the anger welling up inside. He drained his beer and brought the empty bottle down with a pronounced thud. "I think it's time for me to head home. I have a lot to do tomorrow." He turned to leave.

"Hey, now, I'm sorry if I was rude, sweetie. Sometimes I shoot my mouth off when I shouldn't," Monique said in her sweetest voice as she reached for Chris's arm.

Chris stopped and turned toward her.

"I've had a few too many drinks tonight to be safe on the roads if I have to drive myself home. Can you give me a lift?" she asked, batting her false eyelashes. Then she added with a pout, "Besides, it's your fault for buying me all those delicious appletinis."

Chris was trapped. All he could do was tell her to get her jacket and purse. They walked to his car as she prattled on and on about this person and that and all the dirt about them she could muster. Several times she teetered on her stiletto heels, forcing him to take her arm for safety. He wondered if she really was drunk or just playing the part.

Chris opened the door for Monique when they reached his car. As she settled into the passenger seat, she suddenly made a sour face, reached behind her, and pulled a doll's hairbrush from under her rear end. Not realizing that Chris was watching, she scowled and threw it on the floor, then resumed her drunken grin.

The drive to her house was about three miles long, but to Chris, it seemed like hours. The gossip now turned to interrogation as clearly pointed questions oozed out of Monique in her silkiest voice.

"How long has it been since you and your wife were together?"

"Did you date a lot of girls when you were in college? How many? Did you like the blondes, or brunettes, or maybe even redheads, best?"

"What's the craziest place you've ever done it in?"

"How old were you the first time you ever did it? Who was it with?"

"What's the sexiest movie you've ever seen?"

"If you could sleep with any celebrity, who would it be?"

Chris did his best to dodge the questions, but after asking each one, Monique provided her own answers, which she intended as an erotic turn-on, but they only made Chris drive faster. Finally they arrived at a modest, but very neat, two-story cape in a new housing development.

As Chris yanked up the parking brake, Monique leaned across the console and reached for him. Anticipating her move, and not wanting to get stuck in the car with her, he quickly shut off the engine and stepped out of the car. He helped her out of the passenger seat and, once again, she wobbled on her high heels.

"Please help me up the front stairs, honey, won't you?" she pleaded.

Chris reluctantly obliged. She giggled and leaned against him as they made their way to her front door. He turned his head away from her to avoid the sour smell of alcohol on her breath. Chris reached for the door to open it for her and felt her hand firmly grasp his belt buckle. Her other hand reached down and stroked the front of his pants with slowly increasing pressure.

"I think it's time we stopped fooling each other," she whispered. "I want you and I can feel that you want me, too." Chris couldn't contain the bulge in his pants, and he couldn't tear himself away as she continued to stroke his stiffening crotch.

She continued in her low, silky voice. "Come on inside and I'll show you some things you've never seen before, lover boy.

And if that isn't enough for you, I'll do anything you ask me to do—I mean anything. And remember, I'm a girl who keeps her promises."

Chris could feel his plan to cut and run dissolve as Monique ran her hand up and down the fabric of his trousers that barely contained his erect penis. Suddenly that part of his anatomy was overriding the warning voices in his head and his better judgment.

Just as Chris was about to succumb and give in to Monique, the porch light came on, the front door swung open, and a pudgy teenage face appeared, wreathed in wild, curly brown hair.

"Hey, mom," the teenager bellowed. "A guy named Brian Sargent has been leaving messages for you all night. He says he needs to know right away if the Johnsons are going to take his offer or not. Hey, who's that guy?"

Monique turned and shrieked in a voice that would shatter glass, "I told you to be in bed by eleven o'clock and not to come downstairs for any reason. Now get up to your room and don't come down until tomorrow morning. I'll deal with you then." She quickly regained her composure and turned back to Chris, but it was too late.

Chris had used the interruption to regain his senses and scamper down the front stairs to his car. As he got into the driver's seat he called, "Good night, Monique, thanks for the good time."

Once he was on his way home, he thought, Wow, that was close. I could have ended up in bed with that desperate woman.

He shuddered and resolved to be more careful in the future. As he drove, he thought about the people he met and found himself wondering about the old veteran. There was something wise and likeable about him, although he was obviously a little bit crazy. Still, it was nice of him to say that Chris was a good man and a good father who's trying to do his best for his daughter, but could he actually sense the future?

Suddenly Chris realized that he had never said anything to the old man about his family.

Chapter 5

THE OLD MAN turned down sports talk radio as he heard the front door close. The conversation about the latest Red Sox player trade was interesting, but he had other things in mind. Tonight was bowling night for the men's Bible-study group, so the owner of the journal would be away for at least two hours. The old man had often thought about what the rest of the journal contained during the past few days. Although he was keenly aware that he was prying into another's private life, he couldn't resist his curiosity. More and more he found his imagination turning toward the contents of the journal as he waited for his chance to learn more about how this strange story was connected to Holy Rosary Parish.

He rose from the recliner, stretched his back, and tiptoed into the other person's bedroom. All was neat and orderly, so it took a few minutes of searching through the desk drawers before he found the leather satchel with the journal inside. With eager but careful hands, he turned the pages until he found where he had left off reading.

"The little boy grew up strong, bright, and precocious. He was adored by his doting grandparents and his devoted mother. When he was home, his father took him for long hikes in the woods and thrilled him with stories of brave knights, ancient armies, and the past glories of the Germanic people.

But as the tide of war began to turn against the fatherland, the leadership of the SS became impatient for results from the Ahnenerbe. Several times Major Bachman was summoned to Berlin to appear before Himmler himself to report on the progress of his investigations. The major's superiors made it quite clear that, unless his section produced results soon, he would be reassigned to an SS infantry unit. Knowing that he would be of greater service to the fatherland as a scholar than as a combat leader, Major Bachman increased his efforts to uncover long-forgotten religious practices and employed unique, more direct research techniques. He traveled farther and farther from home for longer periods of time, leaving his young wife and little son behind.

Major Bachman investigated every piece of information that he could glean from Gestapo interrogation reports, which led to interviews with all types of traitors, degenerates, and criminals across Europe. The major's travels brought him to the internment camp at Struthof, where a heretic monk who had aided the Resistance was brought to him. During the Gestapo's initial interrogation, the monk had hinted that he was aware of secret religious practices but had been unable, or unwilling, to elaborate before he lost consciousness.

Major Bachman began by trying to reason with the heretic, but the man insisted that he knew nothing. The major attempted to be kind and reasonable, offering cigarettes, extra rations, even special quarters in the camp. But still the stubborn monk professed ignorance of any special religious practices. With regret, Major Bachman discretely exited the questioning room as he instructed his driver to persuade the traitor to be more cooperative. The major hummed to himself to drown out the sound of thuds and curses and cries that echoed through the halls. When all was silent, he returned to the questioning room to find the monk tied to a chair, his robes torn, blood running down his face, one purple eye swollen shut. Major Bachman wiped the traitor's face with his handkerchief, offered him a cup of water, and instructed the driver to carefully write down everything the man said.

The monk told Major Bachman that he had been the caretaker of the library at the cathedral at Aachen, where he had become interested in the history of the church in medieval times. While reading a ninth-century manuscript, he learned of a German monk named Karl of Rothenburg who was alleged to have special powers to punish sinners and vanquish the enemies of the church. The text described a ritual involving a sacred book, a holy relic, and the blood of innocents. According to other chronicles of the time, Karl of Rothenburg fled from Germany to Austria in advance of the invading Huns. Although the priest couldn't be sure, he believed that the ancient book describing the ritual could be found in a monastery in Austria, provided it had been safeguarded through the intervening centuries.

Major Bachman pushed his driver to travel around the clock as they raced from Germany to Austria. After fruitlessly visiting several monastic libraries throughout Austria, he eventually arrived in Salzburg and located our monastery on a plateau high above the Salz River. Dusk was settling after a drizzly autumn afternoon when the major and his driver climbed the stairs to the monastery. The driver pounded the butt of his pistol on the heavy oaken door of the outer courtyard and commanded us to open the door in a harsh shout. I was saying my evening prayers in the garden among the wilted stalks of the sunflowers when I heard the noise. I was the first to reach the door. As I unlatched it and swung it open, I found the barrel of a pistol thrust into my face. It was held by a brutish-looking thug dressed in a gray wool uniform with a scowl on his face.

Perhaps it was utter surprise or perhaps it was the inspiration of the Holy Ghost, but I reached up, grasped the pistol barrel in my hand, and said, "Put that away, friend, you are among your countrymen and brothers here." I then saw a figure wrapped in a long black leather coat with the collar pulled up and the brim of his black uniform hat almost riding on the bridge of his nose. Oddly enough, the officer smiled, then barked,

"Put away your pistol, idiot. We are not barbarians." Then he tugged off his gray kid gloves, extended his hand, and said, "I am Major Gerhard Bachman of the SS. Whom do I have the honor of addressing?"

After introducing myself, I escorted the major and his driver to the abbot's quarters and, in keeping with my station within the order, I withdrew to the dining hall for my evening meal. Although we usually observe a ritual of silence during our communal meals, I was besieged with whispered questions from my fellow monks.

"What are they doing here?"

"Is it true they threatened to shoot you?"

"Have they come to take over the monastery?"

Midway through my soup and bread, I was summoned to the abbot's study. The visitors were seated at the abbot's table and had just finished their evening meal. "Brother Siegfried, I assume you have met Major Bachman and Corporal Schroeder," the abbot said, motioning me to a chair next to him.

"Major Bachman is a scholar of medieval religious practices," the abbot continued. "He has asked to examine our library of ancient texts. I have granted my permission for him to remain with us as our guest and to study for as long as he wishes. He is a fellow Catholic and an officer of the fatherland and, as such, he is our brother and protector. I ask that you serve as his guide and companion during his time with us. Please ensure that he is comfortable and that he has access to all texts and manuscripts in our library."

I muttered my assent, bowed to the abbot, and motioned for the visitors to follow me to the guest quarters.

Our work began in earnest before dawn the next morning. Much to my surprise, Major Bachman appeared at mass in the chapel with our community of brothers. He was carefully dressed in his spotless black uniform with the polished leather belt and black boots. I noticed that his Latin pronunciation was perfect as he responded to the priest's prayers. I offered to have his breakfast brought to his quarters, but he insisted on sharing our meager fare of coarse brown bread and strong black tea at the long table with the brothers.

After breakfast, we descended the circular stairs to the lowest level of the ancient stone structure where the library was located. Because it is the repository of the monastery's most precious treasures, the library was housed in the place within the monastery that would be defended with the very lives of the monks. I lit several kerosene lanterns and heard the major gasp when he saw the thousands of dusty, spiderweb-covered books, manuscripts, and scrolls. I showed him the index to the volumes and proceeded to gather the texts that he requested from the shelves where they hadn't been touched for centuries.

The major said very little as he pored over each book or manuscript, and I could tell from his expression and the way he cast the texts aside when he was done that he wasn't finding what he was seeking. The second day proceeded very much like the first until, while we were eating our cold sausage and bread at lunch, I asked, "What is it exactly that you're looking for, Major? Perhaps I could help you find it." But he just looked at me, smiled in a sad way, and said, "Thank you, Brother, but I'll know it when I find it." With that, he continued to scan the texts that I brought. I asked him again as we finished our work on the second day, but he reassured me that he didn't need my help.

As noon approached on the third day, I could see that the major was becoming irritable in one moment and despondent in the next. He had removed his uniform jacket and belt, loosened his tie, and cradled his head in his hands as he examined the fiftieth or sixtieth text I had brought him. Finally he slammed the book shut and pounded his fist on it as he covered his face with his hands and sobbed. I reached across the table and placed my hand gently on his head. "Please let me help you, my friend," I whispered.

He uncovered his face and looked at me intently for a long moment. Then he said, "If I tell you something, Brother, can I ask that you keep it secret? Just as if I told you in the darkness of the confessional, can I trust you to tell no one?"

I thought for a moment and pondered his question. Although this wasn't a confession, I reasoned that I would still be bound by the rule of secrecy. I nodded

P. G. Smith

to the major and promised that I would not reveal what
he was about to tell me."

Just then, the doorbell rang, and the old man was jolted from
his reading. Oh, Lord, it must be someone looking for a mass
card or something, he thought.

"I'm coming, please be patient," he called out, barely hiding his annoyance. He quickly replaced the satchel and journal,
but as he hurried to answer the door, he didn't notice that a
small pencil had fallen from the desk drawer and now lay on
the carpet.

⇥⬛ ⬛⬸

Saturday was Ronnie's favorite day of the week. She could
sleep as long as she wanted to and when the sunshine peeked
through her window, she could pull the puffy pink quilt up
over her head and snuggle in forever with her favorite doll.
On Saturday she would hear her dad singing old songs in the
kitchen while he made chocolate-chip pancakes for her. He
wasn't such a good singer, but he sure knew how to cook great
pancakes. When he was finished cooking, he'd tiptoe into her
room, pull the covers away from her face, and whisper, "Rise
and shine, my princess, a new day awaits you." Then he'd tickle
her until at least one of them tumbled off the bed onto the
floor.

On Saturday Ronnie didn't think about her mom as much
as she did on a regular day, when sometimes she'd cry in the

early morning darkness but wipe her tears away on her sheets before her dad could see that she'd been crying. She knew it wasn't wrong to cry. It was just that she didn't like the way her dad looked when she cried. He looked so sad, it was almost like he wanted to cry too, even though he always scooped her up in his arms and hugged her tight and whispered, "Don't cry my sweet, sweet girl. Everything will be okay." She just didn't ever want to see that sad look on his face.

It was an unwritten rule—on Saturday she could wear whatever clothes she wanted to wear and play with whatever toys she wanted to play with. Her dad said that she had to brush her teeth in the morning, but she didn't have to take a bath or even fix her hair if she didn't want to. Saturday belonged to Ronnie and her dad.

Chris also loved Saturdays for similar reasons, although he did choose to take a shower and comb his hair. True, most of the day was spent on the little time-consuming chores of life, like picking up the dry cleaning, taking the trash to the dump, and grocery shopping. But having Ronnie with him all day long made everything more bearable. Even nasty little tasks, like cleaning the toilet, became less distasteful when she was there to cheer him up or make him laugh.

They had just finished picking up the week's groceries at the supermarket, followed by their usual Saturday luncheon of cheeseburgers and fries at McDonald's, which reminded Chris that he really needed to find a gym soon. He noticed that Ronnie was unusually quiet as she stared out the window at something that clearly caught her attention. After a few moments she looked up at him and said, "You know what would make me happier than anything in the whole world, Daddy?"

Chris, quite aware that he was about to wade into dangerous waters, cast caution to the wind and asked, "What is it that would make you happy, honey?"

"If we could just go look at the kittens over there," Ronnie said, wearing what she believed to be her sweetest expression while pointing across the street. There on a ragged piece of cardboard tied to a tree were the words "Free Kittens" scrawled in purple crayon. "All we have to do is go over and look at them, Daddy. We wouldn't have to get one unless you wanted to. Can we please just go and look at them?"

Like a cod firmly hooked on a fishing line, Chris sighed, dumped the fast-food tray, and walked across the street with Ronnie, knowing full well that he was probably about to become a pet owner.

A half dozen fluffy little cats were crawling around on the front lawn of a two-story cottage that looked like someone had built themselves without the benefit of power tools. The herd of kittens was under the supervision of a red-haired girl missing her two front teeth who diligently carried out her task of keeping her charges out of the street. As Ronnie ran toward the kittens, a jet-black kitten scampered over to her and rubbed his downy tail against her ankles. She scooped him up and hugged him tight, his soft fur tickling her chin.

"Are the kittens really for free?" Ronnie asked the little girl with the red hair.

"Yup, Momma says we gotta get rid of all of 'em except one, and I like this one the best," she said, holding up a frisky calico that she had just plucked inches from the curb.

The two little girls chatted about the two kittens and then Ronnie turned to Chris as she hugged the squirming black cat a little tighter. "Please, Daddy, please can we take this little kitty home with us? I promise I'll take good care of him, and he's even free, so it won't cost you anything. Besides, Brother Adelard says that every child should have a pet. Oh, please, Daddy?"

Chris looked into his little girl's pleading blue eyes and knew that there was no way in the world that he could refuse her at this moment. He stroked her golden hair, petted the downy little kitten, and said, "If you promise to take good care of him, then okay."

Ronnie, clutching the kitten with one hand, reached up with the other and pulled Chris's face toward hers. She pressed her lips against his scratchy, unshaven cheek and gave him a big, smacking kiss. "I love you, Daddy," she blurted out as she rubbed her nose in the kitten's black fur.

Chris looked away for a second, then dug a twenty-dollar bill out of his pocket, which he stuffed into the red-haired girl's hand.

"Hey, Mister, these cats are free," she said with surprise.

"That's okay, you might need to buy some more cat food," he called as they walked away.

On the car ride home, Ronnie chatted away to her new kitten and repeatedly hugged him until Chris cautioned her that too much hugging might not be all that good for such a tiny cat.

"What are you going to name him?" Chris asked.

"Blackie, of course," replied Ronnie without looking up.

As Chris pulled into the driveway and Ronnie rolled up the back window, he detected a faint scent like a blend of ammonia and rotten eggs.

"Ronnie, did Blackie mess in the backseat?" he asked.

"Only a little bit, Dad," was her cautious reply.

He realized that perhaps he should have saved the twenty bucks for upholstery cleaner.

If the truth were known, Chris would rather sleep late on Sunday mornings and lounge around in his pajamas reading *The New York Times,* like he did in the city. But he had chosen to send Ronnie to a Catholic school, where religion was a daily subject, and going to church on Sunday was a big part of religion. He also realized that Ronnie was bright enough to detect hypocrisy and would probably make his life miserable if he lounged around all morning.

So he rolled out of bed early enough to get himself shaved, showered, and somewhat decently dressed for the nine o'clock mass at Holy Rosary Church. He walked out into the kitchen to find Ronnie sitting on the floor with Blackie on her lap. The kitten was mischievously clawing and biting the pink ribbon on the front of Ronnie's dress while the little girl pretended to scold him.

Chris remembered the day just last spring when Mimi had brought the dress home and Ronnie had been so delighted. He thought back for a moment to the Sundays that the three of them had spent together in Central Park, but then quickly reminded himself that the past was gone, just like his wife. Still, at least Ronnie had a mother back then—a woman in her life to help her pick out pretty dresses. Chris barely managed to keep her in underwear, school uniforms, and matching socks.

"It's time to go or we'll be late, princess," he said gently.

"Okay, Dad, but can we take Blackie to church with us?" she asked.

"I don't think that God would like to have a kitten in church, honey, do you?"

"Brother Adelard says that God loves all his creatures. Can't we just try it and see if he can sit still?" she pleaded.

"No, I'm afraid not," he said firmly. "Besides, the backseat still stinks from Blackie's last car ride. Now get your slicker, it's kind of drizzly outside."

Ronnie obediently set the kitten down on the floor and went to the closet for her shiny yellow raincoat. She had done pretty well this weekend, but she also knew when her dad meant business.

Chris drove to church slowly with his headlights on because of the thick fog that enshrouded the deserted streets. Familiar buildings and trees turned into gray forms lurking in the mist as the Volvo crept down the roads.

As he walked up the wide granite front stairs, Chris glanced up at the steeple that topped the old gothic church. He was surprised that he couldn't see the ornate gold cross on top, and he shivered in the cool damp of the early morning.

It was good to get inside the church where soft candlelight cast a warm glow over the worshipers and organ music played softly in the background. Ronnie waved to Jeanine Brisebois, who was racing through the prayers of a quick rosary before mass on a set of silver beads that matched her freshly coifed hair. They chose an empty pew in front of her and sat down, drinking in the quiet and the faint aroma of incense. Ronnie turned to Jeanine and said, "Bonjour, Grand-mère," at which the old woman smiled and patted her gently on the cheek.

"Where did you learn that?" Chris asked in a whisper.

"Brother Adelard is teaching me French," Ronnie replied proudly.

Chris looked around the old church as he waited for mass to begin. The ornate carved wood interior was at least a hundred years old and had turned a deep brown over time. The massive stained-glass windows reflected saints and angels in brilliant reds and blues, with the names of prosperous Ashton Falls families of another time displayed underneath on discrete brass plaques. Chris wondered if the donors found themselves in heaven today, or not.

Because the pews were not even half full, when the priest and the altar boys made their entrance, they seemed to grow smaller and smaller as they walked up into the cavernous altar where a sorrowful Jesus looked down on them from his massive cross. Father Costello turned to the congregation, welcomed them, and began the opening prayers.

Father Costello was a stocky, energetic man in his mid-sixties, whom Chris had met shortly after Ronnie began attending school. He had impressed Chris as a good guy right from the start.

Chris recalled the first time they met. The old priest was working out in the rectory garden when Chris approached him and asked where he could find the school's main office. Father Costello straightened his faded blue baseball cap and peered at Chris from behind thick glasses. Then he began the interview.

"They say you're the new power plant manager from New York City. Is that right?" asked the priest with a twinkle in his eye.

"That's right, Father. I just moved up to Ashton Falls with my daughter. That's actually why I need to find the school—"

"Mets or Yankees?" Father Costello shot back quickly.

"Uh, excuse me, Father, neither. I was actually born and raised in South Boston," Chris replied.

"Good, then are you prepared to swear allegiance to the Boston Red Sox, Curt Shilling's bloody sock, Fenway Park, Ted Williams's bat, and all that is holy and good in the baseball world?" the priest asked with mock solemnity.

Finally catching on, Chris replied with an emphatic "I do so swear."

"Then I welcome you to Ashton Falls, Maine, and Holy Rosary Parish," the priest said, while blessing Chris in an exaggerated way. "It's a good thing you're not a Yankees fan or I'd send you packing out to St. Michael's Parish up in Bangor."

Chris didn't know Father Costello all that well, but he could detect that the priest was preoccupied this morning. He seemed to be rattling off the prayers of the mass in a perfunctory manner and frequently made errors as he read. Maybe it's the weather, Chris thought. I suppose even priests can get the blues.

When the congregation took their seats for the sermon, Father Costello chose to read a letter from the bishop about the upcoming fund-raising campaign. As he read, he mopped his brow, although it was quite damp and chilly in the church. At the end of the letter, he took off his glasses and looked out into the congregation as his voice took on a low, somber tone.

"Our readings today remind us that we are surrounded by evil. We may even find it raising its ugly head in the most unexpected places, wearing the most unlikely costumes. Evil may hide in a business, or a school, or even a church. It can wear a policeman's uniform, a suit and tie, or a mother's apron."

Father Costello paused as he scanned the congregation. "The psalm we heard earlier carried a warning to be wary, as well as the promise of the good Lord's protection. The Good Shepherd tells us, 'Yeah, though I walk in the Valley of Death, I shall fear no evil for you are at my side.' We must always remember that there is evil all around us, yes, even here in a lovely town like our own Ashton Falls. But we must also trust in our Savior, the Good Shepherd Jesus Christ to protect us from the most vicious evil in the darkest moments, and we must pray that each day He will deliver us from evil. Because if we do not have His love and protection, we are lost, my brothers and sisters, truly lost."

At that the old priest closed his eyes and prayed silently for several moments before putting his glasses back on and resuming the mass.

Wow, I guess he's having a really bad day, Chris thought.

Just like when he was a child at mass, his attention started to wander after the sermon. He looked down at Ronnie and their smiles met. She turned back to watching the priest—clearly doing a better job of paying attention than her father. Chris noticed a man's toupee three pews in front of him and couldn't help staring at the line high on his neck where the brown synthetic hair decidedly did not blend with the natural gray hair underneath. Chris heard a baby crying in outrage to his right and concluded that the infant was understandably indignant at being dragged out on a miserable morning like this. As he glanced over toward the baby, his eyes settled on the long brown hair of a young woman in a tan trench coat sitting just to his right. He noticed that she was very pretty and very alone. Just then she turned, and her glance met his. He quickly looked away with considerable embarrassment, but glanced back to see that she was smiling, ever so slightly. He had seen her before somewhere and knew that he'd like to see her again. Checking out women in church, he chided himself - I will most certainly burn in hell.

Finally mass was over. Jeanine and Ronnie chatted as they filed out of church and stepped out into the fog together, but the old woman had to leave them to serve coffee in the parish hall. Ronnie grabbed Chris's hand and pointed. "There's Brother Adelard, Dad. Let's go over and say hello."

Chris spotted the brother at the far edge of the lawn in front of the church. Brother Adelard reached into his pocket and offered treats to two ferocious looking black dogs as he stooped to stroke their heads. Not wanting to take a chance on the friendliness of the dogs, Chris led Ronnie toward the car, saying, "I don't think this is a good time to interrupt Brother Adelard. Besides, Blackie will miss us and we need to finish up the weekend's chores." As if reminding himself, he added with a sigh, "Tomorrow is the beginning of another work week."

Chapter 6

"I GUESS IT'S no surprise that Casino Night at the American Legion wasn't exactly your idea of a great night out," Jeanine Brisebois said with a laugh as she sat at Chris's kitchen table.

Chris was washing dishes as he told her about his date at Casino Night. Needless to say, he left out a few details.

"Oh, the stories I could tell about some of the people you met, Christopher," she said as she sipped her tea.

"Speaking of people in town, was there something wrong with Father Costello at mass?" Chris asked, turning from the sink. "He seems like such a good guy, but he was in a bad way last Sunday."

"Well, if the truth be known, there's been no love lost between Father Costello and Brother Adelard ever since Adelard came down from Canada. At least that's what Alice O'Brien tells me, and she cleans the rectory twice a week," Jeanine reported with a knowing look. "Now God forgive me for speaking ill of one of His holy men, but I don't blame Father Costello for not liking that snooty, stuffed shirt of a brother. I know he watches little Ronnie for you after school, but there's something about him that just gives me a funny feeling, if you know what

I mean." Then she added with a chuckle, "I better be careful talking about a man of God like that, or something will strike me down." Despite her lightheartedness, the old woman then blessed herself and piously looked up to the ceiling.

Before Chris could speak up in Brother Adelard's defense, Ronnie burst through the door from the back porch clutching Blackie. "Daddy, Daddy, those two big dogs from down the street are in our yard, and they're trying to get Blackie."

Chris stepped out onto the porch where two menacing Dobermans, the dogs he saw at the church, looked up at him, growling expectantly. They clenched their sharp white fangs and glared at him with piercing black eyes. He waved his arms and shouted at the dogs until they eventually scampered away, looking back from time to time with fear and hatred. Chris made a mental note to find their owners and straighten this out before the dogs hurt somebody.

The canine crisis had diverted Jeanine from her news report, and she was now stroking Ronnie's hair. "I'm going down to Kittery tomorrow to get a head start on my holiday shopping. The Golden Age Club always takes a trip to the outlets there every fall after the tourists are gone. I get some great bargains for my boys' Christmas presents. By the way, I put a chicken pie in the oven. It should be ready in ten minutes or so," she said, pointing to the oven. "Well, time for me to go. I have to see *Wheel of Fortune* or my day isn't complete. And remember, I can babysit any time if you need to get out some night."

Chris thanked Jeanine for her generosity as Ronnie set the table and put some fresh cat food in Blackie's bowl. Chris took the pie plate out of the oven. Funny, I don't remember Jeanine putting the pie in the oven, he thought as he savored the first mouthful of one of the best chicken pies in the state of Maine.

On Fridays the lines were always long at the bank, but Chris really needed to cash his paycheck before the weekend. Like many of the old, slow systems he dealt with every day, the power plant hadn't straightened out his direct paycheck deposits. The business manager, who was well into his sixties, didn't have much experience with "that electronic stuff," but he promised to look into it as soon as he could find some time. Chris made a mental note to be sure he helped the business manager find some time.

So there he stood late on a Friday afternoon, shuffling ahead every few minutes. To make matters worse, he had been stuck in a long, pointless meeting with the union steward, a heavyset shop mechanic who loved to hear himself talk. Chris glanced at his cell phone, checked the time, and realized that he was, once again, late to pick up Ronnie on another Friday afternoon.

There was so much to do at night—dinner, laundry, dishes, Ronnie's bath, and finally her bedtime story. Lately he had been falling asleep right there beside her on her bed. Then he'd wake up around midnight and drag himself into his own bed. He was beginning to feel like the attendant on a merry-go-round that never stopped—every day was the same tedious routine. God knows he loved Ronnie; she was all he had in the world. But sometimes, like tonight, he longed for an evening out with other adults.

As he shuffled forward in line he tried to remember the last time he had been to a ballgame, or a bar, or a restaurant that had a wine list and no crayons in a cup at the hostess station. With longing he remembered the good friends, good laughs, and good beer in New York that marked the end of every workweek.

The canned music was starting to get on his nerves. He counted the stains on the olive paisley carpet. With growing irritation, he watched some elderly man in a fur hat count out every dollar before he left the teller's window. He wanted to shout, "Why the hell don't people like you do their banking during the day when normal people are working?"

Finally he reached the teller's window. He slid his paycheck and deposit slip forward without comment. As he waited, he looked around and noticed the woman sitting at the customer service desk behind the counter.

It was her. There was that pretty woman with the long brown hair and the little smile from church. This is where he had seen her before. She looked so prim and proper in her black business suit and rimless glasses with all that hair tucked up into a bun, but she sparkled when she smiled and he knew he had to meet her. He straightened up his tie, squared his shoulders in his suit jacket, and hoped that his five o'clock shadow wasn't too noticeable.

"Sir, sir, here's your cash and receipt," the teller said with some irritation. "Is there anything else I can do for you?"

"Yes, as a matter of fact, I'd like to open a certificate of deposit," he said, thinking quickly, all the while hoping that he had enough money for the minimum deposit.

The teller examined him for a long moment as if to say, "What kind of a jerk opens a bank account on a Friday afternoon with only a half hour left until closing?" But she kept her thoughts to herself and muttered, "I'll see if Miss Mercier can assist you."

Miss Mercier, he thought as he sat in the waiting area. Maybe this is my lucky day.

He saw the object of his attention walking toward him. Suddenly he was gripped by panic and doubt. He hadn't done anything like this in at least seven years. Why was he doing this when he was already late to pick up Ronnie? What was he going to say to her? What if she was already in a relationship? What if she was a lesbian?

"Hi, I'm Jennifer Mercier," she said as she offered her hand. "Come on in and let's see if we can open this account quickly for you so you can enjoy your weekend."

Chris managed to stammer out his name and squeeze her warm, delicate hand in his clumsy, sweaty mitt. In one long moment he noticed that her exquisite red nails perfectly matched her lipstick, she had no rings on her left hand, and her low, sultry voice could melt an iceberg.

She quickly began to ask for Chris's personal information, which she entered into her computer in a very business-like manner. Chris spat out the necessary information, but his mouth was dry and he felt like he was in high school again. He seized the chance to secretly study her as she concentrated on the computer screen.

Her eyes were the deep green of the sea on a summer's day, and wisps of her long brown hair curled slightly as they reached her shoulders. She pursed her full lips as she focused on the computer screen, and he noticed that her healthy complexion didn't seem to be enhanced with makeup. She wasn't stunningly gorgeous, but Chris was fascinated by her intelligent, natural beauty that he found incredibly attractive and a little intimidating at the same time.

When he answered her questions about employment, she sat back in her chair and looked at him more closely. "You're the new manager at the power plant, aren't you? My brother works for you. Bruce Mercier, have you met him?"

"I'm sorry, I guess I haven't had the chance to meet as many people as I should." Chris was beginning to regain some of his composure, but he felt like he just got the first test question wrong.

Jennifer was now peering at him more steadily. "I've seen you before somewhere, haven't I?"

Chris looked down for a second, then up at Jennifer sheepishly. He felt like she had caught him in his true purpose. "Maybe. I think I see you at church—Holy Rosary Church."

"Of course, I saw you Sunday at the nine o'clock mass with that adorable little girl with the gorgeous golden hair. Is she your daughter?" Jennifer suddenly remembered where she was and caught herself. "Oh, forgive me for prying."

"That's okay, and yes, the little girl is my daughter, Ronnie."

"You're so lucky to have such a beautiful daughter." Jennifer studied his face for a long moment and then resumed her professional manner. "We really must get back to your account or they'll lock us in for the weekend." Chris wondered if that would be such a bad thing.

Jennifer took the rest of his information and printed out the forms as Chris drank in little details like the single pearl that hung around her neck, the lock of brown hair that just wouldn't stay up, and the gentle curves under her black pantsuit. If there was anything less than wonderful about Jennifer Mercier, Chris couldn't see it or didn't care to notice. She smoothed the forms out before him on the desk.

"Please just sign here where I've marked the lines with an *X*," she said as their hands brushed ever so slightly. Even her fingertips felt soft and warm. She stood up quickly after he signed the forms, handed him his account booklet, and stuck out her hand, saying, "It's awfully nice to meet you, Mr. Murphy. You should get an e-mail confirmation of your account no later than Monday morning. Do you have any other questions for me?"

At first he thought it was a stupid idea. Then he thought, What have I got to lose? He took her hand, straightened up to his full height, and blurted out, "Yes, I do have one question. Will you have dinner with me tomorrow night?" He regretted it immediately and braced himself.

Jennifer's eyes opened a little wider. First she seemed startled, then her cheeks turned deep red. But slowly she smiled and said quietly, "I really do have plans for tomorrow night."

That's it, thought Chris. What a foolish thing to do.

"I'm really sorry to put you on the spot, but—" he began to say before she cut him off.

"But I'd love to have dinner with you next Friday night." Her green eyes sparkled as she blushed again, ever so slightly.

"Great, I'll pick you up at seven o'clock," he said with as much composure as he could muster. He turned and walked out of the bank, not daring to look back in case Jennifer was laughing at him.

Chris left the bank as gracefully as he could, holding in his whoop of joy until he was safely in the car. Then reality set in. He was almost an hour late to pick up Ronnie and he had neglected to get Jennifer's address or phone number. He really was pretty awful at this dating business.

Chris raced through the clear autumn twilight singing out loud to the songs on the radio as the last rays of orange sunlight disappeared behind the western hills. Yes, he was late to pick up Ronnie, but he also had a dinner date with a beautiful woman next Friday night.

The car jerked to a halt in front of the red brick school. He noticed that the first floor lights were still on. Chris threw open the front door, stepped into the hallway, and his feet flew out from under him, landing him flat on his back in the middle of the floor. He looked up to see the saintly face of a statue of the Blessed Virgin Mary looking down at him as if to say, "Oh, you poor fool." Bringing one of his hands up to his face, he rubbed his fingers together and sniffed them—there was no mistaking the sticky sweet ammonia smell of fresh floor wax, and his suit was covered with it.

As he pulled himself up, he checked for any damage, but found that only his pride had been bruised. He then realized that he was being watched from the shadows of the hallway. A young man, or boy—it was difficult to tell his age—approached him cautiously. He was dressed in black, from his combat boots to his sleeveless Lynyrd Skynyrd T-shirt. The little man gripped the mop handle tightly with his fingerless black gloves and said, "Who are you?"

Chris's first thought was to scream at the custodian for the slippery floors, but he realized that the school had long since been closed, and he noticed that the janitor had the almond-shaped eyes and round features common to people with Down syndrome. He responded tentatively as he straightened himself up. "I'm Chris Murphy. Who are you?"

The little man's face broke into a grin. "Everybody knows me, I …" Then remembering something that he had once been taught, he formally reached out his hand and said, "I am Joseph Wilson, pleased to meet you," as he mechanically pumped Chris's hand. "Call me Joe." Then his face darkened as he asked, "Why did you ruin my floor? What are you doing here so late?"

Again Chris's anger rose as he thought about telling Joe what he thought of his floor, but he checked himself. "I'm here to pick up my daughter, Ronnie Murphy. She's with Brother Adelard. Do you know where they are?"

Joe smiled at Chris, who couldn't help but notice his crooked teeth. "Oh, you're Ronnie's dad. She's a nice little girl."

"Yeah, that's right, Joe, can you tell me where she is?"

"She's downstairs with Brother. He doesn't like me very much." Then the janitor lowered his voice to mimic Brother Adelard. "He says, 'Joseph, I am going downstairs to pray. You must not disturb me for any reason.'" Then he whispered, "I don't like Brother very much."

Chris assured Joe that he had to go downstairs to get Ronnie or Brother Adelard would become very angry indeed, so the janitor agreed to show him where they were. Chris followed Joe down the long, dim corridors as Joe chatted about rock music, professional wrestling, and how much he liked Father Costello. At least that's what Chris assumed he was talking about, because he could only clearly understand about every third word in the lopsided conversation. Finally they came to a black iron stairway that led downstairs. When they reached the basement, Joe flicked on a switch that lit a single bulb hanging from the ceiling, pointed to an old wooden door about halfway down a stone-lined corridor, and quickly scampered back up the stairs.

As he neared the heavy oak door, Chris noticed the stifling scent of burning wax as if many candles were burning somewhere nearby. Brother Adelard suddenly appeared in the dim light of the hallway holding Ronnie by the hand. Ronnie reached out for her father's hand. "I thought you'd never get here, Daddy," she gently scolded him.

"I'm truly sorry that I'm so late tonight, Brother Adelard." Chris started to make up an excuse about working late, but decided that he couldn't lie to a man of God. "I was delayed and I really appreciate your willingness to care for Ronnie until this late hour."

The brother straightened his long black cassock and smiled with an expression that lacked either warmth or humor. "I am pleased to be of assistance to you. Veronique was joining me in my evening prayers, which is a custom that has suited me well since my youth. As always, Christopher, it is my humble pleasure to serve the Lord in any way I can," he stated, choosing each word carefully. Then he turned and placed a thin, white hand on Ronnie's head. "Good night, Veronique, may God watch over you this weekend. Now, if you'll excuse me, I must return to my devotions." Chris detected a hint of irritation in Brother Adelard's voice. "I'm sure you can find your way out." At that he entered the chapel, again closing the door behind him. Chris thought he heard the click of a bolt sliding into place after the door swung shut, but by then Ronnie was scampering up the stairs.

Once outside, the sparkling stars and the cool, clear air were a welcome relief from the stale air of the basement and the odor of floor wax that clung to Chris's suit. He held Ronnie's little hand as they walked to the car. "What did you and Brother Adelard pray for tonight, princess?"

Ronnie glanced up at him furtively. "Brother Adelard says that prayers are like secrets with God. You're not supposed to tell anyone." Then she said in a whisper, "But I prayed for you tonight, Daddy. Did anything good happen for you?"

Chris stopped, suddenly remembering his visit to the bank. Scooping Ronnie up in his arms, he gave each of her cheeks a slobbering kiss. "Yes, princess, something wonderful happened today. Thank you for your prayers ... and thanks to Brother Adelard, too," he added.

Chapter 7

INSTEAD OF THE raw dampness of the previous Sunday, this weekend Chris and Ronnie basked in sunny warmth. It's known in New England as Indian summer, when the season hangs on for one last visit accompanied by brilliant red, gold, and orange foliage illuminated by dazzling sunshine. Because every New Englander knows that the cold winds and snows of winter are just around the corner, Indian summer is precious and glorious, if all too fleeting. Like most Mainers, Chris was feeling good on Sunday, and his upcoming dinner date on Friday also went a long way toward lifting his spirits.

But, just as Indian summer fades into the chill of autumn, so the glorious weekend was destined to fade into the dull routine of preparing for another workweek as Sunday afternoon came around. Still, Chris was determined to stretch the pleasure of the weekend for all it was worth, and the fading golden sunshine found him raking the newly fallen leaves into big piles by the side of the street. Jeanine Brisebois had asked him if he would help get the leaves out so the public works crew could pick them up on Tuesday. Chris figured it was the least he could do, considering the many kindnesses that Jeanine had shown Ronnie and him.

He pushed the leaves into knee-high piles while Ronnie and Blackie jumped in and rolled around with shrieks and giggles as he buried them in yet another wave of gold and red leaves. Ronnie emerged from the pile seconds later, her cheeks the color of ripe apples with fragments of leaves tangled in her hair and sweater. Blackie hopped and dashed in the leaf piles seeking some imaginary prey. Chris watched his little girl and her kitten frolic, and he deeply regretted that the sun was sliding down behind the horizon. He wished there was a way that he could freeze this moment and savor it a little longer. He turned toward the garage to put away the rake, calling over his shoulder, "Stay away from the street, princess. It's getting dark."

Chris hung up the rake on the garage wall and was just picking up the last of the Barbie toys that Ronnie had been playing with earlier in the day when he suddenly heard the sharp snarling of dogs coming from the front yard. As he headed for the yard, he heard the screech of car tires and then Ronnie's piercing shriek. His heart skipped a beat, and he screamed Ronnie's name as he sprinted for the front of the house.

Ronnie was standing rigid by the curb, sobbing in agony. He threw his arms around her and squeezed her tight, relieved that she wasn't hurt, but frightened by her crying. "What is it? What is it, honey?"

She buried her face in his chest and whimpered, "Blackie … Blackie." Then she pointed into the street.

An old rusty Toyota sedan was pulled up to the curb a few feet away. The exhaust sputtered unevenly as the teenage driver stood behind the car and looked at something in the street.

Then the ashen-faced boy tentatively approached Chris, nervously wiping his hands on his Bruins T-shirt. "I'm really sorry, Mister. I didn't see it. I swear to God I couldn't see it until it was too late. I'll get the little girl another one if you want me to, or I can give her some money to buy a new one. I'm wicked sorry." The words spilled out all at once.

Ronnie ignored the young driver and continued to sob bitterly, her face buried in Chris's shoulder. Chris fought back the urge to lash out at the careless teenager, to curse him for not paying attention, to strike out at him for taking something precious from his little girl. Instead, he took a deep breath and calmly said, "It's getting dark, and he was a black kitten. It's not your fault." At that Chris carried Ronnie into the house. He sat her down on the couch, got her a juice box from the refrigerator, and gently picked the leaves from her hair. The little girl quietly cried as she sipped on the juice box. When her tears finally stopped, he gently kissed her cheek and whispered, "I'll be back in a few minutes, princess." He turned on the television to a cartoon station and headed out to the backyard.

Chris found a shovel in the garage and scooped up the mess of black fur and bloody pulp from the street, trying not to look at what remained of Blackie. Then, digging a hole in the far corner of the backyard, he buried the cat and covered the grave with stones and pieces of bricks. As an afterthought, Chris quickly fashioned a cross out of two sticks and some duct tape, and planted it into the soft mound of earth.

When Chris returned inside, Ronnie was still sitting on the couch where he had left her. She was staring blankly at the wall above the television screen and quietly sobbing. He sat down next to her and pulled her onto his lap. After a few moments, she looked up into his face through swollen, red eyes and asked, "Where's Blackie now, Daddy?"

Chris hesitated, then replied softly, "I buried him in the backyard, honey, but he's really up with God."

Ronnie asked through her sobs, "Can I go see him? I mean, can I see his grave?"

Chris had hoped that he could wait until morning for Ronnie to see the grave, but, since she was asking, perhaps it was better for her to deal with it now. So he held her hand and silently led her to the fresh grave in the backyard, which was barely visible in the falling darkness.

"Sweetheart, Blackie's body is here in the ground, but his soul is up in heaven. He's God's little kitty now. He has all the cat food he wants, and all the toys he can play with, and lots of kitty friends," he whispered as he crouched beside her and gently stroked her hair. "And he'll never forget how much you loved him."

The little girl stared intently at the grave, no longer crying. "Maybe we should say a prayer for Blackie, Daddy," she said in a weak, faraway voice.

"Okay, princess, that's a good idea," Chris said and then began, "Our Father, who art in heaven …"

Ronnie folded her hands and joined in the prayer, her voice getting stronger with each line, until she drowned out Chris's low whisper as they reached the end of the prayer. "… and deliver us from evil, amen."

Chris put his arm around her in the darkness, and they walked back toward the house. Ronnie felt stiff and rigid to him. "I wish that kid had been driving slower," he said.

"Those mean dogs chased Blackie into the street, Daddy. They killed him," Ronnie said in a flat tone of voice. "It wasn't that boy's fault. Those dogs killed Blackie."

A shiver ran down Chris's spine. It was getting quite chilly now that darkness had completely fallen. With his arm around Ronnie, they came back into the bright, warm house, but there was something about his little girl that made him uneasy. He wished that she was still weeping.

As the week went by, Ronnie couldn't seem to forget about Blackie's death. Chris could see that she had almost fully retreated inside herself as she played quietly with her dolls in the evening. He tried in vain to draw her out, to please her, to bring back her laughter. She didn't want to talk about getting a new kitten, and even a surprise trip to the toy store did nothing to lift her spirits.

It wasn't so much that she was angry or depressed, it was her silence that troubled him. He had never known her to be so withdrawn, so unreachable, before. Even when Mimi left, Ronnie had cried, and she had asked questions, and talked about it, and cried some more. Together they had worked it out a little, but now he felt shut out. There was nothing that he could do or say to make any difference to her.

After several days of wondering how she was feeling, he decided to be straightforward with her. At bedtime he tucked in her blankets, kissed her forehead gently, and sat down on the edge of the bed.

"Ronnie, dear, it hurts me to see you so sad about Blackie and know that there's nothing I can do to make it better," Chris said as he smoothed the pink bedspread over her. "Are you sure you don't want another kitty, or maybe some other kind of pet, like a bird, or some fish?"

Ronnie thought for a moment, then said quietly, "No, Daddy, nothing can ever replace Blackie."

"It's not good to think about sad things all the time and not do anything about them," he whispered as he stroked her hair. "You really need to find something to help you forget."

"I'll never forget about Blackie," she blurted out in a voice tinged with anger. "Brother Adelard helps me pray about Blackie and that makes me feel not so sad." A strange look came over her face as if she'd said something wrong. She turned her face to the wall and began to softly whimper.

Chris stayed and rubbed her little shoulders until her breathing told him that she was asleep. The odd reaction after she talked about praying didn't go unnoticed, but he was too pleased to see her cry to pay it much heed. Chris was no child psychologist, but he knew that Ronnie's tears meant that she was letting out some of her pain. Maybe tomorrow she would talk a little more and let him in a little more. But tonight he was very tired and he realized, for the first time, that Blackie's death had taken a lot out of him, too.

Across town, the old man finished his supper and carefully crept up the stairs. He chuckled to himself when he realized he was tiptoeing. After all, the men's Bible-study group was having their annual dinner down in Portland, and he knew he would be all alone for the next few hours. Nevertheless, he quietly entered the bedroom, switched on the desk lamp, and searched for the old satchel and the leather-bound journal. He carefully turned the yellowed, brittle pages until he found where he had left off reading.

"Over the next several hours, Major Gerhard Bachman told me about himself, his mission, the purpose of the Ahnenerbe, and the urgency of his quest to find the ritual of Karl of Rothenburg. He also shared his deep love for his beautiful wife, Marte, and his cherished son. With a touch of embarrassment, he confided his fear that reassignment to an infantry unit would mean that he'd never see them again.

As he spoke, the major became more animated and human. It was as if a heavy cloak had been lifted from his shoulders. I realized that this man, now baring his soul before me, was what I had hoped to be all my life. If my body had not been afflicted with the deformity that prevented me from growing straight and strong, perhaps I would have become just like this Teutonic knight, scholar, father, husband, and warrior who now revealed his hopes and fears to me.

The more Gerhard shared his thoughts, the greater the bond between us grew. The dinner bell brought us both back to the present moment. I promised to keep his secrets on the pain of death, and I have revealed them in this text only to ensure that his son understands

that his father was a true knight and hero. I also promised to pray that the next day's search would bring us to
the manuscript of Karl of Rothenburg.

After dinner I visited Brother Sebastian, one of
the oldest members of our order. I found the elderly
monk in his tiny room silently praying the rosary on his
heavy black beads. The room was nearly pitch black,
and I was only able to see the old monk by the light of
a slender crescent moon through the narrow window.
I then remembered that Brother Sebastian was almost
totally blind. He had been in charge of the library for
many years until his sight began to fade. After apolo-
gizing for interrupting his evening prayers, I asked the
old man if he had ever heard of a manuscript written by
Karl of Rothenburg.

Brother Sebastian thought for a moment, then
reached out and took my hand in his smooth, soft palm.
"I do remember something I was once told about several
manuscripts that were brought here in the early Middle
Ages," he said in a voice that was barely louder than a
whisper. "It was said that they came into our possession when monks from other monasteries fled the Huns
during the Dark Ages and took refuge here. I think
Rothenburg was a town in which one of the monasteries was located," he continued. "But I must warn you,
Siegfried, some of these manuscripts contain curses and
spells and other nonsense from a time when our church
was just emerging from the darkness of pagan beliefs."

The old man gripped my hand tighter. "Our Lord works wonders in response to our prayers, but He would never lend his power to foolish spells and curses. If there ever was any effect from these rites and incantations, it was the result of the Evil One's power, not the grace of our good Lord."

Trying to hide my eagerness to find the manuscripts, I casually asked Brother Sebastian where they might be found.

"If you really must see them, they're kept beneath a loose floor slate under the reading table in the center of the library." The old monk then explained, "You see, we needed to keep them away from those who might try to use them to discredit the church or get into some other mischief." I thanked Brother Sebastian and gently kissed his hand. As I stood up to leave, he said, "Be careful, Siegfried. I don't hold much stock in the stories that were told about these manuscripts, but handle them with caution. Perhaps there may be some dark force that has been dormant throughout all these centuries. Sometimes what is dead is best left buried." I wished the old monk a peaceful night, but knew I had to see for myself if the ancient rituals really had the power to punish sinners, heretics, and enemies of the church.

The next morning, Gerhard and I wasted no time as we searched for the loose slate in the library floor. We found the spot in the floor quickly, but it took two of us with all our strength to slide back the heavy slate. Beneath a dark opening in the floor was a lower room, probably a medieval crypt for some knight, with shelves holding scrolls and books covered with cobwebs and mold. There was a ladder in place that enabled us to climb down into the dark crypt.

We scanned the ancient texts with a flashlight and smiled at each other in triumph as we began bringing the manuscripts up into the light where we could examine each one. There were court transcripts from the Inquisition, books of incantations to keep away the Black Plague, and scrolls of prayers that would save the dying from damnation in exchange for the donation of their worldly possessions to the church. Clearly this was a depository of manuscripts that had the potential for great embarrassment to the church if they fell into the wrong hands. After spending hours poring over dozens of texts, most of which were superstitious foolishness, Gerhard once again became discouraged.

Wondering aloud if there were any manuscripts we had overlooked, Gerhard climbed back down into the dark crypt and searched every inch of it. In a small alcove, he found a solitary volume in a dusty woven sack. Moments later I heard him call out to me as he reached up through the opening and passed the dusty sack up to me.

We quickly untied the top of the sack, which almost fell away from the book. I'll never forget the first time I saw it—bound in rich, polished leather, with gold embossed letters and scrolls along the spine and across the cover that read *"Precis Intemporaliter Damnare,"* or "Prayers for the Damned." The book looked like it had just been bound, and it even retained the rich scent of new leather. What was even more surprising was that it felt warm in my hands although the air from the crypt was cold and damp. I passed the book to Gerhard, who quickly studied the first few pages.

"This is it!" he shouted. "Look, Siegfried, here it is. 'I, Karl of Rothenburg, reveal these secret prayers to vanquish the pagan barbarians and those who would attack our church and harm true believers.'"

As I leaned over to view the manuscript, he seized me in a jubilant embrace and my heart soared. Together we closely examined the manuscript. Page after page told of Karl's devotion to the holy martyrs of the church and recounted the cruelties and sacrileges of the Huns, but told us nothing of any ritual.

Suddenly Gerhard turned a page to reveal a gruesome illustration of Christ hanging on the cross in the final moments of his life. The following page was beautifully decorated with the most vivid blue, red, and gold letters that seemed to float above the parchment.

The words described, in exact detail, the sequence that would curse an enemy of the faithful to eventual death. For hours we read with intense interest how a consecrated priest, while holding Christ's Crown of

Thorns dipped in innocent blood, would recite the incantation that would strike down an enemy of the church whom the priest had touched. After describing the ritual in detail, the writer told of the misfortunes that had befallen the first victims of the curse. I quickly dismissed it all as just more of the impossible superstitious nonsense that we had been reading all day and shook my head.

However, Gerhard looked at me with fire in his eyes. "Don't you see, Siegfried? We've found it. This is exactly what we've been seeking." He grasped the book in both hands as he rose from the table. "This will give us the power to strike down the enemies of the church. We will vanquish Stalin, Churchill, and even that pathetic cripple, Roosevelt. This will change the course of the entire war and ensure the victory of our Reich."

"But, even if this ritual actually had the power to curse our enemies, where could we possibly find Christ's Crown of Thorns and a source of innocent blood?" I asked.

Gerhard smiled. "The SS has many resources and connections, my friend. As soon as I get a message to Himmler, I will take possession of the Crown of Thorns relic kept at the cathedral in Cologne." He continued as he paced back and forth. "As for innocent blood, well, it may be somewhat distasteful, but don't we have access to young children in our relocation camps? After all, with the considerable trouble the

Jews have caused us, their children can do their small part to serve the fatherland."

I was still having difficulty understanding how the elements needed for the ritual could all be combined. "Even if we possess the relic and gain access to innocent blood, how will we get consecrated priests who will be able to get close enough to the world leaders and generals we wish to strike down?"

Gerhard grabbed my arm. His piercing blue eyes radiated. "This is your opportunity for greatness, my friend. This is your call to become a warrior priest commander." He took me by both shoulders and stared into my eyes. "You will recruit and train an army of consecrated priests who will infiltrate the enemy's command centers. We will dispatch our soldier-priests to Moscow and London and Washington. And in the end, when victory is ours, Siegfried, you will become the first priest-field marshal of the new Reich."

Gerhard turned away from me and placed his hand on the book. "Just as Karl of Rothenburg came here to fight back the invasion of the Huns, so you and I will turn back the communists and heretics and atheists, and our counterattack will begin here in this sacred place. They are the true enemies of our holy church and our fatherland, which must be defended at all costs." He continued as he raised up the book. "We must remember that our Reich is descended from the Holy Roman Empire. Although our Führer does not yet embrace our holy church, one day Adolf Hitler will return to the sacred faith of his childhood. One day all will see that the Master of the New Reich is the spiritual son of Charlemagne."

Gerhard's handsome face glowed with passion for this new crusade, and flames touched my soul. I could envision myself beside an airfield, blessing a squad of warrior-priests dressed in camouflage uniforms. I would raise my hands over their bowed heads as they prepared to board aircraft and parachute into hostile lands where they would vanquish the enemies of the church.

Maybe I would finally live up to my father's legacy and, perhaps, exceed his martial achievements. In that instant, I saw that my true vocation might be fulfilled in this new mission. "Where will we begin, Major?" I asked with anticipation, straightening up as best I could.

Gerhard explained that he and his driver would depart at first light for the cathedral in Cologne. While he located the relic from the Crown of Thorns, I would search the city's orphanages for a source of innocent blood. We agreed that it would be best to hide the old book in the cellar hole and we swore to tell no one until he returned with the relic.

Before we went our separate ways, Gerhard embraced me. Then he suddenly knelt before me with his head bowed and said, "Please give me your blessing,

Brother Siegfried, and pray that the good Lord will guide our steps and give us the strength not to falter as we seek to vanquish those who would harm our church."

I placed my hands on his handsome blond head and whispered the prayer for travelers in Latin and I added, "And may the Prayers for the Damned save our fatherland from the stranglehold of sinners." The major jumped to his feet, smiled with confidence, and headed off to find his driver, his shiny black boots leaping up the stairs two by two."

The old man took off his glasses and wiped his eyes with his handkerchief. Looking up to the ceiling, he whispered, "My God, what have I stumbled into?"

Chapter 8

CHRIS ALMOST FORGOT about his Friday night date with Jennifer because of his deep concern about Ronnie. At first he thought that maybe he should just postpone their plans, but something inside him said that he needed this night out with this charming woman.

Jennifer laughed when he called her at the bank to get her address and cell phone number. He could picture her at the other end of the phone line, and he imagined her radiant smile as they talked. It pleased him to know that he could make her laugh, but he quickly reminded himself that this was just a first date.

Jeanine arrived a little early on Friday night and began to play Chutes and Ladders with Ronnie at the kitchen table. That was good, because Chris hadn't said much to Ronnie about his plans for the evening. It felt awkward and strangely dishonest when he thought about telling his daughter that he was going out on a date with someone who wasn't her mother. But he told himself again that this was just a dinner date—they weren't going to a motel. And besides, Mimi walked out on him. It wasn't like he deserted her.

Chris had made a reservation at the restaurant that Peggy recommended as the best in Ashton Falls. He had chosen his best gray suit, still in plastic wrap from the cleaners, a new white shirt, and a really expensive red silk tie. As he got dressed, the jitters started. What would he talk about? What if they didn't hit it off? What if they hit it off and finished dinner too early? He laughed at himself for thinking like a high-school freshman on his way to his first dance and quickly finished dressing.

He pecked Ronnie on the cheek and told her to be a good girl for Grand-mère.

Without looking up from the game, Ronnie said, "Have a nice time with your friend, Daddy." He suppressed a fresh rush of guilt. Jeanine gave him an impish wink and told him to have fun and not worry about getting home too late.

With butterflies racing around his stomach, he pulled up in front of the address that Jennifer had given him. It was a modest two-story brick home in a neighborhood of other neat two-story brick houses. As he started up the leaf-covered front walk, Jennifer came bouncing down the front stairs wearing jeans, a pink sweater, and a short denim jacket. He immediately realized two things—he had forgotten to tell her where they were going, and she looked so good that it took his breath away.

Before he could even open the car door for her she was laughing in a nervous way. "Oh, I'm so sorry. I should have asked where we were going to dinner," she giggled as she held her hands over her face in embarrassment. "You look great and you must think I look like a slob. I'll go back inside and change."

Chris recovered quickly. "No, you look wonderful, I mean it." He quickly took off his tie and unbuttoned his collar. "See, I knew I was overdressed."

She looked him straight in the eye with just a hint of a smile, laughed again, and muttered, "Oh, I can't believe I did this." He loved the sound of her laugh and the way her sea-green eyes sparkled.

Once they were inside the car, there was a moment of awkward silence. Chris spoke first. "Look, I'm the new guy in town. Why don't you show me around Ashton Falls tonight? And since I screwed up the dinner plans, you can pick the restaurant." He hoped he had gracefully adjusted to the uncomfortable situation.

"Do you like Italian food?" she asked.

"I love it."

"Good. Go to the end of the street and take a left at the lights. Our first stop is Giovanni's Villa."

The restaurant was a dimly lit little place with red-and-white checked tablecloths, and it was nearly empty except for Chris and Jennifer. Frank Sinatra music played softly, and the rich scent of garlic and fresh bread greeted them. The hostess was an elderly woman in a black dress who waddled and chatted incoherently as she led them to their table. The chairs didn't match and the menus had traces of tomato sauce on them, but Jennifer looked even more beautiful in the light of the flickering candle set into the straw-covered Chianti bottle.

His fears about conversation were unfounded. They talked effortlessly about their jobs, the news, and sports during

P. G. Smith

the calamari and salad. Chris was surprised to learn that they shared a common interest in history halfway through the lobster gnocchi, which was the best he had ever tasted. Jennifer happily promised to show him the historic sites of Ashton Falls after dinner.

Once the waitress cleared away the dishes and poured the coffee, Jennifer rested her chin on her folded hands, looked directly at Chris, and asked the question that he most dreaded.

"So what's a big-city boy like you doing in a place like this, all alone except for his adorable daughter?"

He had to give her credit for being direct. There was no way to dodge the question, so he answered her as succinctly as possible. He couldn't sugarcoat the story, but he tried not to come across as bitter when he got to the part about Mimi walking out on them.

Jennifer listened without interrupting him, then said softly, "Your poor little girl. It must be awful for her without a mother, but she's lucky to have such a great father."

Chris reached out and patted her hand gently. "That was kind of you to say that," he whispered. Then he pulled himself upright, looked directly at Jennifer, and said, "Now, it's your turn. What is a beautiful, intelligent, classy woman like you doing in this land of pickup trucks, chain saws, and bingo halls?"

Jennifer blushed. "You don't really want to know, do you?"

"Oh yes, I do," Chris shot back with a twinkle in his eye. "I had to tell you my life story, so now it's your turn."

"Well, where do I begin? Despite my thick glasses, crooked teeth, and lack of any self-confidence, I managed to get a scholarship to Boston University after I graduated from Ashton Falls High. So there I was all alone in downtown Boston, which terrified me." She sipped her wine and smiled in a sad way. "Because I had no social life and no money to go play anywhere, all I could do was study. So, I graduated summa cum laude from BU and got accepted into the Harvard Business School MBA program."

Chris whispered, "Wow, I had no idea I was dining with a genius," and leaned a little closer.

"Well, hold on, Chris, this story isn't over." She continued, "When I was at Harvard, I met Martin, who was witty, brilliant, and handsome—much like my present dinner companion." She smiled. "But there was a lot about Martin that I didn't know. Anyway, we both graduated with our Harvard MBA diplomas in hand and set out together to make our fortunes. I became an analyst with Neponset Investments, and he landed a high-paying job at the Boston office of Allied International." She took a sip of coffee, glanced at Chris, and said, "Oh, I'm so sorry for going on and on. I must be terribly boring."

Chris reached across the table and gently grasped her hand. "Please go on."

"We were doing really well for a few years. We had a townhouse in the North End overlooking Boston harbor. When we could find time for vacations, we flew to Paris, or Barcelona, or Cancun—wherever we decided to go on a whim. Believe it or not, I was driving a bright red BMW Roadster on my half-mile commute to my office. Unfortunately, I trusted Martin with handling our finances because he was a much sharper investment expert than I was, or so I thought. I didn't realize until a check bounced, they canceled our credit cards, and an apologetic man came to repossess my sweet little BMW that Martin had some issues. When I confronted him, he admitted that he had made some risky investments. He also finally confessed that he had a serious cocaine habit and had been having an affair with a cocktail waitress on Cape Cod." Jen paused to wipe the corner of her eyes with her napkin.

"I'm sorry, Jen," Chris stammered. "It must have been awful for you."

"I think the worst part was that I was hoping to start a family with him," Jen continued with a sad little laugh. "I was even planning on putting a deposit down on a beautiful little white house with a picket fence in the suburbs. But I lost everything in bankruptcy court and I didn't waste any time in divorcing poor, sad Martin."

Jennifer laid her spoon carefully next to her empty coffee cup and looked intently at Chris. "But, you know, for all the warts this little town has, I'm thankful that it welcomed me back and gave me a soft landing. I have a decent job, good friends, a wonderful father and brother, and sometimes, handsome men come into the bank and invite me to dinner." She smiled as she reached across the table and tentatively laid her hand on his.

They sat that way for a few moments, then Chris said, "Hey, is it too late for that tour of Ashton Falls?"

"Nope, I can show you all three points of interest and have you home before the sitter falls asleep," she laughed, quickly dabbing the corners of her eyes once more.

Chris paid the check and helped her on with her jacket. As they stepped out into the cool night air, she shivered. He instinctively put his arm around her and drank in the warm sweetness of her perfume. Jennifer said something about how clear the stars and the crescent moon were. They both looked up, and she leaned her cheek on his shoulder, just for a moment. He was trying to decide whether to kiss her or not when they reached the car. Like a coward, he unlocked the door and held it open for her.

Jennifer directed Chris past the "new" Ashton Falls High School, a one-story cinder-block affair that may have looked modern in the seventies, but now just looked kind of drab. Jennifer claimed that she had been a field hockey sensation back "in the day" when she played for the Battlin' Bobcats.

They drove on and stopped outside the town's oldest house, a weathered shingle saltbox where Josiah Ashton had fought back an attack by half the Abenaki nation while his wife gave birth to twins and reloaded his musket, or, at least, that was the way Jennifer told the story.

Jennifer pointed out the statue of General Isaiah Strong Livingston, local Civil War hero, on the common in front of the pizza place. So far, he was the most famous resident of Ashton Falls. Then they drove on through the sleepy town center, past the bars and the gas station and the bowling alley, until they came to the church.

"And this is where I went to grammar school, and now I go here on Sundays to look at cute guys and their daughters," she said with a wink. "But seriously, do you want to hear the story

P. G. Smith

about why they call it Holy Rosary? It's kind of interesting and kind of spooky."

Chris pulled the car up in front of the church and said, "I'm all yours."

"Way back in the 1850s our Yankee neighbors decided that they were losing too many jobs to the Irish and French-Canadian immigrants, so they formed a secret political party called the Know Nothings. The goal of the Know Nothing movement was to get rid of all the immigrants flooding America and return it to the land of good old white men, their subservient women, and those who served them. They were a secret society, which is where the name came from. When a member of the party was questioned about his membership, he was instructed to say 'I know nothing.' Despite their innocent-sounding name, the Know Nothings weren't hesitant to play rough from time to time. The Know Nothing party was particularly powerful here in Maine, where they actually tarred, feathered, and left a Catholic priest for dead up in Eastport. They tried to burn down churches and parochial schools throughout Maine. Here in Ashton Falls there was a Catholic church right over there where the school stands now.

"Anyway," she went on, "the stalwart Yankee Know Nothings in Ashton Falls figured that, if there was no church, there would be no Irish or French Canadian immigrants. So, one quiet autumn evening, they decided it would be a good idea to burn down the town's Catholic church. The legend has it that the parish priest, Father Pierre Simoneau, saw the church in flames and ran into the burning building to try to save the tabernacle. He was trapped inside, and the next day, when they sifted through the ashes, all they could find were his rosary beads. Hence the name of the church—isn't that creepy?" Jennifer shivered as she concluded her story.

Chris chuckled, but the story made him oddly uncomfortable as he realized that Ronnie's school rested on the ashes of this macabre episode in local history. However, he wasn't going to let a holy horror story ruin a good evening, so he said, "Come on, there must be at least one more spot of interest in this lovely old town."

Jennifer looked at him slyly and said, "Maybe there is one more place I could show you. Take the road to the right that heads up that steep hill."

They drove for at least ten minutes until they came to an unpaved clearing on top of the hill that overlooked the cascading Micmac River. The stars and the moon blended with the twinkling lights of the town below. Chris turned off the engine. He noticed that they were surrounded by absolute silence.

"My guidebook says that I'm supposed to tell you about how this river powered the early mills," Jennifer said softly as she turned toward him.

"I don't think I care about the mills very much," he said as he put his arm around her and drew her close. Chris slowly bent his head toward hers and felt the softness of her lips against his in the darkness. Their breathing quickened as they kissed again and again, the passion building with each successive kiss. He was intoxicated by the aroma of her skin, her hot breath, and the sweet taste of her kiss. His left hand slipped inside her jacket. He could feel the warm fullness of her breasts as she pushed against him.

As the fire within him grew, Chris kissed her neck and inhaled the garden scent of her perfume. His left hand unbuttoned her blouse as she moaned and thrust herself against him. Slowly his hand slid down across her silky belly and slipped under the waistband of her jeans.

Then suddenly there was a flood of blue swirling lights and a white beam glared through the fog on the passenger-side window. Jennifer pulled her jacket tightly across her body, covered her face with her hands, and instantly began to sob. Chris rolled down his window.

Another beam of white light penetrated Chris's window and a gruff voice said, "Time to move on, kids, I mean folks. Ma'am, are you all right?"

Jennifer kept her face hidden and replied, "Yes, officer, I'm fine. Thank you for asking."

Chris rolled up the window, too shocked and embarrassed to say anything. Once he had driven a short way down the road, the police car pulled off down a side road. He turned to Jennifer and said, "I'm so sorry. Are you sure you're all right?"

She pulled her hands away from her face, and he could see that the sobbing was really stifled laughter. "I haven't been so embarrassed since I was sixteen," she shrieked, "and the best part is that the cop was Jack Thibodeau. I graduated from high school with him!" At that she doubled up with laughter. Chris found that her laugh was contagious.

"Get me home, Chris, before I wet my pants," she begged. "This always happens when I laugh too hard."

He pulled up in front of her house. She quickly pecked him on the cheek. "I had a great time tonight. Now call me, or awful things will happen to your bank account." At that she dashed out of the car, slammed the door, and ran up the front stairs of her house.

"Wow, what a screwed-up date," he thought as he watched her, wondering what time he should call tomorrow.

The old man was obsessed with the story in the journal. Every moment that he was alone in the house, he calculated whether or not he had time to sneak into the bedroom down the hall and read more of Brother Siegfried's writing. Tonight the other occupant of the house announced at dinner that he would be visiting a sick woman over in Brunswick, so the old man shouldn't wait up for him.

As soon as the old man heard the front door close and the car drive away, he crept into the bedroom and took the journal from the drawer. His eager fingers turned the pages and he continued his reading.

"While Major Bachman was in Cologne securing the relic from the Crown of Thorns, I cautiously approached several of my fellow monks to begin to recruit my warrior-priests. Two members of our congregation, Brother Gunther and Brother Joachim, expressed interest in fighting for the fatherland if the situation became desperate. I planned to initiate them in the rite of the Prayers for the Damned as soon as the major returned.

During this time it seemed that the enemy increased the intensity of his nighttime air raids. At the monastery, we passed many anxious hours in prayer as we huddled together in the library. I wondered if somehow the Russian Bolsheviks and their godless American friends knew that a most mysterious and powerful weapon of war was hidden away in a monastery in the fair city of Salzburg.

After the sirens sounded the wailing "all clear" signal, many of the brothers and I grabbed satchels full of emergency medical supplies and hurried down the long, winding path that led to the heart of the city. The ominous orange glow and the sickening odors of singed flesh and burning oil fumes were a sad preview of the horrors that awaited us. We did our best to minister to the physical and spiritual needs of the poor wretches who fell victim to the shower of death and destruction that rained down from the skies at night, but often our efforts were in vain. In the end, all we could do was offer our prayers for the souls of the dead.

Gerhard had been gone almost two weeks when we left the relative safety of the monastery on our nightly errand of mercy after the explosions had ceased and the "all clear" was sounded. This night we could see the police waving onlookers away from the ruins of a small German military convoy that had suffered a direct hit.

At first I didn't consider that my friend might have traveled in a convoy, but when I recognized the twisted, charred body of Corporal Schroeder lying by the side of the road, I was seized with panic. I pushed my way past the police until I found the smoldering remains of a staff car, and there in the backseat was my friend, my partner, my hero, Major Gerhard Bachman.

I could just barely reach him by leaning through the wreckage of the rear door. He was bleeding heavily from a deep gash over his right ear and his leg was bent under the seat at an alarming angle, but his eyes were open and I could see that he recognized me. As I bandaged his head and tried to stop the oozing blood, he groaned, reached into his pocket, and pressed a small velvet bag into my hand. "Siegfried, take this relic and carry on our work, our crusade."

I cradled his head in both arms and assured him that we would vanquish our enemies together when he recovered from his wounds. But he shook his head and whispered, "It's too late for me. In moments I will receive my heavenly reward and be with our Lord." Then he grabbed my arm with surprisingly strength. "I beg you, Siegfried, promise that you'll take care of my beloved Marte and my sweet little boy." I nodded my head and promised that I would care for his family. Then he plucked the new Iron Cross medal from his uniform and gasped, "Make sure my son knows that his father fought to protect the fatherland and the church until the end." He made a choking sound like he was clearing his throat, then slumped back on the car seat. I took the medal from his hand, then ran for help to get him out of the twisted wreck.

When I returned with two hulking firemen, we managed to pull away the automobile's door. But when the firemen carried the major's body out of the mangled wreckage and laid him on the ground, they just shook their heads. I lifted up his head and looked into his glassy eyes. Although my tears blurred my vision, I could see that he had an expression of complete tranquility and peace on his face.

We buried Major Gerhard Bachman of the SS on a drizzly morning in our monastery's cemetery. All the brothers were present and the abbot said the funeral mass, dressed in glowing white and gold vestments. As the brothers raised their voices in a harmonic chant, I could see that several of them had tears running down their cheeks. Although they didn't know Gerhard well, I think they mourned for a young father taken during a cruel act of war. They mourned for a young widow now abandoned. They mourned for a beautiful child who would grow up fatherless. And, most of all, they mourned for our fading Germanic empire, which was now clearly losing the battle against atheists and Bolsheviks.

Many of us prayed over the fresh earth of his grave for several hours with our hoods pulled over our heads against the chilly, raw wind. I begged our Lord to receive Gerhard's soul in heaven, but I prayed even more fervently for guidance and protection as I resolved to set out on the hazardous journey that I knew was my duty to God and Gerhard.

At first the abbot shook his head and insisted that he would never approve of such a fool's errand. He said that I was in the throes of grief and would see reason if I prayed and rested for a few days. But I went to my room and loaded up an old knapsack with canned goods and bread that Brother Otto gave me from the refectory. I filled a large jar with clear drinking water, packed my small Bible and breviary of prayers, and borrowed a pair of hiking boots from Brother Melchior.

Finally I slipped the pistol that I had quietly taken off Gerhard's belt before they prepared him for burial. It was an elegant shiny black luger with rich walnut grips carved in an intricate checkered pattern. On one side of the grips there was a silver inlaid eagle atop the swastika of the Nazi party. Underneath the symbol was a tiny silver plate engraved with the words "Gift of H. Himmler." I paused for a moment, knowing that a monk probably shouldn't be carrying a lethal weapon, but I jammed it into the bottom of the pack and fastened the straps.

When all was ready for the journey, I still had an important task to tend to. I took a lantern and, when

I was certain no one would observe me, I descended into the library, lifted up the loose stone, and climbed down the ladder into the crypt. In the alcove next to the Prayers for the Damned, I carefully set down the small red velvet bag that Gerhard had given his life to bring to me. The mysterious book and the relic would lie in wait in the crypt until I completed my mission.

I returned to the abbot's chambers and knocked on the door with insistence. He opened the door just a crack and looked at me with annoyance.

I cleared my throat and said, "Reverend Father, I know you cannot bless me as I undertake this journey. I have therefore come to say farewell. I do not wish to be disobedient, but I must go and keep my promise to a dying warrior. If you forbid me to return when my mission is complete, I will understand."

The abbot sighed, opened the door, and beckoned for me to sit down. "I understand that you must listen to what your heart and your conscience tell you to do. Although I do not agree with your decision, I wish you luck and God's protection on your journey. And when your mission is complete, you will return to this monastery, because it is, and always will be, your home."

Then he placed his hands gently on my head and whispered the prayers of blessing. He motioned for me to stand, embraced me powerfully, and kissed me on both cheeks. He looked into my eyes with sadness and said, "Godspeed, Siegfried."

Before dawn the next morning, Brother Otto served me a special breakfast of sausage, bread, and the last of our precious eggs. I knelt in the chapel for one last prayer and set out for Alsace. I was fortunate enough from time to time to catch a ride in German Army transport convoys as I made my way west. The old men and boys in mismatched uniforms were always pleased to have a holy man ride along with them as a sign of God's favor and protection. They freely shared their coarse brown bread as we bounced and jolted over the pockmarked roads. In return, I offered prayers for their safety and read psalms from the Bible. Even if they were Protestant, or had no religion at all, they must have believed that the prayers of a deformed Catholic monk couldn't hurt their chances for survival in the battles to come.

When I reached Munich, there was chaos everywhere. Buildings smoldered from the previous night's air raid. Ambulances raced here and there with their sirens blaring. Weary, stern policemen lurked on every corner eyeing each passerby carefully in search of deserters, saboteurs, or enemy sympathizers. I found the train station and, with the help of a sympathetic Panzer sergeant, was able to climb into a freight car loaded with tank repair parts bound west for Stuttgart. Soon the train was rolling down the tracks and, although my nose burned from the stench of diesel fuel and oil, the clicking and rocking of the freight car eventually lulled me into a deep sleep.

I awoke to a high-pitched whine that grew into an earsplitting shriek followed by the staccato thump of bullets striking home in the darkness. I struggled to my feet, but I was suddenly thrown against the side of the railcar as it twisted and rolled until it came to a shuddering stop. I rummaged through the debris around me and found my rucksack. Kicking through the shattered boards of the railcar's side, I crawled away from the train's wreckage into the relative safety of the forest. In the leaping flames left behind by the bombing, I could see burning lumps that used to be human beings, the wounded dragging themselves away from the blazing train, and some poor souls who just stood helpless, still in shock from the explosions. And still the death machines swooped down from the dark sky for one more pass with their machine guns spitting fire. I burrowed into the earth, but not before I saw the white stars in blue circles on the wings of these angels of death illuminated by the flickering flames of hell.

When I could safely come out of the cover of the forest, I did my best to ease the suffering of the wounded, but I administered more last rites than medical care. As a dismal dawn arrived, I was able to climb into the back of an ambulance loaded with charred, moaning men, mercifully drugged into semi-consciousness with morphine. The ambulance took me southwest for about fifty miles to a field hospital. I asked the driver if there were any vehicles traveling west, but he said nothing moved past this point except combat vehicles because of enemy patrols. I thanked him, shouldered my rucksack, and jumped down from the ambulance. As my feet touched the hard earth I noticed that my boots were stained red with the dried blood of my German brothers. I continued my journey on foot.

For almost a week I made my way through the forests of western Germany. Several times each day I confronted desperate, frightened German soldiers who warned me about the dangers ahead and begged me to go back, but I trudged on under cold, cloudy skies. Soon my meager food supplies were gone, and I laughed to myself that the good Lord had blessed me with a lighter rucksack. At night I lay down on piles of leaves and pine boughs and tried to sleep. Frequently I woke up shivering and prayed feverishly that I would arrive in Colmar in time to care for Marte and her little boy.

Early one morning, I stiffly began my day's journey down a country road that passed by the blackened ruins of once productive farms. Suddenly I heard the sound of voices from the woods up ahead to the right. I quickly dashed into the tree line until I could determine if the voices were those of our German warriors or the enemy.

As silently as I could, I crept through the forest toward the sound of the voices. Finally I could make out the form of a standing American soldier who was yelling something over his shoulder to his comrades as they were loading up onto their vehicles. The idling engines of the tanks and diesel trucks created a loud din. I crept a little closer and saw that there were three German soldiers kneeling at the American's feet with their hands on their heads. Two were bareheaded, grimy teenagers who were sobbing. I could see the tears cutting through the dirt on their cheeks in little rivers. The third was an older man whose wrinkled face was set like flint as he resolved himself to his fate. Quickly I thought of what I could do and then remembered the pistol in my rucksack.

As I fumbled with the pistol and attempted to load a bullet into the firing chamber as quickly as possible, the American drew a pistol from his belt and placed it next to the first teenager's temple. The American savored the anguish of the German boy as he slowly cocked the pistol and taunted him, forcing the boy to repeat over and over, "Heil, Hitler." The American's charade gave me just enough time to cock the luger, creep closer, and take aim with shaking hands. I closed my eyes and squeezed the trigger. The explosion almost knocked the pistol out of my hands.

My shot missed the American, but it startled him enough that he was now shooting at me instead of the three kneeling Germans. The angels must have protected me because the bullets whizzed harmlessly over my head. The American came closer, firing as he stepped toward me.

Mercifully shielded by the bushes around me, I raised my head and fired again. This time my bullet struck the American in the thigh and he dropped to the ground, losing his pistol as he fell. In seconds, the older German soldier was on top of the wounded American, pounding him again and again with a rock. I rose up and walked toward the fallen soldier. The older German continued to strike the American's head with the rock until he was clearly dead and his face was nothing more than bloody pulp.

In seconds the three soldiers stripped the American of his weapons, warm clothing, money, canteen, knapsack, and even his socks. Following the older German soldier's instructions, we ran for several kilometers until we collapsed, lungs aching, in a secluded, rocky grotto. There we eagerly shared the contents of the American's pack—two cans of fruit, a chocolate bar, and a packet of crackers. No saints' day feast had ever tasted so good to me. After our meal, the soldiers divided up a half pack of cigarettes and decided who would take possession of the rifle, pistol, and bayonet.

As the soldiers sorted the ammunition for the weapons, I rummaged through the other contents of the American's pack. To my delight, I found a map of the region. I also saw a stack of folded papers bound up in olive drab cord. I untied the cord and realized that they were handwritten letters. Crinkled photos fell out of the stack of letters. There were pictures of a pretty young woman at the beach, leaning against a shiny automobile, and holding a beautiful baby in its christening dress. I stared at the photos in my gunpowder-stained hands and I wept.

The soldiers urged me to come with them on their journey to the east, toward Germany, to safety. But I briefly told them of my mission that lay to the west. Before we parted, they each thanked me and wished me good luck in my quest. I beckoned them to kneel, and I placed my hands on each of their heads as I said the prayers of blessing. When I reached the older soldier, I muttered the words of absolution and told him his sins were forgiven. He looked into my eyes knowingly and whispered his thanks.

I continued my journey alone and the tears flowed as I contemplated the violation of my vows as a priest— I was responsible for participating in the brutal death of another human being. I came upon a small clearing in the forest where a ray of sunlight shone on the grassy bank near a clear pool of water. I knelt on the smooth grass in the beam of sunshine. Then the voice of our Lord spoke to my soul as I looked to heaven, and the skies began to brighten. First He asked me what would have happened to the three Germans if I had not taken action. Then He told me that it was no sin to act as an instrument of His vengeance to prevent evil men from harming His people or His church. Suddenly bright, warm sunshine surrounded me and the surface of the pool of water sparkled like precious diamonds. I cast off my robes and waded into the surprisingly warm, clear water. I ducked my head under the surface and emerged clean, refreshed, purified.

After two more days of hiding from both German and American patrols, I reached the Black Forest town of Freiburg. Despite my resolve and my faith, I was footsore and weak from hunger, but the town was completely deserted. Suddenly I heard a voice in the darkness speaking in a language I couldn't understand.

I stopped in my tracks and reached into my rucksack. My hands closed around the butt of Major Bachman's luger, but I prayed that I wouldn't need to shoot another human being ever again. A freckle-faced American soldier, who couldn't have been more than a teenager, approached from the shadows. When he saw me, he slung his rifle over his shoulder and smiled.

I didn't understand what the American was saying, but his broad smile and his careless movements seemed friendly. I slowly shifted my hand from the luger's butt to its barrel. Then I put both hands up as the young soldier approached. I motioned to the pistol and tried to pantomime an eating motion in an attempt to offer the pistol in exchange for something to eat.

The soldier took the weapon and turned it over in his hands, amazed at his good fortune in getting his hands on a Nazi officer's sidearm. I pointed toward my mouth again in an eating gesture. The soldier grinned and handed me a chocolate bar that I stuffed into my mouth, disregarding my dignity in the presence of an enemy soldier.

The soldier took me to a nearly bombed-out school building that the Americans were using as their headquarters. They fed me noodles and sausage and beans and bread and coffee until I thought I would burst. A German-speaking American officer came and sat with me as I finished my third helping of food. The American asked me many questions about the condition of roads and towns in the Black Forest. I answered carefully, but honestly. After all, the sooner the Americans advanced to the east, the better the chance that they would arrive in Salzburg before the Russians.

After the officer finished taking notes, I explained that I needed to get to Colmar as soon as possible. The American shook his head, but I explained my mission to care for the widow and child of a fallen German officer. The American looked at me intently for a long time, then showed me a photo of his wife and young son. In the end, I was granted a pass to travel inside American lines and I was able to hitch a ride in the back of a cargo truck to a road junction just outside Colmar.

Despite my pathetic limp, I almost ran down the road to Colmar, the end of my journey. When I reached the outskirts of town I saw the red, white, and blue of the French tricolor everywhere. Church bells pealed, children banged spoons and cooking pots together, and the town band played *La Marseillaise* over and over, each time a little more off-key. Everywhere people were drinking wine, kissing each other, and dancing in a celebration of freedom and liberation.

When I neared the town center I heard a different sound, the angry growl of a mob. I could smell the choking fumes of burning gasoline and rubber, and soon I saw the black smoke rising from a German staff car in flames. People were racing into the town hall with wild, crazed looks and hurling books, flags, and furniture onto the fire. Off toward the fountain I saw a crowd gathered around a man in a beret who was angrily shouting. I could just make out the French words for "whore" and "traitor."

I watched in horror as the man, who was clearly drunk, grabbed a beautiful young woman, pulled her up on the fountain stairs with him, and roughly began to hack her long blond hair away with evil-looking sheers. I struggled to push through the throng of people hoping to stop this madness, but the crowd roared in a frenzy. When the man in the beret was finished, the young woman sobbed as clumps of stubble clung to her bleeding scalp and the mob howled with anger.

Suddenly a teenager on the outskirts of the crowd grabbed a broken brick and flung it at the woman with all his might. I gasped as the brick struck home, raising a horrible gash on the woman's forehead. She fell from the stairs, striking her head on the pavement. The crowd parted as a pool of blood spread around the woman on the gray stones.

The mob fell silent and people began to disperse— some silently, some making the sign of the cross as they silently prayed in remorse, some shaking their heads saying, "She got what she deserved, the Nazi whore." When I reached the bloody, broken form of the woman, she was lifeless. As I lifted my tear-filled eyes to heaven in the prayer for the dead, the last of the mob drifted away.

I found myself alone kneeling on the pavement, my robe damp with the woman's blood, as a chilly wind swept across the empty town square. When I saw the cross around the woman's neck, I feared that this poor woman was Marte Bachman. I raised my hands to the sky and cried out in grief for this innocent woman and in fear that I had arrived too late —Had I failed in my mission and my promise to a dying warrior?

As I slowly regained some composure, I noticed a faint whimper and looked to my right. I was startled by the unflinching stare of a blond little boy, his clear blue eyes absorbing the scene, but thankfully not comprehending all that he saw.

I stooped in front of the boy and hesitatingly whispered in German, "Are you Major Bachman's son?"

The little boy replied, "Ja, I am Adelard."

I folded him in my arms and wept bitter tears for both of us."

The old man heard the sound of a car door close and voices on the street. He quickly replaced the journal in the satchel, but never noticed the fine dusting of powder that an unseen hand had placed on the flap of the satchel to see if it had been disturbed.

Chapter 9

AFTER NIGHTS IN October when temperatures dip well below freezing and the ponds wear a skim coat of ice until noon, there comes an afternoon in northern New England when people can open their windows just a crack and let in the soft, warm breeze one last time. The sun shines with almost the intensity of summer, and despite the golden leaves lying all about and the clear realization that this is just a brief respite before winter's chill, spirits soar in the last sweet dance of summer.

Chris couldn't concentrate on work. He told Peggy to hold his calls and cancel his afternoon meeting with the production team. Shoving a few files into his laptop bag, he made some well-placed comments about feeling a cold coming on and headed out the door. It would be a nice surprise to pick up Ronnie a little early for a change.

As he headed toward Ronnie's school, he noticed people in shorts and T-shirts washing cars, mowing lawns, or just sitting on front porches. It was almost as if everyone had to get in one last taste of summer before it became just a memory. When he reached the school, he had to park two blocks away because of all the other parents' cars in line to pick up their children. He took off his jacket and tie and tossed them into the backseat, then sauntered off down the street to the school.

He glanced over toward the rectory as he strolled and spotted a cherry-red 1969 Ford Mustang in the driveway. Joe, the janitor, was leaning against a tree near the driveway and gyrating to the music on his iPod. The sight of the vintage car brought back a flood of memories.

The Mustang was identical to the one his father had spent hours restoring. Chris didn't have many fond memories of his father, but the hours when they worked on the Mustang together were perhaps the only good times that Chris recalled spending with his father. Every now and then Chris was able to borrow the car for a special dance at the high school. His father would put up a fuss, but in the end he'd wink and say, "Just be careful how you handle it, hotshot, and be careful what you do when it's parked."

Chris couldn't resist the urge to go get a closer look at the car across the street. He waved to Joe, who returned the greeting but chose not to interrupt his musical enjoyment and kept on dancing, if that was what his movements could be called. Chris inspected the car closely, admiring the leather upholstery and chrome accents, and appreciating the fine condition in which it had been kept.

"What do you think of my baby?"

Chris was startled by the sudden appearance of a smiling red-haired man in jeans and a greasy T-shirt who slid out from under the rear of the car. "It's absolutely gorgeous," Chris replied with admiration as he ran his hand over the gleaming hood. "My dad had a '69 Mustang, but it never looked this good."

"I look at her as both transportation and a hobby all rolled into one," said the red-haired man, wiping the grease off a wrench. "But I still get a rush from the looks I get when I pull away from a stoplight."

"Yeah, Dad's Mustang did wonders for my popularity in high school," Chris said with a grin, "especially with the girls. Although I always found the backseat to be a little cramped for entertaining, if you know what I mean. By the way, my name is Chris Murphy. I was just picking up my daughter from school. I didn't mean to interrupt you."

The red-haired man stuck out a grease-stained hand. "I'm Jack Scanlon. Always happy to meet another Mustang lover." Then he reached out and tapped Joe on the shoulder. "Time to go to work, old buddy."

Joe removed one of his earbuds and said, "Okay, Father, can I help you again tomorrow?"

"Only if the second floor shines like a mirror and the boys' room faucets are sparkling," Jack said as Joe gave him an enthusiastic high five.

Chris instantly regretted his remark about the backseat of the Mustang. "So you're a …"

"Yes, but sometimes I'd rather just be a car guy than a parish priest. And, incidentally, the comment about the girls in high school was perfectly all right. I'm new here and so far I've met all the altar boys, their parents, the ladies' altar society, and, in an hour and a half, I will be introduced to the choir. Don't get me wrong, they're all wonderful people, but it was kind of nice to be mistaken, even for a few minutes, as just some guy who likes to work on cars."

Chris smiled in sympathy. "Well, Father, I've got to get over there and pick up my daughter, but it was nice talking to you." He reached out to shake the priest's hand again.

Jack gripped his hand firmly. "Please call me Jack, and don't be a stranger. If you get a chance, the new priest could use some background information about the parish, and I might even let you take the Mustang out for a spin with me."

Chris arrived at the school library just as Ronnie and a half dozen other children in plaid uniforms were sitting down at well-worn oak tables in the library to begin their homework. Brother Adelard was sitting at a large desk in the front of the room, his back ramrod straight as he examined a leather-bound book in front of him. Ronnie jumped up from the table and ran to Chris. Brother Adelard's silver head jerked in surprise, but he smiled when he saw Chris scoop Ronnie up in his arms.

"Christopher, how nice that you could come early to take Veronique home," Brother Adelard whispered. "We have shared her sadness at the loss of her beloved kitten. An early afternoon with her father is such a nice surprise for her." A murmur rose from the other children in the library, but the brother sternly raised his finger to his lips to restore silence and order.

Chris gathered up Ronnie's knapsack, lunch box, and several papers with stars and stickers of witches on them. Taking her by the hand, he headed down the long hallway. As he reached the front door, he glanced back and waved at Brother Adelard, who was framed in the wooden doorway of the library, gazing after them.

Ronnie almost seemed like her old self again as they laughed and chatted over ice-cream sundaes at Friendly's. It had been so long since Chris had seen any signs of life or spontaneity from her. Lately she kept falling into long periods of silence, and sometimes he caught her looking off, at nothing at all, with a strange, grim intensity that he'd never noticed before. When he would ask her what she was thinking about, she would usually give him a forced smile and reply, "Oh, nothing, Daddy, nothing at all." The day that cat was killed something had changed inside of his little girl.

But Chris was particularly pleased when, after scooping up the last bit of marshmallow sauce, Ronnie hopped down from her seat, tugged at his shirt, and said, "Let's go home and play outside, Dad."

They arrived home just as the sun was flooding the backyard with pale golden light. The warmth of the day was fading fast. Ronnie ran into the house to put on her pink hooded sweatshirt. Chris went to the garage to grab a rake and began to build a mountain of red, orange, brown, yellow, and green leaves. Ronnie ran down the back stairs and leaped into the leaf pile with a shriek of delight. Chris showered her with another heap of leaves and jumped into the pile, growling like a wild animal. Ronnie's giggles filled the air as she fought off her wild, tickling father.

After they were both exhausted from wrestling in the leaves, Chris hugged her close, breathing in the innocent perfume of her hair mixed with the earthy scent of autumn leaves. He remembered how Blackie's death had spoiled their last sunny afternoon together and quickly dismissed the memory.

He gently released his embrace and struggled to his feet. Suddenly he heard a strange sound, like animals growling in the distance. The sound grew louder and louder as whatever it was drew closer. Ronnie jumped up from the leaf pile and looked at Chris questioningly.

The growl became a roar and was punctuated by hideous shrieking as if someone, or something, was in unimaginable pain. Without thinking, Chris ran to the front of the house, toward the terrible sound.

Down the street, roaring, shrieking, with their fangs bared, spun the two black Dobermans, locked in combat. From time to time one of the dogs would back off momentarily only to lunge at the neck or belly of the other and begin the horrible assault again. Both dogs were bleeding heavily. A trail of bright red blood and clumps of fur marked the path of their battle.

Neighbors had come out of their houses and looked on in horror. One man began to run toward the dogs with his garden hose, but they spun out of his reach. Soon the dogs appeared to run out of strength, and the ferocity of their battle ebbed. They rolled up in the street in front of Chris's house and stopped, a pool of blood growing underneath them. The man with the hose cautiously approached the heap of bright red blood and black fur, and said, "Well, I'll be damned. They're both dead."

At that some of the neighbors walked over to inspect the hideous sight.

Chris, too, had observed the spectacle with morbid fascination. Now he came to his senses and realized that Ronnie had watched the whole gruesome episode. He turned to her and was surprised to see that she had a sort of smile on her face as he scooped her into his arms and carried her away from the bloody carcasses in the street.

"I'm sorry this ruined our beautiful afternoon, princess," he said as he set her down and smoothed the last of the leaves out of her hair. "Those dogs must have just gone mad or something."

Ronnie turned and looked at him directly. "Those dogs were punished for what they did to Blackie." Then she took his hand and turned toward the house. "Shouldn't we start cooking dinner soon, Dad?"

She turned on the television in the living room and started watching one of her favorite late afternoon cartoons. Chris took hamburger patties from the refrigerator and began frying them on the stove. From time to time, he peered into the living room. Ronnie just peered intently at the television and giggled from time to time at the crazy antics of the cartoon animals.

"Do you want cheese on your hamburger and some chips?" Chris asked gently.

"Sure, Daddy, that would be great. I'm starving," replied Ronnie without taking her eyes off the television.

She never mentioned the incident again that night, and Chris certainly wasn't going to bring it up. Ronnie gobbled up her cheeseburger and chattered constantly until it was time for bed.

After Ronnie was asleep that night, Chris opened a bottle of beer and sat down at the kitchen table. He was puzzled by Ronnie's reaction to the horrible dogfight. Maybe in Ronnie's mind the dogs were somehow paid back for their part in Blackie's death, and maybe that made it easier for her to come to terms with the loss of her pet. Kids are funny, he told himself as he finished the beer, and his thoughts turned to Jennifer.

He felt like a teenager again as he stared at his cell phone trying to summon up his courage. He thought about having another beer but decided that wouldn't be the best combination in these circumstances. He hadn't wanted to seem too eager, so he had waited three nights before calling. He was so nervous, he couldn't even leave her a voice mail.

He knew he had to try again tonight, but he feared that she might not want to have anything to do with him after the awkward and embarrassing way their first date ended. He knew that he really wanted to see her again, but wasn't sure how to handle the conversation.

Jennifer answered the phone.

"Hi, Jennifer, this is Chris Murphy from the power plant." His tongue felt like it was coated in baby powder. Why did he say 'from the power plant'?

"Chris Murphy? From the power plant, you say." She was toying with him, and he knew it. "Let me see if I remember anyone by that name."

"This is also the same Chris Murphy in the police log from last Friday night," he said, catching on.

"Oh, I have no idea what you're talking about, because I have nothing to do with criminals," she said.

"Well, you see, it really wasn't my fault because I had a terrible tour guide for the Ashton Falls History Town Tour," he said. "I'm planning to write a letter of complaint to the Chamber of Commerce."

"Perhaps the next time you hire a tour guide, you should consider paying a little bit more and checking references," she shot back.

"Fine," he replied, "do you know any tour guides who are available this Saturday night who are of sound character?"

"Well, I do have one, but she's going to the movies with a friend," Jennifer said.

Chris's heart sank. "Who is she going to the movies with?" He knew he shouldn't, but he asked anyway.

"Some guy from the power plant … named Chris Murphy."

He smiled. "What, no tours this Saturday night?"

"No, Chris, let's just have a normal first date," she said, her voice softening and taking on a serious tone. "I really like you, but I'm afraid we started off on the wrong foot last Friday."

"I actually had a wonderful time, Jen, but I admit it was a little wacky," he said.

"Okay, the movie starts at seven o'clock, so pick me up at six thirty. We'll have dinner afterwards at Gilligan's Pub, so don't wear a jacket and tie." She spelled out the instructions carefully.

"Well, I can see who's in charge here," he remarked.

"That's right," she said. "And, one more thing …"

"What's that?"

"Don't keep me in suspense after the date, wise guy," she admonished. "You call me the very next day. Got it?

"Yes, ma'am," he replied. Then he made a smooching noise in the receiver and said, "See you at six thirty on Saturday."

He put his phone down on the kitchen table and chuckled to no one in particular.

The rest of the week went by quickly. Ronnie was back to her playful, happy self, no longer falling into long bouts of silence. Chris had a new spring in his step every time he thought about Jen.

He was a little embarrassed to ask Jeanine to come to the mall with them on Saturday. After all, she had already agreed to babysit on Saturday night, but Ronnie really needed some new outfits, and he really needed a woman's judgment to help pick out a new outfit of his own, even if the lady providing the judgment was well into her seventies. Mimi had always bought his clothes for him because he was a fashion nightmare when left to his own devices. The memory of Mimi and their shopping outings in Soho brought an odd mix of regret, longing, and anger that he didn't have the time or energy to sort out.

Thankfully Jeanine was available on Saturday morning and seemed quite pleased to be asked for her grandmotherly expertise. They drove down to the mall in Portland and spent the time chatting about work, school, recipes, and, of course, the latest happenings in Ashton Falls. In the end he brought home two pairs of khaki pants and three casual shirts, in pastel colors, at Jeanine's insistence. He wasn't really quite sure what Jeanine picked out for Ronnie. All he knew was that they each carried a full bag and the credit card receipt was a little frightening.

Jeanine arrived a few minutes early to babysit for Ronnie that evening as usual. Chris noticed that the old woman seemed a bit quieter and a tiny bit older than she had earlier in the day.

"Are you okay tonight, Grand-mère?" he asked as he put his arm around her.

"Oh, thank you for asking, Chris." Jeanine leaned against him. "My friend Louise called to tell me that an old classmate of ours passed away last night."

"Oh, I'm sorry to hear that, Jeanine," Chris said. "Were you close?"

"Well, he was a dear friend when we were in school," she explained. "But he went away to Vietnam and he was never the same when he came back home."

An odd feeling came over Chris. "How did he die?"

"They found him on the railroad tracks by the station this morning. The night train must have struck him. You see, he often slept near the railroad tracks at night. As I said, he was a bit strange." She dabbed her eyes with a tissue. "They say it was an accident, but I don't know, I just don't know."

Chris rubbed her back. "Was his name Truman?"

"Why, yes, did you know him?" She looked at Chris with surprise.

"We met at the American Legion on Casino Night," Chris explained. "He seemed like a nice old guy."

"He was, and he gave the best part of himself for our country," she said as she straightened up. "Now he's gone, but he'll always be a handsome seventeen-year-old football star to me." She blew her nose and dabbed her eyes one more time. "Now where is my little friend Ronnie?"

"Jeanine, I can cancel my date—"

"I won't hear of it," Jeanine scolded. "A girls-only night is just what I need." She smiled and gave his arm a reassuring squeeze.

As Chris finished dressing in his new khakis and a lavender plaid shirt that he wasn't quite sure about, Ronnie called to him from the living room where she was making Halloween decorations for the porch.

"Dad, do you know where the scissors are?"

Chris was just splashing on some aftershave. "No, honey, why don't you check in one of the kitchen drawers?"

Then Jeanine's voice chimed in, "No, they're in the bathroom medicine cabinet, right in front of you, Chris."

Chris opened the medicine cabinet and, sure enough, there were the scissors. He brought them out to Ronnie. Jeanine met his puzzled glance and said, "I saw them there last week when I was looking for a Band-Aid for Ronnie. She had a nasty little cut on her finger that looked like it was going to get infected."

That was a little strange, Chris thought, but he couldn't waste time on the incident or he would be late to pick up Jen.

When Chris pulled up in front of Jen's house, she didn't come out to meet him. Instead he knocked on the door, which was answered by a burly man in his sixties who grasped his hand in a firm, vigorous handshake and motioned for him to come inside.

"Good to meet you, Chris," the older man said. "I'm Gus Mercier, Jennifer's father. Can I get you a drink?"

"No, no thank you, Mr. Mercier," Chris responded warily, wondering if the offer was a test of his judgment.

"Please sit down and call me Gus. I understand that you're the boss over at the power plant," Mr. Mercier continued. "My son Bruce tells me that things are running quite a bit better since you arrived."

Was this another test? Chris responded, "Bruce is being kind. There's still a lot of work to be done over there until we're operating the way we need to be."

"That's the spirit," Gus grinned, "constant improvement. I retired from the shipyard in Bath a few years ago—I worked there as a foreman for more than forty years—and that was always what kept me going. Constant improvement."

"What are you doing now, Mr. Mercier?" Chris asked.

"To tell the truth, I'm having a little trouble adjusting to retirement," he said. "I volunteer at the Salvation Army and stay active in the VFW, but ever since Jennifer's mother passed away two years ago, the place has been kind of lonely. That's why it's a blessing of sorts that Jen's back here with me."

"I bet that wasn't what you said when my hair dryer blew out the circuit breaker for the whole second floor," Jen said, making her entrance down the stairs. Chris sucked in his breath for a moment. She was absolutely stunning in a fitted white blouse and tight black skirt. Her hair was pulled back and she wore a strand of tiny white pearls that stood out against her tanned skin. He stood up as she entered the living room, and he noticed that she was taller than usual. Looking down, he noticed her elegant black high heels. Payback for my suit and tie on the first date? he wondered.

"All right, Daddy," she said, "you've bored him enough. Now he's all mine."

"Okay, okay, have a nice time tonight, you kids." Gus blushed a little as Jen pecked him on the cheek.

She whispered in his ear, "Don't wait up and don't worry, Daddy. I'm a big girl."

As Chris shook Gus Mercier's hand, it dawned on him that Jen was all he had in the world. He wondered how he would feel when Ronnie was walking out the front door with some young man. The thought was oddly sobering.

The rest of their date was everything that it should be. The movie was a light comedy—nothing too deep or disturbing, but entertaining nonetheless. Dinner was a simple, but classy affair at a local pub with an upscale menu and a well-heeled clientele. Throughout the evening, Chris was a perfect gentleman, and Jen, while always entertaining, seemed somehow subdued.

When they pulled up in front of her house, Chris leaned over to kiss her. Jen kissed him in a tender, but clearly one-time manner.

Chris brought his lips up to hers again, but she turned her head away.

"Do we need to drive up to the falls again?" asked Chris with a touch of sarcasm.

"Come on, Chris, we're not sixteen," replied Jen with some annoyance.

"I don't get this, Jen," Chris shot back. "Last week we were practically ready to sleep together, and this week I can barely get you to kiss me."

"I told you that I wanted this to be like a genuine, not messed up, first date," she answered, her temper rising. "If you just want a piece of ass, pal, you need to go elsewhere."

"There's no other place to go," Chris shouted. "I couldn't find a better looking piece of ass in the whole state of Maine, so I'll just stay here, thank you."

They both stopped and looked at each other with puzzled expressions, then Jen giggled. "Did you hear what you just said? It made no sense at all."

Chris put his arm around her. "I'm just a dumb guy, Jen, and you know, sometimes we don't think straight in matters of the heart. I really like you and I'm finding that my feelings for you are getting stronger every time I see you or talk with you. Look, I even go to church on Sunday mainly to see you."

"Then you need to understand that I want to take it slowly because I'm falling ... I really care for you too, Chris, and I don't want to start our relationship off on the wrong foot before we even get to really know each other." Then she kissed him long and deep.

"See you in church tomorrow, and don't forget to call me this week, you jerk," she said as she stepped out of the car and ran up the front stairs to the house.

Chris started up the engine and went to pull away from the curb, but had to wait a few moments because the windows were all fogged up on the inside.

Looking through the curtains of a darkened second-floor window, Gus Mercier noticed the Volvo's foggy windows and smiled to himself.

Chris and Ronnie arrived late for church the next morning, so they had to sit in one of the back pews. That meant that Chris had a clear view of Jen during the entire mass and didn't hear more than a few of Father Scanlon's words because he couldn't keep his eyes off her. After mass was over, he waited in front of the church to see Jen, thinking that it was about time she met Ronnie.

As Jen stepped out of church, she dropped her umbrella. Brother Adelard darted over to retrieve it, taking her hand and smiling as he returned the umbrella. She raced down the stairs to where Chris and Ronnie were standing.

"Ronnie, I'd like you to meet a friend of mine," Chris said as Jen approached. "This is Jennifer."

"I've been wanting to meet you," Jen said as she grasped Ronnie's hand. "Your daddy talks about you all the time and says the most wonderful things about you."

In the innocence of childhood, Ronnie looked up at Chris and asked, "Is Jennifer the friend that you go out to dinner with, Daddy?"

"That's right, honey."

Then Ronnie looked at Jennifer and up at Chris and observed, "She's pretty."

Jen jumped right in. "You're pretty, too, Ronnie, and your dad tells me that you're also very smart."

"Brother Adelard says that I'm the smartest girl in the first grade," Ronnie reported in a matter-of-fact way.

"Well, Brother Adelard is a very smart and nice man himself, so he should know," said Jen.

"Daddy, can I go out to dinner with Jennifer and you sometime?" Ronnie asked, looking up at her father.

"Well, it's kind of late when Jennifer and I get home, Ronnie," Chris replied, "but maybe we could take a day trip someday." Then he added with a sly look at Jennifer, "Jennifer grew up in Maine, and she's a wonderful tour guide."

Not to be outdone, Jen shot back, her eyes smiling, "I would love to take you on a little trip someday, and maybe we could bring your dad, if he promises to behave. Where would you like to go?"

"We read a story in school about a lighthouse," Ronnie said. "Can you take me to a lighthouse?"

"I know just the place out on the coast. And there are lots of good shops in the harbor," Jen replied, "so we'll tell your dad to bring lots of money with him."

Ronnie giggled, "That sounds like fun. When can we go?"

"How about next Saturday, Dad?" Jennifer asked.

Chris nodded and said, "Sounds great."

Jen stooped down and shook Ronnie's hand again. "It was very nice to meet you, Ronnie." Then she turned to Chris and said, "See you next Saturday, and don't forget to call sometime this week." Then she turned and walked toward her car.

Ronnie looked after her. "She's almost as pretty as Mommy. I like her."

"I do too, honey," Chris said quietly.

Chapter 10

IN THE MIDDLE of the night, one of the old, rusting chemical tanks at the power plant began to ooze a foul-smelling, green liquid. In the darkness, the toxic sludge slithered down the embankment near the Micmac River. By the time the plant maintenance team detected the leak, hundreds of gallons had seeped into the soil dangerously close to the river. Federal and state environmental protection agencies were quickly notified according to regulations.

Soon an army of technicians swarmed over the plant and its grounds in their white coverall suits with all sorts of meters and probes, checking on containment, recovery, and disposal procedures. During the following days there were meetings with contractors at all times of the day and night. Thankfully, Jeanine was able to babysit for Ronnie at night when Chris had to stay at the plant.

Late in the week, Chris received a call from the Ashton Falls Town Manager's office requesting that he attend a mid-morning meeting with the town manager. Although Chris had briefly met Big Bill Benson at the American Legion, he asked his secretary, Peggy, about him. Chris had a sense that this wasn't going to be a simple, friendly meeting.

"He's quite a guy," Peggy told him as she sipped her Diet Coke. "He's called Big Bill for lots of reasons. He was born and raised in Ashton Falls. Big Bill was the quarterback of the state champion team in the seventies, and he's probably lived his whole life here, except for his time in the Marines. He knows everybody in town, has done favors for half of them, and probably has some dirt on the other half, which he's not afraid to use if it suits his purposes." Then she added, "I'd be very careful at this meeting if I were you, Chris. Big Bill knows how to stick it to people with a smile on his face."

Chris set off for the meeting prepared for the worst.

The Ashton Falls Town Hall looked like time had frozen it in 1900. The three-story stone building resembled a small castle with its two conical turrets that reached to the sky, but the flaking paint around the window frames showed that the town was having trouble keeping up with the needs of the aging palace. As Chris walked up the broad granite stairs in front of the building, he noticed the bronze plaques bearing the names of the town's sons and daughters who had given their lives in wars from the Revolution to Iraq and Afghanistan. There were a lot of names up there.

As Chris opened the front door, he spotted a cherry-red 1969 Mustang parked on the other side of the building. There can be only one car like that in Ashton Falls, he thought. I wonder what Father Scanlon is doing here?

The town manager's secretary greeted him courteously and explained apologetically that Big Bill was running a little late. Chris sat down in a dusty old mission oak chair outside the office door. He looked for something to read but could only find

P. G. Smith

copies of the Ashton Falls town report, a *Field & Stream* magazine, and *The Old Farmer's Almanac* from last year. Luckily there was a copy of today's *Portland Press Herald* on another chair.

After scanning the headlines and reflecting on his annoyance at this waste of time, Chris became aware of the raised voices inside the office. From time to time, one voice boomed out, only to be answered by a lower, bitter snarl, then a quieter voice would take over for a few minutes. This pattern was repeated several times until the door finally opened and Father Scanlon, accompanied by Brother Adelard, stepped out into the hallway. Chris could clearly see that Brother Adelard's face was flushed and he had dropped his customary veneer of composure and good humor.

"Hey, Mustang Man, it's good to see you again," Father Scanlon said, thrusting out his hand. "What brings you here?"

"Probably the same kind of business that brings you here," Chris said, shaking the priest's hand.

"I certainly hope that you fare better than we did, Christopher," Brother Adelard stated gloomily.

"Hey, listen, Chris," Father Scanlon said, "please call me at the rectory and we'll go out for a drive. I mean it."

"Okay, Father," Chris said. "See you this afternoon, Brother."

The secretary cleared her throat, escorted Chris into the inner office, and motioned to another dusty oak and leather chair, explaining that Mr. Benson would be right in. Chris felt like he was waiting for the dentist. As he sat there, he surveyed Big Bill's office: there were photos of Big Bill and Donald Trump,

156

Big Bill and Tom Brady of the New England Patriots, Big Bill and his family, Big Bill and David Ortiz of the Boston Red Sox, and Big Bill and a huge fish. But the biggest photo, right over his desk, was an enlarged photo of a smiling Big Bill, in camouflage, and a dead, bloody moose. Chris couldn't help but notice all the certificates and citations, neatly framed and displayed so the person in his seat could admire them. On the wall to the left was the head of a sorrowful buck on whose antlers hung a Red Sox cap. Perhaps it was meant to be whimsical, but the message was clear: "Play ball with Big Bill or you could end up with your head on his wall."

At length, Big Bill burst through the door. He clamped his hands firmly on his hips, thrust out his barrel chest, looked Chris up and down, and said needlessly, "No need to get up, just make yourself comfortable, uh, Mr. Murphy." Then, forgetting that they'd met before, he put out his hand and said, "Oh yeah, I'm Big Bill Benson." Then he crushed Chris's hand in his iron grip. "Sometimes I forget because everybody around here knows me," he said as he settled onto a corner of the desk under the head of the deceased buck.

Chris spoke up, "What can I do for you, Mr. Benson? I understand that you wanted to see me." He studied the town manager who perched on the corner of his desk, one leg nonchalantly dangling. Chris had a better chance to see the man now than he did in the dim light of the American Legion. Big Bill certainly earned his name. He was probably close to six and a half feet tall and he was solidly built, with a flattop haircut and a neatly trimmed brush of a moustache. His lined face and steel-gray hair indicated that he was in his fifties, but he projected strength and energy, and, Chris thought, a hint of hidden venom.

"Well, Mr. Murphy, I don't like to beat around the bush," Big Bill began. "You're a relatively young man for such an important position at the power plant, and I have to compliment you on that. But you probably have never worked in a small town before, and you've certainly never worked in this small town before."

Chris nodded his acknowledgment as Big Bill looked down at him from his perch on the desk. But he still didn't know where this was going.

"Things are done differently here than they're done in the city," Big Bill continued. "Sometimes we do business by a handshake, rather than formal contracts with lawyers and such. That's the way it's been done here for more than three hundred years, and it's worked pretty well, now, hasn't it?"

This is pretty windy for someone who doesn't beat around the bush, Chris thought, but he said, "Please go on, Mr. Benson."

Big Bill's eyes narrowed and he leaned toward Chris. "Right now, you've got alligators crawling up your asshole, son, and I'm in a position to feed 'em or help chase 'em away, if you see what I mean."

"I'm afraid you've lost me," Chris said, although he was getting a pretty clear sense of where this was going.

"Then I'll make myself perfectly clear." Big Bill lowered his voice. "Although officially this conversation never took place. You've got the EPA, Conservation Trust, and every other fucking tree hugger group in the world in your shorts because of your little chemical spill. Now I, on behalf of the town government, can scream bloody murder about the environmental damage to our town caused by your company's carelessness or violation of regulations—and you know there are at least a few counts. On the other hand, I can call up to Augusta and ask our state representatives and senators to put in a good word for your company, because it's such an important part of the town and a good corporate citizen."

Chris took a deep breath. He didn't want to have anything to do with some kind of backdoor deal with Big Bill, but he knew if he rejected the idea outright, Big Bill would be on the phone to the EPA before Chris left the parking lot. So he said, "Our company always seeks to be a good community partner, Mr. Landry. How can we work more closely in partnership with Ashton Falls?"

"Ashton Falls expects a few little league sponsorships, donations to the PTA, contributions to the firefighters' fund, that sort of thing."

"I'll check with our community relations representative to make sure that those things are happening," Chris replied.

"But what I expect," Big Bill said as he leaned closer to Chris and stared at him hard, "demonstrates real commitment to our partnership. A few 'special customers' will need to have the power meters on their homes adjusted, or perhaps just read differently. There also may need to be a few rate adjustments for some small businesses in town. Nothing major, nothing costly, nothing illegal, just a few considerations to demonstrate friendship and good faith for my assistance in saving you from the alligators."

Chris was furious, but he contained his temper. He wanted to lunge up from his chair and grab Big Bill by his big throat. This was extortion and blackmail, but he knew he needed to keep his mouth shut—at least for now.

Chris stood up. "Thank you for this enlightening conversation, Mr. Benson. Our company is committed to being a good neighbor to the Ashton Falls community. Please call on me if I can be of service to the town."

Big Bill grinned as he crushed Chris's hand once more and said, "Oh, you'll be hearing from me, all right, you can bet on that."

While Brother Adelard and Father Scanlon were at Town Hall, the cleaning lady was busy vacuuming and tidying up the rooms in the rectory as she did once every week. When she finished Brother Adelard's bedroom, she closed the door, lugged the heavy vacuum cleaner down the stairs, and started on the dining room. Over the high-pitched whine of the vacuum, she couldn't hear the old man step into Brother Adelard's bedroom, reach into the desk, and begin reading.

> "I carried the little boy on my hunched back most of the way from Colmar through the front lines of Germany to the nearly ruined city of Salzburg. As I scrounged for food, begged for rides, and bluffed my way through checkpoints, I kept up a cheerful façade

with little Adelard, never letting on that I was as frightened and heartbroken as the little boy must be.

Often at night Adelard asked if he would ever see his mother or father again, and sometimes he cried. I held the boy close, gathering all the loose folds of my robe around the boy to keep him warm. Then I would tell him stories about my favorite saints, the wonders that await us in heaven, and the kindness of the Blessed Virgin Mary until the boy drifted off to sleep. Looking at the sweet little face of the sleeping child, I often ran my hand gently along the boy's soft cheek and stroked his silky blond hair. Then I would look up into the twinkling stars and pray, "Lord, thank you for bringing this angel into my life."

After weeks of travel, we arrived at Salzburg as the sun was painting the snow-covered Alps with a faint lavender glow. I held the little boy's hand tightly as we made our way up the long, winding path to the monastery. Little Adelard couldn't help himself from looking over his shoulder at the mighty Hohensalzburg Fortress that seemed to radiate rose-colored light from its perch over the rushing Salzach River. The little boy had never seen something so beautiful, just like a magic castle in a fairy tale.

The abbot was both relieved and impressed that I had successfully completed my errand of mercy, but when I discussed my plans for Adelard to remain at the monastery, the abbot would hear none of it. He was adamant that the monastery was no place for a little boy. No, he insisted that every child belonged in a family with a mother and a father.

I returned to my cell and cried as I contemplated saying good-bye to Adelard. I even considered breaking my vow of obedience, taking the child, and fleeing. But where could I go? What kind of life would that be for an orphaned little boy who most needed security and stability in his life?

A plea to the good people of Salzburg was sent out through the local parishes to find a good home for a war orphan. Weeks went by until eventually a certain Frau Mueller inquired about the war orphan. She was a fat, slovenly woman who reeked of alcohol and body odor. She told the abbot that she and her husband would be willing to take in the orphan, but they already had many mouths to feed in their home. Perhaps if the monastery could help them with the little boy's food and upkeep, they could welcome him into their family. The abbot, wishing to get Adelard into a good Catholic home, agreed to pay the Muellers a small monthly allowance to help feed and clothe the child. And so, little Adelard packed up his few belongings, took the woman's pudgy hand, and reluctantly walked down the hill into the scarred town.

I was inconsolable. I spent my days and nights in silent prayer and fasting. I spoke to no one and accepted comfort from no one. The abbot called me to his room to explain that it was futile to resist God's will. I simply nodded and bowed my head.

After Adelard left our monastery, my thoughts returned to the Prayers for the Damned. Although Major Bachman had passed away, the ancient rite still offered me the chance to do our Lord's work in a special way. And so, I began to visit the city's jails and darker corners in search of unrepentant sinners. I also arranged to visit the emergency treatment center at the hospital by offering spiritual comfort to those who were injured. When I was lucky enough to be near a newly admitted child, I could sometimes sneak a bloody bandage under my robes, but my access to innocent blood was intermittent. I only took Brother Gunther and Brother Joachim, whom I knew I could trust, into the knowledge of the ancient rite, fearing that others might not be discrete. Soon the three of us gathered whenever the conditions were right to cast the vengeance of the Lord upon sinners.

Sometimes as I walked through the city, I would stand on the street outside the Muellers' house in the faint hope that I could catch a glimpse of Adelard. Although I never saw him there, often I could hear the shrill voice of Frau Mueller shrieking at the children and I feared for my little boy. But I fought back the urge to storm into the house and take him back to the loving shelter of the monastery. The abbot had forbidden me to have contact with Adelard, explaining that it would make it that much harder for him to start a new life, and I believed that the abbot was right.

Then one spring evening as dusk drew a gentle hush over the city, I was walking in the monastery garden among the tender green shoots saying my evening prayers. Suddenly I heard a soft whisper. It was Adelard, who was hunched down in the gloom outside the monastery gate. I opened the gate quickly and took the little boy into my arms. I kissed the boy's tearstained face and noticed that his cheeks were scratched and bruised. As Adelard wept, he told me about the harsh conditions and the beatings he endured until he decided to flee from the Muellers' house. He begged me to take him back, to keep him safe.

After pledging to God and Adelard that I would never allow him to be taken from me again, I took the little boy straight to the abbot's room. I threw open the door, and, pointing to the marks on the boy's face, demanded, "Is this the will of God, Abbot? Look carefully—is this God's will?"

From that day on, Adelard was a member of the community of the Monastery of Saint George. He dressed like a monk, worked like a monk, and prayed like a monk. I was his special guardian, his teacher, and his only parent, but he had dozens of uncles who cherished him. The little boy quickly settled into life with his new family, which was safe, predictable, and loving.

Often I would take him to the small graveyard near our chapel, where together Adelard and I would stand near his father's grave and offer our prayers for the souls of his parents. I wanted to be sure that he never forgot his heritage as the son of a brave Teutonic warrior and a beautiful German maiden.

One afternoon as he was helping Brother Simon bake bread, Adelard heard the peal of church bells in the city. Looking up at the baker, he asked why the bells were tolling. The baker looked down sadly at the little boy and explained that there had been a terrible fire in the city that had killed a family trapped inside their burning house. Adelard asked what family it was. "I think the name was Mueller," replied the monk innocently. "I believe they took in orphan children. Thankfully they say many of the orphans escaped from the fire, but the parents weren't so fortunate." The little boy said nothing more, but returned to the dough he was kneading as he tried to hide his smile from the baker. My prayers for Adelard's abusive foster parents had been answered.

Years went by and Adelard grew into a strong, devout, and extremely well-educated young man. The monks gave him the best they had in every way. He spoke fluent German, French, and English, and was able to read and write easily in Latin and Greek. The young man had a mastery of calculus, biology, world history, and was steeped in the works of Aristotle, St.

Augustine, and Thomas Moore. From his afternoon labors with the monks, Adelard could also bake bread, frame a structure, grow vegetables, make wine, brew beer, sew clothing, and cook a fine meal for sixty men. But there was one area of learning in which the young man was sorely lacking.

One day the abbot was walking in the garden with me and asked me what I planned for Adelard in the future. I replied that soon it would be time for Adelard to take the vows of poverty, chastity, and obedience as a full member of the order. The abbot stopped and looked at me sadly. "Brother, only those who know the world can choose to renounce its ways. Our little Adelard is like a caged bird in many ways. When he sees other young people in the city, I notice his curiosity and longing to be one of them." The abbot paused as he saw my anxiety rise. "You have given your all to save this poor lost soul, and you have done well. Look at what a fine young man he has become. But now it's time for him to experience the world outside our walls. If he returns, it is God's will. But he must experience life and see its possibilities—both good and bad—before he chooses to devote himself, his very being, to the monastic worship of our Lord."

This time I realized that the abbot was right. With a heavy heart, I took Adelard down into the center of Salzburg where we bought a suit of clothes, a pair of sturdy shoes, a suitcase, and an umbrella as I explained to the young man that he must set out on a journey to see life outside the monastery. For several weeks the monks prepared Adelard for his journey, instructing him in new subjects like how to ride a train, how to order a restaurant meal, and how to read a street map. As best they could, they tutored him about young women and how to conduct himself properly in their presence.

On a cold, wet morning in April, Adelard embraced me as we said our final prayers at his father's grave. I swallowed the lump in my throat as I watched him pass through the monastery's gate and walk down the long stairway into the city, his stiff new shoes squeaking on the cobblestones. The rain mixed with the tears that streamed down my face just as raindrops washed salty tears into the young man's mouth.

Adelard's first task was to claim any survivor funds due to his mother because his father had died in combat. After countless wrong turns, missed trains, and social miscues, he made his way to the capital city of Bonn. Adelard was quickly learning that his good looks, fine manners, and cultured bearing were opening many doors for him that might remain closed to others. He also carried a letter of introduction from the abbot that provided for food and shelter in any Catholic parish along the way. Finally arriving at the correct government office, he was pleasantly surprised to find that his mother was due a small fortune, nearly a year's wages for a laborer, because of his father's back pay, savings, and life insurance.

Although it took several weeks before he received the money, Adelard had plans when the cash arrived. The young man was fascinated by the libraries, historical museums, and art galleries in the capital city. He eagerly absorbed information about secular culture as well as his Germanic heritage. But his awakened appetite for the sensuous side of nightlife was equally insatiable.

Adelard soon learned that someone with plenty of money can make friends easily, and these new friends were only too willing to lead him further and further down into the murky underbelly of the city while helping him spend his inheritance at an alarming rate. The foolish young man soon fell madly in love with a worldwise prostitute who introduced him to rock and roll, beat poetry, kinky sex, opium, cocaine, and heroin. By the time he realized that his "beloved Beatrice" was using him for his cash, it was too late. His money was gone, he was hooked on heroin, and—after she threw him out on the street—he was homeless.

One thing Beatrice did for him before she threw him out, though, was to acquaint him with her pimp, Gunther. Under the guise of helping out a friend, Gunther found a room in a seedy hotel for Adelard and set him up with a heroin fix. Then Gunther arranged for Adelard to entertain a visiting businessman from

Chicago who was fond of the company of attractive young men and willing to pay handsomely for their services. Because of his cultured manners, Adelard's first customers were high-paying, older gentlemen who appreciated the companionship of a tall, good-looking young man as much as they wanted sex.

But soon, as Adelard's drug habit took its toll on his looks and demeanor, Gunther offered Adelard up to perverts and predators who abused him and forced him into demeaning and bizarre sexual activities. Adelard's soul burned with the rage he felt toward those who used him so badly. And so, within less than a year, Adelard had gone from baking bread in the monastery to servicing sexual deviants in the back alleys of Bonn.

One night, when he was strung out and desperate, Adelard propositioned an undercover policeman on the street. He was arrested, taken to the city jail, and thrown into a cell with other common criminals. By chance, one of the police officers, a good Catholic, recognized him as a former guest of his parish priest and alerted the priest. The following morning, the priest came to the station, took Adelard back to the rectory, and nursed him while he went through withdrawal. A few weeks later the priest paid Adelard's court fees and gave him just enough money for train fare to Salzburg.

Late at night a young man in a ragged suit trudged up the long stairway to the gates of the Monastery of Saint George above the sleeping city of Salzburg. He hesitated, then tapped on the heavy oak door. The door swung open, and the light from inside shone on the young man's gaunt, haggard face. Strong arms reached out to embrace him and welcome him home.

I was overjoyed to see Adelard. My prodigal son was home to stay. Indeed, after Adelard confessed his sins to the abbot, he put on his coarse gray monk's robe again and resumed his life at the monastery, taking on his share of the chores and joining the community for daily prayers. The monks welcomed him back as if he had never left, and Adelard seemed truly happy to be home with the only real family he had ever known.

After several months, Adelard approached the abbot and asked if he could take his final vows to become a member of the order of monks. And so on a wintry Sunday in February, the monks gathered for a high mass in their chapel. The abbot presided, dressed in the glittering white and gold vestments reserved for the holiest days in the church calendar. Adelard, with his monk's hood pulled up over his head, made his way slowly and solemnly down the main aisle of the chapel, eventually prostrating himself in front of the altar. The abbot pronounced the oath of poverty, chastity, and obedience. Adelard uttered his vows and the abbot invited him to rise, remove his hood, and take his place with the other brothers of the Germanic House of Saint Mary in Jerusalem. The monks looked on with pride, but no one was happier to welcome Brother Adelard into the order than me.

On the night after Adelard took his final vows, I went to his room just as he was about to go to bed. "Brother Adelard," I whispered, "you know that I've always loved you as a son. Well, as I get older, I realize that I won't live forever. There is knowledge I need to share with you just as your father and I shared it. Please come with me."

The sound of the vacuum cleaner abruptly ceased, and the old man quickly replaced the journal in the desk. Listening carefully for footsteps on the stairs, he quietly stepped into his own room, turned to the Red Sox game on his television, and sank into his recliner just as if he had been there all afternoon.

Chapter 11

THE REST OF Chris's time that week was taken up in reports and meetings and inspections of the spill site, but, by late Friday morning, the crisis was winding down. Still, Chris was troubled by his meeting with the town manager and couldn't get it off his mind. He considered himself to be an ethical person and was ashamed that he hadn't refused Big Bill's proposition immediately. But, on the other hand, he knew from his interviews after the spill that the maintenance crew had been cutting corners on their precautions in handling chemical waste. If the spill was investigated carefully, there would be hundreds of thousands of dollars in fines and he'd probably lose his job.

On a whim, Chris called the Holy Rosary Parish rectory and arranged to go out for a drive with Father Scanlon in the Mustang later in the afternoon. Chris asked Peggy to cancel his afternoon appointments, which she had started to do anyway.

As she reviewed the final business of the week with him, she said, "The town manager's office called several times this morning. Big Bill would like you to call him as soon as possible."

Chris muttered, "The town manager can go to hell." Then he recovered his composure and said, "Please call the Town

Hall and tell them that I was called away this afternoon on urgent business and that I'll contact the town manager on Monday morning."

Chris stepped out of his office door, and there was Jack Scanlon behind the wheel of the red Mustang, revving the engine. He looked distinctively un-priestlike in a ratty old gray Notre Dame sweatshirt and aviator sunglasses. The priest tooted the horn and Chris jumped into the passenger seat, tossing his briefcase and jacket into the backseat.

"Good to see you, Father," Chris said as he turned the window crank. "I really needed to get away from the office today."

"Will you please call me Jack?" the priest pleaded. "Remember, this is my chance to blow off a little steam, too, and all that 'father' stuff makes me feel like I'm on the job."

"Well, aren't you always on the job, Jack?" Chris asked.

"I guess you're right," Father Scanlan replied, "but I hate being reminded of the fact." At that he stamped on the accelerator and the vintage Mustang roared out of the parking lot, leaving two streaks of rubber on the pavement in its wake. Chris knew he was in for a great ride.

They flew through the Maine back roads for almost an hour, hugging curves, screaming along straightaways by farms and forests, and mischievously scattering piles of leaves as they raced through the sunny afternoon. Jack let Chris have a turn behind the wheel, and Chris found that driving the well-tuned car was almost like sipping a fine wine or savoring a choice cigar. As they neared a roadside bar, Jack told Chris to pull into the parking lot. Feeling the euphoria of speed and freedom, Jack asked Chris if he wanted a beer.

They each grabbed a vinyl-covered stool inside the dim, empty bar. The place reeked of stale smoke, spilled beer, and someone's halfhearted efforts to cover it all up with air freshener. The bartender was a stout middle-aged woman who served up two ice-cold draft beers and returned to her chores in the back room.

As they sipped their beer, Jack asked, "What were you doing at Town Hall the other day?"

"I'm kind of glad you asked," Chris replied, taking a deep breath. "I know it's your day off, but I was going to ask for your advice about my visit with Big Bill."

"Lay it on me, brother, either as a priest or a friend," Jack replied.

Chris then explained, as simply as he could, the ethical vise he found himself caught in by Big Bill's proposition. "So, I guess you could say, Jack, I'm damned if I do or damned if I don't."

The priest downed the rest of his beer and motioned to the bartender for another two beers. "I don't agree, Chris," he said thoughtfully. "If you'll forgive my plain assessment of Big Bill, the guy is nothing but a bully. If you play ball with him, you risk becoming contaminated. If you do the right thing and tell the main office in New York about his attempt at extortion, you'll probably come out of this thing without too much damage. The most important thing of all, though, is that you'll be able to live with yourself. The only way that you're damned is if you get into bed with Big Bill."

Chris nodded and took a swig of beer. He turned to the priest, looked him in the eye, and said, "You're right. Thanks for the advice ... Father."

Jack jokingly punched him in the arm. "What did I say about that 'father' stuff?"

Realizing that he had monopolized the conversation, Chris asked, "What were you and Brother Adelard doing at Town Hall?"

Jack chuckled. "Now there was a scene. The school has some kind of septic problem that Father Costello never got around to having fixed, so Big Bill sent us a letter notifying us that he was fining us for a health code violation. As I'm sure you know, there's not a lot of fat in the parish budget, so Adelard and I met with him to appeal the fine."

"How did it go?" Chris asked.

"Swimmingly. The appeal needs to go to the Board of Health, anyway, and three out of the five members are Catholic, so it shouldn't be much trouble. We just needed to schedule a date for the appeal. But Big Bill tried to lecture Adelard about our school practicing what it preaches to children and following the rules of the town. That got under Adelard's skin, and he shot back with some comparison between Big Bill and Pontius Pilate. Then the two of them started a royal pissing contest complete with biblical quotes, insults, and threats of legal action, until I decided it was best to cut and run."

"I just can't picture Brother Adelard losing his temper," Chris observed.

"He's kind of an odd duck. Behind that European reserve and fine manners, there lurks a man of great passion and intensity. The fire in his eyes when he was arguing with Big Bill would have frightened me if it was pointed my way. Big Bill should be grateful that Adelard doesn't own a gun, at least that I know of." Then Jack added, "The funny thing was, as we went to leave the town manager's office, Adelard was suddenly as composed as ever. He reached out, shook Big Bill's hand, and thanked him for taking the time to meet with us. It was like nothing ever happened."

"Well, maybe he's a little different, but I'm certainly thankful that he takes care of Ronnie in the afternoon," Chris said. "I don't know what I'd do without him." Then glancing at his watch, he added, "And speaking of Brother Adelard, if we don't get going soon, I'll be late again to pick up Ronnie."

Jack downed the last of his beer. "Well, we can't have that."

The two men, acting more like teenagers, whooped as they raced the Mustang through the narrow, twisting roads back toward town with total ignorance of the speed limit. Inevitably, blue flashing lights came up behind them as they passed the sign that read "Welcome to Ashton Falls."

"License and registration, please," said the gruff cop who appeared at the driver's window. He also asked Chris for his license. Chris could see his partner in the rearview mirror, positioned behind the car, his hand on his holster.

"We're in deep shit now, my friend," said Jack, rubbing his forehead. "You may not be surprised to know that I have many speeding tickets, but the bishop gets particularly upset when I'm called into court for reckless driving charges. Maybe it's time to pray."

The policeman returned moments later, removing his sunglasses. Chris thought he recognized him from his tour of the falls with Jen, which only served to increase his own anxiety. The officer smirked at Jack. "Well, Father, you have an interesting driving history, to say the least, but I guess we can leave it at a warning this time." Jack breathed an audible sigh of relief. Then the cop added, "Just remember this, Father, the next time I'm in the confessional."

On Saturday, Ronnie was out of bed before dawn. Chris woke up to her little face, inches from his nose, as she gently shook him. "Wake up, Daddy, wake up or we'll be late to pick up the pretty lady who's taking us to see the lighthouse." As he opened his eyes in the predawn darkness, he noticed that she was already fully dressed with her yellow L.L. Bean jacket zipped up and ready to go.

He shook his head as he asked himself, Has it been that long since I took her anywhere other than school, church, or the grocery store? He quickly dressed and called Jen to make sure that she was ready.

He had called Jen earlier in the week to work out the details of the trip, but all she would say was, "Pick me up by seven thirty on Saturday morning. Dress Ronnie in warm clothing. Bring plenty of cash, and don't plan to be back until late Saturday night. Oh, and trust me, you're going to have a great time."

When they arrived at Jen's house, she came out to the car with an armload of blankets and umbrellas, followed by Gus carrying a blue cooler.

Chris got out of the car and opened up the back of the station wagon. "Are you coming with us, Mr. Mercier?" Chris asked with good humor, although he certainly hoped he didn't get an affirmative response.

Chris helped settle the cooler into the wagon and was relieved to hear the old man reply, "Nope, I've got too much to do around the house today." Then he added with his hand on Chris's shoulder, "But I'd watch my wallet if I were you today, my boy. My daughter has big plans, and they're not cheap."

Jen hopped into the car, her face flushed and pink with the exertion of loading the car and coordinating all the details of the trip. She gave Chris a peck on the cheek and immediately turned her attention to Ronnie. "Okay, Miss Ronnie, this is your day," she began. "We're going to start off with a visit to the nicest lighthouse in Maine, just as you asked. Then we'll have a picnic on the shore, and maybe a boat ride, and lots of shopping, won't we, Dad?"

Chris nodded his agreement as Ronnie giggled and gushed, "This is going to be the best day ever!"

Jen struck up a conversation with Ronnie and the two of them chattered away about dolls, and school, and clothes. Chris noticed that Ronnie was far more animated talking with Jen than she was with him, but he also realized that he was unable to talk about most of the things that Jen was now effortlessly and enthusiastically discussing; "girl talk" was a magical and wonderful thing. This is just like the old days in New York, he thought, but then corrected himself. No, this is a lot better than the old days in New York.

He drove on as the warm sunshine cut through the early morning fog, listening to the incomprehensible chatter of two people he was crazy about.

Jen refused to tell Chris where they were headed, simply saying, "Take a right at the next set of lights," or "Head north on Route 1." He drove on through green forests, catching a glimpse of the sea from time to time. He was a little bit curious about their final destination, but he didn't really care where the road might lead him. He was just happy to be out on a fine fall morning with his two favorite girls.

Finally, after almost two hours on the road, Jen directed him into a gravel parking lot. In front of them was a magnificent whitewashed lighthouse perched on a cliff over the surging ocean. Chris could hear the crashing surf as he turned off the Volvo's engine.

"This is our first stop," announced Jen, "Pemaquid Point Lighthouse."

Ronnie jumped out of the car. "This is it—a real lighthouse! Just like the one in the book that Mrs. Campbell read us in school."

Chris held Jen's hand on his left and Ronnie's hand on his right as the little girl pulled the two adults up the path and into the lighthouse. He could smell the chilly, salt air from the sea as the breakers crashed against the rocks below, throwing spray skyward, the foam retreating into the gray-green ocean.

Ronnie was fascinated by the rushing sea as Jen explained, "The lighthouse is here to warn sailors to stay away from the rocks. So that's why the light flashes up top and the foghorn blows every few minutes." No sooner had she finished speaking then the loud groan of the foghorn deafened them, and they all laughed.

"But can't the sailors see that their ship is getting near the rocks?" Ronnie asked.

"Not always," Jen replied. "When the fog is thick, especially at night, sailors sometimes don't know where they are. In fact, that boulder over there was placed in memory of the people who were shipwrecked here a long time ago, before there was a lighthouse."

Chris marveled at Ronnie's fascination with every detail of the lighthouse and the keeper's house. He also appreciated Jen's patient answers to all of the little girl's questions. In fact, Jen and Ronnie were so absorbed in their conversation about the lighthouse that Chris felt like he was just tagging along. He studied Jen closely and thought how beautiful she looked in her bulky Irish-knit sweater as the wind blew her shimmering brown hair this way and that.

They explored every room of the keeper's house as Ronnie retold the story about the little girl who had to keep the light burning because her parents were too sick to do it. They waited at the base of the lighthouse until it was their turn to climb the narrow, steep circular metal stairs that led to up to the light itself. When they reached the top, Chris gazed out for miles over the rolling sea that smashed into the Maine coast and recoiled to strike again. The late morning was brightening, and he could see faint swaths of blue sky here and there through the gray fog blanket. Ronnie darted from one side of the light to the other, pointing out seagulls and ships. Jen leaned up against Chris and kissed him quickly when she thought Ronnie wasn't looking. Her lips were cool and the tip of her nose felt like ice, but her cheeks glowed with the chill and her smile warmed him to the soles of his feet.

After a while Ronnie agreed that she had seen about all she could see at the lighthouse. Chris started up the car while Ronnie and Jen took a quick tour of the gift shop on the other side of the parking lot, after coaxing some cash out of him. Ronnie outran Jen back to the car, waving a pink bracelet made of sailor's rope on her right wrist. Jen climbed in breathlessly after her.

"What is that?" Chris asked indignantly.

"Every special trip requires souvenirs," Jen patiently explained. "Besides, I warned you that this trip wasn't going to be cheap. Now let's get going. I have a special spot for our picnic."

The late morning sunshine had just about burned off the mist as they traveled through the countryside. They passed through small New England villages where stately white-steepled churches looked down on town commons carpeted with golden leaves that sparkled in the autumn sunlight. They drove along roadways that skirted the coastline and watched as lobstermen pulled their traps up out of the rolling sea. Jen directed Chris down a coastal road that was barely wide enough for two cars to pass each other and pointed to a parking spot. He could see a rocky stretch of shore with small pockets of sandy beach interspersed between the boulders. Seagulls circled overhead, the brilliant sunshine glowing on their white wings. Some of the houses that overlooked the shoreline were already boarded up in preparation for the winter snows.

"This is Ocean Point, my special place for a picnic on the rocks," Jen announced. "Mom and Dad used to take us here when we were little. In the summer, it's always crowded with tourists and the rich people who own these houses, but in the fall … well, we have it all to ourselves."

Chris unpacked the cooler, and they tiptoed over the rocks until Jen settled on the top of a smooth, flat rock that was nicely heated by the sun. The sea breeze was fresh and cool, but the bright sunshine warmed their faces. Jen enlisted Ronnie in the effort to set up the picnic, and the little girl scampered off to find four large rocks to hold down the corners of the red plaid blanket. Then Jen tasked Chris with opening the bottle of wine and finding a level spot to fill the wine glasses. She even brought a glass for Ronnie's orange soda. The cooler seemed bottomless as Jen unloaded peanut butter and jelly sandwiches, an Italian grinder, two types of potato chips, cheese and crackers, a chef's salad, and an assortment of cookies. After she had laid it all out, she said, without any sense of irony, "Now don't forget to save room for dinner because they have the best seafood restaurants up here."

When they all had eaten their fill, Ronnie climbed down into one of the tiny pockets of beach between the rocks where she happily dug in the sand with a piece of driftwood. Chris took off his denim jacket, rolled it into a pillow, and stretched out on the rock, warming himself in the sunshine. Jen repacked the cooler, then took off her hooded parka and laid it beside Chris. She curled up next to him with her head on his shoulder. He breathed in the subtle aroma of her perfume as her hair tickled his cheek and the sun shone bright on his face. After savoring the moment, he turned to her and said, "Have I said thank you yet?"

She nuzzled closer and asked, "For lunch?"

"For that, and for this day, and for being so nice to both Ronnie and me, and for coming into our lives, and for being you," he said, lifting up his head.

She didn't answer. She just kissed him gently, looked into his brown eyes, and ran her fingers through his hair.

Ronnie shrieked from below, "Hey, you guys, come and see the starfish I found. It's really cool and it almost has all of its legs."

They sat up and the precious, warm feeling, for now, sailed out to sea on the light offshore breeze.

They packed up the car and drove a few miles into Boothbay Harbor, which, Jen explained, was a crowded spot at the height of tourist season, but in the fall it returned to being a pleasant, slow-paced little fishing village. Chris parked the car in the town parking lot that was adjacent to a long wooden footbridge, which Jen informed him was the longest wooden footbridge in the world, or at least in Maine, or certainly in Boothbay Harbor. A white, stately church stood watching over the far side of the harbor, the gold cross on its steeple glittering in the sun. Jen explained that President Kennedy worshipped there when he

P. G. Smith

vacationed in Maine. Sailboats glided across the shimmering harbor as lobster boats chugged from colorful buoy to colorful buoy in the afternoon sunshine. Chris was enchanted by the place. Before he had finished looking out over the harbor, the two girls trotted off hand in hand to the shops by the wharves.

Even before they set foot into the first shop, however, Jen walked up to a small ticket booth next to a sign that said "Harbor Cruises." She chatted with the old man in the booth for a few moments, then came over to Chris. "We're going for a boat tour of the harbor at three o'clock, but don't worry, I worked a deal. It'll only cost you sixty dollars," she said, reaching out her hand and smiling sweetly.

Chris pulled out his wallet and grumbled, "I thought we were riding on the boat, not buying it."

Ronnie was delighted about their upcoming cruise, which departed in less than an hour, but Jen said that there were a few things she would need. First they stopped into the T-shirt and sweatshirt store on the waterfront to find a Maine sweatshirt, because Jen assured Chris it might be cold out on the sea. They settled on a pink hooded one with flowering blueberries on it. Next it was up to a gift shop near the waterfront to find the perfect scarf, which would ward off even more chills on the high seas. A green plaid one was selected for a reasonable price. Jen led the way next door to yet another gift shop, which boasted a collection of snow globes, figurines, plastic lobster boats, beer mugs, and other necessities of life. Jen spotted a set of red plastic binoculars and a white sailor hat with "Boothbay Harbor" in blue letters. The first item, she explained to Chris, was an absolute necessity on a harbor cruise, and the second item was just because every kid on their first boat cruise should have one. Ronnie added a snow globe with the Pemaquid lighthouse at the cash register. Time was running short as Jen and Ronnie hurried across the street to a candy shop. Jen selected a large bag of old-fashioned, red-hot cinnamon fireballs, reasoning to Ronnie that, when you get really cold, you can pop a fireball into your mouth, and as your mouth burns, you forget about how cold the rest of your body is. Chris just shook his head and reached into his wallet again.

There were only ten other passengers on the *Monhegan Lady*. The big tour boat blasted her horn and backed out of her berth to set out on her cruise around Boothbay Harbor in the clear afternoon sunshine. Ronnie wanted to sit out on the deck, so Chris and Jen found two seats by the stern as Ronnie gazed over the side with her new binoculars. Thankfully Jen thought to bring the blanket because, ten minutes into the hour-long cruise, the adults were huddled under the blanket, shivering from the strong sea breeze.

The truth of the matter is that harbor cruises are very exciting for the first half hour or so, but after that each island looks the same, the squawking seagulls become less interesting and more annoying, and the drone of the diesel engine lulls one into a sort of trance. Ronnie, however, never tired of pointing out the lighthouses, approaching boats, and other sights of interest. At one point she even claimed to have spotted a great white shark, which was probably just a curious dolphin. Jen and Chris pulled the blanket closer around them and admitted to each other that they wished the voyage was about an hour shorter.

At length, Chris decided that a little drink might perk things up, so he stepped inside to the bar. A bored teenager lackadaisically retrieved a plastic cup of beer and a glass of merlot in a plastic thimble at prices that would easily have purchased a full bottle and a six-pack on dry land. As he stepped gingerly toward the outer deck, trying not to spill a precious, expensive drop, he stopped and leaned against the doorway for a moment.

Ronnie was sitting on Jen's lap while she brushed her golden hair and arranged it, using little blue dolphin hair clips that she must have picked up in one of the shops. Chris watched from a distance as the two of them giggled and Jen cradled the little girl's face in her hands. As he tiptoed toward them, he heard Jen say, "You tell your Daddy that anytime you need somebody to fix your hair, he should just pick up the phone and call me and I'll come right over."

"Is that a promise?" Chris asked, stepping forward with the drinks.

"You bet," Jen answered, squeezing his hand.

The sky had turned from blue to a light gray and the sun had all but disappeared as the tour boat glided into its home berth. Ronnie hopped about, ready for the next adventure on this magical day. Chris and Jen unrolled themselves from the blanket and stretched their stiff limbs, ready for a nap or at least another drink. The weary adults limped down the gangplank and up onto the dock as Ronnie scampered ahead. Stepping onto the sidewalk that led to the parking lot, Ronnie almost barreled into a heavyset middle-aged woman pulling in a sandwich-board sign in front of a tiny, cramped storefront. The sign said "Just in Time for Halloween! Psychic Readings, Palm Readings, Tarot Cards, Off-Season Rates!"

Chris apologized for Ronnie's exuberance and the woman, who was dressed in a long, flowing dress with sparkling moons and stars on it, said with a husky, accented voice, "Oh, no problem. I had little kids once, too." Then she added, pointing to Jen and Chris, "Hey, why don't you come in and have your palms read? I tell you both the future for the price of one. You can't get a better deal than that in the whole harbor."

Jen looked up at Chris and shrugged. He turned to the woman and said, "Why not?"

She ushered them into a tiny parlor that reeked of incense mixed with mothballs and stale cigarette smoke. Then she motioned to two green velvet chairs, pulling up a little stool for Ronnie. The walls were decorated with pictures of the zodiac, the pyramids, and other mysterious images. There was also a large, ornate statue of the Christ child dressed in royal garments in the corner overlooking the proceedings.

The woman turned to Chris and reached out her hand. "I always ask for payment ahead of time in case the reading tells you things you don't want to hear. Twenty-five dollars will do." Chris reached into his wallet and paid the woman with a grimace that he hoped she didn't see.

Ronnie piped up, "I want to have my palm read, too."

Chris looked at the woman, who said, "For the child it is only five dollars." With a sigh and an air of resignation, Chris reached into his wallet again, which was quite a bit slimmer than when they had set out that morning, and handed over a five-dollar bill.

The woman placed lighted candles on either side of Ronnie's little hand, stroking it gently. Then she began to chant and moan, opening and closing her eyes. She stopped abruptly and stared at a fixed point on the ceiling, crossed herself, and peered intently at Ronnie's palm.

"I see many things," the woman whispered. "I see that you like to play with dolls and are very smart at school. I see that you are a little bit sad about someone or something that you miss very much. I see that you love your father very much and are happy to have a new friend." Then the woman went off into a rambling, overwrought performance about the future. "I see that you will grow to be very beautiful one day and become very successful. I see that you might become a doctor, or a teacher, or an important businesswoman, but only if you work hard in school. In time you will meet the love of your life and maybe have beautiful children. All of these things are certainly in your future."

Ronnie looked up at Chris, her face flushed with delight. "Wow, Daddy, this lady is right about everything—even about Blackie and Jen. And she says that I'm going to be a doctor or something and be happy when I'm big."

The woman sat back and smiled, obviously pleased with the result of her work. Then she took Chris's and Jen's left hands and gently laid them side by side between the candles. "At first I thought you were husband and wife when you came in, but the little girl's palm told me different. Let us see what the future holds." Chris shot a nervous glance at Jen.

Again the psychic took a deep breath, staring at the ceiling as she muttered her incantations. She abruptly sat forward and stared at the two palms. "I see deep bonds growing here, like roots of a tree entwining. I see healing from past sorrows, each one helping to heal the other. For the man, I see a problem at work that will be resolved soon. For the woman, I see only love that grows stronger every day." The woman smiled at the two of them, then continued. "Now let us see what the distant future will bring." She peered intently at Jen's palm and muttered something, then looked over at Chris's palm. She quickly looked back and forth between the two palms, crossing herself and muttering a prayer in a strange, foreign tongue.

Pushing back from the table, she blew out the candles and turned on the lights. The fortune-teller looked at them with obvious distress. "I am sorry. I could not see anything in the future. Perhaps it is because I am tired, or perhaps the light is not right." She looked away from them as she reached into her cash box. "Here, I give you your money back." Then she reconsidered and said, "You come back in the spring and I give you a discount. Just say that you were here near Halloween and I remember." Standing up, she hastened them to the door without looking directly at them. "It's late and you have a long way to travel, so bye-bye, and come back the next time you're in the harbor." Once they were out of the tiny shop, she closed the door behind them. They saw the lights go out and heard the door latch click as they started to walk away.

Jen spoke first. "That was bizarre."

"It was all a trick to get us to come back again," Chris said. "You heard that silly business about a discount next spring. What a bunch of nonsense!"

They had forgotten that Ronnie was listening. "Does that mean that the lady was lying about me becoming a doctor and getting married when I'm big?" the little girl asked.

Chris stopped and picked her up. "That was the only thing that woman said that made any sense at all," he said as he kissed her cheek.

They quickly forgot all about the fortune-teller as they turned toward a restaurant at the end of the pier. The neat gray-and-white building was decked out with colorful lobster buoys and boasted an extensive seafood menu. Jen announced that this was their last stop. By now evening had fallen and it had become quite chilly, but they decided to eat outside anyway, where tall kerosene heaters magically warmed the open air.

Jen insisted that Chris order fresh native lobster and coached him through the proper way to eat a Maine lobster. She handed him a device that looked like a pair of pliers to crack the shell, a pick to remove the tender white meat, a small bowl of liquid butter in which to dip it, and a white vinyl bib with a large, angry-looking lobster on it to prevent him from dribbling on his jacket. The experience was a culinary delight for Chris, but served as an even better source of comic relief for Jen and Ronnie, who chose the clam chowder and grilled cheese respectively.

After dinner was over, they made their way back to the car, the girls still teasing Chris about his sloppy lobster eating. Jen decided to keep Ronnie company in the backseat, so she gave Chris permission to use his GPS for the quickest route back to Ashton Falls. As he pulled out of the parking lot, he noticed the first stars in the evening sky, sparkling like tiny jewels.

Jen entertained Ronnie by teaching her all the camp songs that she could remember as Chris drove through the darkness. Even Chris sang along to old favorites like "The Wheels on the Bus," "This Old Man," and "Bingo Was His Name-O." Just about the time they got to the third chorus of "He's Got the Whole World in His Hands," Ronnie's voice faltered and eventually died out, and, looking in the rearview mirror, Chris noticed that Jen had nodded off to sleep, too. He kept glancing back at the two most beautiful women in the world—his angels.

As Chris drove on through the black Maine countryside, he smiled remembering the visit to the lighthouse, the picnic on the rocks, and the sunny boat ride. But his thoughts returned to the fortune-teller's strange behavior.

Maybe it was just a business trick, he thought. But she accurately detected something about Blackie and Mimi in Ronnie's palm. What had she seen in his palm and in Jen's? Shaking his head, he dismissed the whole thing as theatrics and silliness. Turning to the rearview mirror again, he glanced at the two sweet faces in the backseat, periodically illuminated by the headlights of oncoming cars.

"At least they're real," he whispered to himself, "and this day was real." And he smiled.

Chapter 12

As the Volvo made its way down the Maine coastal roads on Saturday night, Father Costello and Brother Adelard were finishing their dinner in the rectory. Father Scanlon was away visiting his sister in Bangor, so it was just the two of them sharing sporadic conversation as they finished their hot dogs and baked beans.

Sopping up the last of the brown molasses sauce with a bit of hot dog roll, Adelard glanced across the table and casually said, "I think I'll go over to the school tonight. There are a few things I need to catch up on." Then he added, "Don't wait up for me, Father. I'll bring my front-door key with me."

Father Costello replied, "I think I'll turn in early tonight. I haven't slept well lately." He `gathered his plate and silverware and added as he turned to the kitchen, "I'll take care of the dishes tonight, Adelard. You can get started on what you're doing over at school."

Once the dishes were washed and dried, the old priest climbed the stairs to his room. He turned on sports radio loud enough to drown out any noise and crept down the hallway to Adelard's bedroom. He knew that this invasion of privacy was wrong, but he also knew that there was something dark, something ominous, something he needed to know in the final pages of the diary. He gently opened the bedroom door, turned on the desk lamp, and quickly opened the journal.

"I led Adelard down several staircases into the cellar of the monastery. Then I took a candle and matches from behind a cask, lit the candle, and pushed open a small wooden door that appeared to be nailed shut. Inside was a long, narrow corridor that was dimly lit at the far end. Adelard stooped as he followed me through the dank, chilly passageway.

The passage opened up into a small windowless chamber that was lit with many candles. Inside were statues of the great martyrs of the church around a simple wooden altar. On the altar was an ancient leather-bound book on a pure white cloth. Beside the book was what appeared to be a sharp, curved twig with several fresh drops of blood on the point.

Two older monks, each with his face shrouded in his hood and his hands folded in prayer, stood on either side of the altar. I turned to Adelard and said, "This is the sacred rite that your father made complete for us. The ancient rite of *Precis Intemporaliter Damnare*, the Prayers for the Damned. It has given our Teutonic warriors power to turn back the Huns, triumph over the Saracens, and defeat the enemies of our Holy Father in medieval times. But its power was lost for centuries when godless men scattered our most precious relics and threatened to close our churches during what has been wrongly called the Enlightenment.

"It was your father, Adelard," I continued, "a true Germanic knight, who brought us the missing element to revive this powerful and most holy rite. This ancient ritual has restored our ability to seek out and destroy the forces of darkness in our world." Pointing to the leather-bound book, I continued, "This book contains the Latin prayer that has been carried down through the centuries to this very day."

My hands trembled as I picked up the sacred thorn damp with blood. "This thorn, which was once bathed in the blood of our Lord, has been dipped in innocent blood. If a member of our brotherhood recites the prayer precisely and raises the thorn to heaven, he has the power to strike down a sinner whom he names three times in the ritual, provided the hand that holds the sacred relic has touched the body of the sinner.

"Through the years we have worked tirelessly to punish murderers, pedophiles, thieves, blasphemers, perverts, communists, and those who would abuse children, like the Muellers. We hunt those who do the work of the devil and strike them down. Sadly, it was too late to save our fatherland, but it is not too late to give us the power to, once again, triumph over the enemies of our Lord."

I crossed over to the altar, gently ran my hand over the book, and carefully picked up the sharp, bloody thorn. "Now you know our deepest and most precious secret. Tonight is the night you must decide, Brother Adelard. Do you wish to join us in the brotherhood of *Precis Intemporaliter Damnare*? Do you wish to gain the powers of the Prayers for the Damned?"

Adelard was enthralled and immediately stated that he wished to join the brotherhood. The silent monks approached him slowly and stood on either side. I then said, "First you must bear the marks of our Lord's wounds from His Crown of Thorns dipped in innocent blood. Do you wish to take on His suffering?" Adelard nodded, and I motioned to the two other monks who lifted Adelard's robe over his head.

I gently but firmly grasped his hands and held his palms up and open to heaven. I approached the young monk and held the thorn up in front of his eyes. Then I quickly plunged the bloody thorn into his palm. Adelard trembled like a jolt of electricity shot through his hand. He tried not to scream in pain. I repeated the process in Adelard's other palm, then both feet.

As I plunged the thorn for the final wound into Adelard's side, the young monk collapsed onto the floor and lost consciousness. Moments later he awoke to find himself being propped up by the two silent monks. He looked at his hands, feet, and side, but there were no marks. The monks helped him back into his robe. "Welcome to our brotherhood," I said as I embraced Adelard. The other two monks also embraced him. "Now stand next to me at the altar and learn. There is an abortionist in Munich who is an enemy of our Lord. Brother Joachim visited him last month and warned him to cease his evil deeds, but he did not listen. Tonight we will pray that the Lord's vengeance will be done to him."

Brother Adelard learned the secrets of the Prayers for the Damned well, and soon the powerful rite drove his thoughts and occupied his waking moments. He read the local newspapers and police reports, scouring them for the names, addresses, and details of the enemies of our Lord.

Brother Adelard convinced the abbot to allow him to start a Sunday school for orphans so he had access to a steady supply of innocent blood. Soon the hospitals and doctors in the Salzburg area were receiving more frequent reports of freak accidents and mysterious illnesses that were afflicting pimps, prostitutes, drug addicts, and petty racketeers, as well as outspoken atheists and communists. As his secret crusade gathered strength, he became increasingly introspective and had minimal contact with his fellow monks. His days were spent in prayer and reflection. My spiritual son had become a true warrior-priest, a crusader for our Lord, intent on punishing those who would harm his church or its holy people.

Finally, when the abbot called Adelard to his room and demanded to know..."

Suddenly, the dim light from the hallway was blocked by a figure in the doorway of the bedroom. Father Costello's fingers froze as he looked up in dread.

"I hope you have enjoyed the story of my life," said the dark form in a heavily accented voice.

Father Costello stepped back from the desk in panic.

"No, Father, stay where you are," Adelard purred in a mock soothing tone. "I have a few questions for you."

The old priest tried to stammer an apology, but the words wouldn't come.

"What do you plan to do now? Call the police? Call the bishop? And just what would you say?" Adelard began to mimic the old priest's Maine drawl. "Well, bishop, I violated Brother Adelard's privacy and invaded his private property and read all about his sad life and his strange ability to curse our enemies."

Adelard turned on the lights as Father Costello blinked in the harsh glare. Adelard continued, "And when the bishop wants to see your proof, Father, do you think you would be able to locate the diary?" Adelard's low chuckle sounded more like a growl. "I think not ... I think not." Suddenly his eyes narrowed as he stepped out of the doorway and barked, "Now get out of my room."

As Father Costello bolted through the doorway, Adelard called after him, "Oh, Father, one more thing—I'll be praying for you."

The raindrops softly splashed on the golden maple leaves and tapped gently on Chris's bedroom window. He awoke with a start. As the mists of his dreams evaporated, he realized with relief that it was Sunday and that he wasn't late for work. He glanced at the clock and knew that he had to hustle if he and Ronnie were going to make it to church. It was a struggle, but Chris and Ronnie managed to get themselves out the door in time for the nine o'clock Sunday mass. The stubble on his face showed that Chris hadn't had his usual time for morning grooming, and Ronnie's hair looked a little like a bird's nest after a nor'easter.

When they arrived at church, Chris wasn't expecting to see Jen, who had stumbled out of the car at her house last night barely awake, but he certainly hoped she'd be there. And there she was, looking radiant and rested, in her usual pew on the right side of the church. Chris started to guide Ronnie toward the pew on the left side in which they ordinarily sat, but he hesitated, then led Ronnie to where Jen was sitting under the softly smiling gaze of the statue of Our Lady of the Rosary. People might talk, but what the heck, he said to himself. Jen looked up at him and beamed, her sea-green eyes twinkling as they met his. Ronnie stood close beside her, and Jen squeezed her little hand affectionately.

Father Costello sat in his chair on the altar and stared at the floor. His face was drawn and pale after a sleepless night, and it was only years of experience leading the ritual of mass that kept him on track. Fortunately there was an African priest from the missions who gave the day's sermon, so he was spared that challenge. Never before in his life had he been so ashamed, so perplexed, and so very, very frightened.

The old priest's misery wasn't apparent to Jen and Chris, who were lost in recollections of the day before with fleeting thoughts, and half-formed prayers, of what the future could bring. After the service was over they walked down the main aisle, Jen greeting the people she had known since childhood as Chris smiled and nodded. "You know that this will start quite a lot of gossip in our little parish," she whispered.

"I really couldn't care less," he responded.

Outside of the church, Jen reached into her purse, took out a brush, and began to straighten out Ronnie's tangled hair in mock exasperation. "You tell your dad that if he wants to sit with me in church, he needs to do a better job on your hair in the morning."

Ronnie giggled at all the fuss and attention.

Chris looked intently at Jen. "I really had a great time yesterday, Jen. We should plan another day trip soon."

"You know, Mr. Murphy, I'm not just available on weekends. In fact, I'm around on most weeknights, and furthermore, I make some mean pasta dishes," Jen replied with a wink. "And I work really cheap. Besides, that child needs a good meal that doesn't come out of a can or the microwave."

"Hey, I resent that!" Chris shot back. "I'm a master chef when it comes to hot dogs, grilled cheese sandwiches, and macaroni." Then he switched his tone. "But when would be the earliest date one could make a reservation for your services, if one was interested in a gourmet pasta dinner?"

"Well, I'd need to check my booking schedule, but I think we could safely plan on maybe ... Thursday night," Jen stated, pretending to search her memory.

"Great, your place or ours?"

"Yours, of course. That way you can take care of the dishes."

"Maybe that's not such a great deal," Chris exclaimed. "Are there any other hidden charges?"

"Yes," Jen replied, "you buy the wine."

"Okay. I'll pick you up at, should we say six thirty?"

"Six thirty's good, but I'll drive over myself with the groceries."

"Do you know where we live?" Chris asked.

"Of course," she said as she started to walk toward her car. "Don't you think I scoped it out when I did your background check?" Then she called over her shoulder, "See you on Thursday at six thirty. Have a nice week ... and don't forget to call me sometime before then, you big jerk."

Neither Chris nor Jen realized that Brother Adelard overheard their conversation and listened with great interest.

After Chris, Ronnie, Jen, and all the parishioners had left the church, Father Costello stood alone on the church stairs as raindrops pelted down on his bald head. He raised his face and his hands to the skies and reiterated Jesus's final words, "My God, my God, why have you forsaken me?" Suddenly he dropped to his knees, clutched at his throat, and fell unconscious into the wet, brown leaves.

Brother Adelard finished extinguishing the candles on the altar and strolled to the rear of the church. Glancing out the door, he noticed the prostrate figure of Father Costello still clad in his bright green vestments. Adelard slowly made his way down the deserted aisles of the church to a small office where there was a telephone. He looked up at the figure of Christ on the cross, smiled, and carefully organized the hymnals on the shelf in the office. When he was certain that the fallen priest was no longer moving, he dialed 911 to calmly report an accident on the front stairs of the church.

When Chris and Ronnie arrived home after church, Chris started to gather the laundry and tend to his usual weekend chores while Ronnie turned on the television and watched cartoons. There was a knock on the door, and Chris opened it to find a rough-looking man wearing a yellow reflective Department of Public Works jacket. The man seemed anxious.

"Are you Chris Murphy?" the man asked, looking down at a large manila envelope.

"Certainly," Chris replied. "Won't you come in?"

"Uh, no thanks," the man responded, as if Chris's question wasn't part of the script. "I'm supposed to give you this personally." He handed the envelope to Chris.

"What is this? Who is it from?" Chris asked, becoming somewhat anxious himself.

"You're supposed to know what it is when you open it, and I'm not supposed to answer any questions," the man stated, considerably relieved that his duty was complete. "See you later.

Have a nice day." At that, he raced down the stairs and hopped into the Town of Ashton Falls pickup truck that was idling in front of the house.

Chris tore open the envelope and scanned the contents. It was a neatly handwritten list of names and addresses, some businesses, some private homes. He turned the paper over, but it was blank on the other side. He looked inside the envelope, but it was empty. Then it dawned on him—this was part of Big Bill's extortion scheme, and these were the addresses whose power meters were to be adjusted. But of course it all needed to happen without Big Bill's fingerprints on it.

Chris stared at the list in dejection. He had managed not to think about Big Bill's blackmail for most of the weekend, but here it was, staring him in the face. Then he remembered his conversation with Father Scanlon last week and knew what he had to do.

Ronnie sat on the floor staring intently at the antics of SpongeBob SquarePants on the television. It really sucks to be an adult, Chris thought as he picked up the laundry basket and headed for the basement.

As soon as he got into the office on Monday, Chris picked up the phone and called the New York office. Elliott was a good guy to work for most of the time, and he had been generous to Chris, but he was also a tough, no-nonsense businessman with plenty of experience in the corporate school of hard knocks. He'd probably seen something like this before and would know what to do. And Chris badly needed advice about how to deal with Big Bill before the situation spun out of control.

At first Elliott's secretary tried to put him off, but Chris convinced her that it was an urgent matter. When Elliott finally answered the phone, Chris could tell that he was somewhat annoyed, but Chris went ahead and explained the situation to him in careful detail. After Chris finished his explanation, there was silence at the end of the line.

"My sources informed me that there was trouble up there, Murphy," Elliot began. "First of all, you should have known that the EPA guidelines for chemical waste handling weren't being followed closely. After all, you did the initial inspection report last spring, so this is a mess of your own creation."

Not exactly what I was hoping to hear, Chris thought.

"The biggest problem we have—you have—right now is the prospect of huge fines or even a shutdown because of environmental regulation violations," Elliott stated emphatically.

"But the spill has been contained. The contaminated earth is being removed. There are no wetland issues, and the environmental safeguards are being implemented," Chris protested.

"It doesn't matter what the facts are, it's the perception that your power plant is a polluter and therefore needs to be punished or shut down." Elliott continued, "You need to use any strategies available to build allies in the town government and the state legislature."

"To include cooperating with blackmail and extortion?" Chris shot back.

"Any strategies available," Elliott repeated.

"You gotta be shitting me," Chris exclaimed.

"Welcome to the real world, son. You're drowning in quick-sand, and now you need to grab any hand out there to get out of it."

"But what the town manager is proposing is illegal. I could go to jail for something like that," Chris protested.

"Any strategies available," Elliott said slowly once again and added, "just don't get caught."

"All right. I guess I need to think this over some more," Chris said.

"Good luck, Murphy, and remember, I'll deny that this conversation ever occurred. I sent you up to Maine to straight-en out that mess, not to drag me into the shit." Elliott quickly hung up.

Chris slammed down the phone and remembered the for-tune-teller's prediction about his problem being resolved. She certainly saw the future clearly, didn't she? he thought bitterly.

Chapter 13

CHRIS TRIED TO avoid calling Big Bill as long as he could. But as much as he tried to bury himself in personnel issues, cash flow trends, production schedules, and the details of cleaning up from the chemical spill, he couldn't forget the bad taste of cooperating with extortion. On Tuesday afternoon he called Brother Adelard to let him know that he would be working late. The brother didn't appear to be put out at all and acted as if the call was expected. Chris thought, Thank God I have him to look after Ronnie.

Ronnie was tired after spending a long afternoon at school, and she actually went to bed early. Chris tossed and turned all night long. His semiconscious thoughts and dreams drifted to blackmail and extortion and the consequences of the scheme coming to light. At one point, well after midnight, he heard Ronnie crying. He cradled her in his arms, and she told him that she had a nightmare about Jesus being mad and coming to their house. He laughed with her and lay down beside her until the peaceful look on her face and her shallow, rhythmic breathing told him she was asleep. When he returned to his own bed, he tried to think of Jen, but as he slipped into sleep, dreams of bribery, blackmail, and jail returned to haunt him.

After getting Ronnie off to school the next morning, he stopped off at the coffee shop on his route to the power plant to get some breakfast and a decent cup of coffee. He pondered the plate of bacon and eggs sunny-side up. It looked like a contorted Picasso face that stared at him and asked, "What are you going to do now, hotshot?" He tried to take a bite of the eggs but found he had no appetite.

The waitress bustled up with a fresh pot of coffee and asked if he wanted a refill. As she poured the coffee, another waitress bumped into her and she missed Chris's cup, spilling the hot liquid across the counter. He grabbed a handful of napkins and an abandoned copy of the *Portland Daily Mail* to keep the spill from rolling off the counter onto his lap. The apologetic waitress retrieved a rag from the kitchen and sopped up the rest of the coffee. She offered to dispose of the soiled napkins and soggy newspaper. Chris handed over the napkins, but before he gave her the newspaper, he glanced at the headline.

Town Manager and Local Youth Die in Vehicle Mishap

Ashton Falls— Longtime town manager William F. Benson, 56, of Ashton Falls and an unidentified minor were found dead early this morning in the cab of a pickup truck in the woods just off Route 202 in Ashton Falls. A Maine State Police trooper discovered the pickup truck containing the unconscious victims at 3:17 a.m. according to the police report. Ambulance crews who responded to the scene were unable to revive Benson and the youth, who were pronounced dead at Midcoast Medical Center.

The cause of death is believed to be carbon monoxide poisoning resulting from a faulty vehicle exhaust system. Maine State Police Captain Roland Johnson stated that the circumstances of the incident are being investigated as in the case of all fatalities, but foul play is not considered a factor.

Benson served as the Ashton Falls Town Manager for 32 years. He was a graduate of the University of Maine, where he was a varsity football player. He also served in the United States Marine Corps and was an active member of the Masonic Lodge. The Ashton Falls Town Hall could not be reached for comment.

The waitress returned and asked if she could throw away the paper, but all Chris could do was stare transfixed at the article and whisper, "Holy shit, holy shit."

She lingered as she wiped up the last of the spilled coffee. "Did you know Big Bill?" she asked tentatively.

Chris nodded and replied, "I guess you could say we had some business dealings."

The waitress scanned the tables nearby, then said in a hushed voice, "The trooper who found the bodies was in here this morning. I don't know if he was supposed to tell, but he said the boy and Big Bill were naked when he found them. I guess there's more to this story than the newspaper's telling us." She gave Chris a conspiratorial wink and hurried off to take a food order from a waiting customer.

Chris stared out the window. How was he supposed to react to this? He felt the urge to run outside and cheer at the top of his lungs, but despite the unexpected resolution to his dilemma, two people were dead. He scratched his head, left a twenty-dollar bill on the counter next to his barely touched breakfast, and headed off to his office, clutching the stained newspaper in his hand.

The rest of Chris's workday was almost surreal. He had difficulty concentrating as his thoughts dwelt on the bizarre turn of events. Several times, people asked him, "Are you all right today, Mr. Murphy?" To which Chris would reply, "Oh, I'm fine, just fine." Only Peggy knew anything about his recent dealings with Big Bill, and she watched him with a knowing look.

Chris managed to get out of the office to pick up Ronnie on time. It had been a great day—his crisis with Big Bill had been unexpectedly resolved, and things were starting to fall into place at the power plant. In fact, it was a nice afternoon—not too warm, not too cool. The sunshine was interrupted from time to time by white puffy clouds that floated across the sky. Chris felt a little guilty thinking it, but it was actually a really good day for him.

Chris parked the car and leisurely strolled toward the school. Somewhere nearby someone was barbecuing chicken or ribs for dinner, and the smoky, sweet scent was making him hungry. Maybe he'd try to cook burgers out tonight.

As he neared the school, he heard a strange noise coming from behind the building. It sounded like a low rumble mixed with the laughter and chanting of several young voices. The more he listened, the more concerned he became. Chris quickened his pace and turned toward the back of the school.

When he came around the corner of the building, he saw Joe the janitor standing in the middle of a circling group of young teenagers. The boys, who were dressed in almost identical black T-shirts and torn jeans, were riding BMX bikes around and around Joe as they laughed and chanted "RE-tard, RE-tard." Joe tried to swing his mop at them, but the long mop was too unwieldy to hit the nimble bikers, who chanted and laughed even louder the harder Joe tried to hit them.

One of the teens, with greasy shoulder-length hair tucked under a backwards baseball hat, jumped off his bike and pushed Joe down from behind. The boy then reached over and ripped Joe's iPod and earbuds away from him before the janitor could lash out. Jumping onto his bike, the teen waved the iPod in the air like a battle trophy and yelled in triumph, "Come on, motherfuckers, I got the retard's music. Now he can't sing his stupid songs."

The gang of boys went to make their getaway up the pathway from the back of the school to the street before Joe could get help. When the kid with the backwards baseball hat saw Chris coming down the pathway, he realized that he was going too fast to avoid the man running toward him. In a split second the boy decided to speed up and try to race by, or through, the oncoming adult.

Chris headed straight for the teen in the lead and, remembering his skills from high-school football, crouched and timed his lunge perfectly. Striking the teen full-on with his shoulder, he knocked the boy off his bike into a chain-link fence. Chris stood over the boy with his fists clenched as he glared down at him.

"Give me Joe's iPod, you little asshole, or I swear I'll smash your brains in," Chris growled.

The boy, whose nose was bleeding considerably, quickly handed over the iPod and immediately wrapped his arms around his head and curled up in the fetal position in fear that Chris would make good on his threat.

"If I ever see you come near Joe again, I'll drag you by your skinny little neck to the police station so they can charge you with theft." Then he added, "By the way, Joe is a better man than you can ever hope to be, you piece of shit. Now get out of here before I change my mind and take you to the police right now."

The boy wiped his bloody nose and raced away on his bike without looking back. By now the other boys had fled around the far side of the building. Chris walked over to where Joe was shaking out the mop as if nothing had happened. Chris handed the iPod to the janitor and said, "I'm really sorry this happened, Joe. Kids can be stupid sometimes."

Joe reached over and hugged Chris. Burying his face in Chris's chest, he sobbed. Then Joe quietly said "Thanks" and returned to picking clumps of dirt out of his tangled mop.

"Why don't you let me take you home, Joe?" Chris offered. "You're in no shape to work tonight. I'm sure Brother Adelard will understand if I explain what just happened out here."

Joe wiped his eyes and shook his head. "No, I'll be all right. I need to mop the floors in the first-floor classrooms or the teachers will wonder what happened to me."

With that, he picked up the mop and headed into the school. Before he let the heavy door close behind him, he turned to Chris and said, "Thank you. You are my true friend."

Looking at his watch, Chris realized that he was, once again, late picking up Ronnie.

Ronnie was waiting outside with Brother Adelard. She pranced around in the afternoon sunshine, scuffing through the leaves, and Chris saw her bring one of the prettiest ones over to Brother Adelard. Chris walked into the school yard and took Ronnie's knapsack off her shoulder.

"How was your day, Daddy?" she asked, presenting him with a speckled maple leaf.

"It was absolutely wonderful, honey," Chris replied. "How was yours?"

"Okay, I guess. Mrs. Hancock was kind of grouchy 'cause some boys in the back of the room were noisy, but Brother Adelard let us all have double recess," she said without taking a breath. "He said that God would want us to enjoy His beautiful sunshine before the winter cold sets in."

"Brother Adelard is a smart man," Chris said. He glanced over toward the brother, who gave him an uncharacteristically animated wave and shouted, "A good afternoon to you, Mr. Murphy. Isn't it a glorious day?"

Chris waved and shouted back, "It certainly is, Brother." Then he shuffled through the leaves as Ronnie skipped beside him on their way to the car.

When Chris returned to the office on Thursday, it felt like the week before Christmas. Word quickly spread that the plant would be assessed relatively minor fines for the chemical spill and the threat of complete plant shutdown, which was everyone's worst fear, had been averted. All the workers in the office went through the day with smiles on their faces and a spring in their step. Peggy seemed particularly chipper and couldn't suppress the smirk when she asked Chris if he planned to attend Big Bill's funeral. Chris couldn't help but feel sorry for the teenager's family, and he felt more than a little guilty about the unconcealed joy that surrounded Big Bill's death. Still, the town manager had been a power-hungry, manipulative son of a bitch who had probably dealt everyone in the office more misery than Chris had received in the past two weeks. And, in the end, if the rumors were true, in addition to being an unrepentant bully, Big Bill had probably been a predatory pedophile for a long time.

Chris gazed out the window at the crystal clear sunlight that set the gold and red maple leaves on fire up on Meeting House Hill. Maybe things are going to be all right here, he thought, and he smiled as he returned to his desk.

As the clock neared four o'clock, Chris grabbed his laptop bag and headed for the door. Peggy looked up with mock surprise. "Well, well, well, where are we going in such a hurry? Got a hot date or something?"

Chris stopped dead in his tracks, glanced back at her with a sly look, and replied, "Maybe I do. See you tomorrow, unless I get a better offer." With that he skipped down the stairs two at a time. He raced over to Holy Rosary to pick up Ronnie, then bolted over to the Duffy's Package Store to buy the most expensive bottle of wine that he could find on the dusty shelves.

When he returned to the car, Ronnie looked up at him and asked, "Shouldn't we have some flowers for Jen at our special dinner?" He sighed and smiled—she was right. Then it was over to the florist's to get whatever they had on hand. At first Chris asked for yellow roses, but the florist talked him into their special, which was a dozen red roses with a red satin bow around the vase. The florist insisted that he write out a card, and he quickly scribbled "Dear Jen, Thanks for bringing joy back into my life. Love, Chris."

He sealed the card, grabbed the vase, and set it in the back-seat next to Ronnie, asking her to be sure that the vase didn't fall over. Just as he was about to back the car out of the parking lot, Ronnie let out a muffled cry.

"Ouch, Daddy, I pricked my finger on the flowers and it's bleeding."

With a sigh, Chris shifted into park and searched the contents of the glove compartment until he found a Band-Aid. Then he got out and went to look at Ronnie's finger. He gently examined her tiny white finger, wiped away a fresh drop of red blood, and carefully wrapped the bandage around her finger. As he looked at her finger, he noticed that there were two tiny punctures in her index finger other than the one that was bleeding. "Honey, the blood has stopped, and the Band-Aid will make your cut go away." As he climbed into the driver's seat, he added, "Why didn't you tell me that you cut your finger before?"

"Oh, that happened at school," the little girl replied, "and it didn't really hurt anyway."

Chris thought there was something strange in her voice, almost like it was another child who answered. But if they didn't get moving, Jen would be waiting on their front stairs, and that wasn't the way he wanted to start off this evening.

As it turned out, Jen did indeed get to the apartment before Chris and Ronnie. After they climbed up the stairs, they opened their door and found the apartment transformed. The mellow sounds of jazz played in the living room, and the rich aroma of spaghetti sauce simmering on the stove wafted from the kitchen. Chris set the flowers on the table and was surprised to find it covered with a white linen tablecloth and set with three place settings of expensive china.

Ronnie ran into the kitchen and Jen scooped her up, giving her a big smooch on the cheek. "Couldn't you get your old, slow daddy here any sooner, Ronnie? Now go change your clothes so you can help me make garlic bread." At that Ronnie skipped off to her room, giggling as she went.

Chris looked on. Jen was radiant. Her cheeks were flushed from the cooking, and it made her green eyes sparkle all that much more. She wore old blue jeans that fit just right and a red fitted blouse just tight enough and unbuttoned far enough to show that dainty strand of white pearls around her neck. It also showed enough cleavage to remind him how much he wanted to find some time alone with her. He walked over and started to kiss her, but she backed away and her eyes pointed to the corner of the kitchen.

There sat Jeanine Brisebois with a grin from ear to ear. "Well, how do you think Miss Mercier got into the kitchen to start dinner? You'll be late for your own funeral, Mr. Chris Murphy." At that the old woman stood up with a groan and said, "That reminds me that I need to start my own supper." She started for the door.

Jen quickly said, "Won't you stay and have dinner with us, Grand-mère? We have plenty of spaghetti and bread, and plenty of my mother's secret marinara sauce."

Jeanine shot a sly look at Chris. "If I said yes, young lady, that fellow over there would never forgive me. He wants all the spaghetti for himself tonight." Then she whispered, "Or at least the cook." Then she hobbled out the door with a chuckle and called after her, "You kids have a lovely evening."

Chris uncorked the wine and poured two glasses. As he handed one of the glasses to Jen, he leaned toward her and whispered, "Now can I kiss the cook?"

But just as his lips reached Jen, Ronnie hopped into the room. "Can we make the garlic bread now, Jen?" And with a quick peck on the cheek for Chris, Jen stepped away to butter the bread with Ronnie and ensure that just the right amount of garlic powder was sprinkled on each slice.

Chris was left to sit at the dining room table, sipping his wine in peace, listening to the mingled sounds of jazz and giggling coming from the kitchen. He smiled and savored the moment.

Dinner was delightful. The food was wonderful, but the laughter and the warmth were the best parts of all. Ronnie re-lived all of the little events that happened on their trip to the coast last Saturday, and Jen told her about the fun things that lay ahead in Boston as they plotted to get Chris to plan another trip, as if he wasn't sitting at the table with them.

During the salad, he thought he felt Jen's hand brush his knee. By the end of the spaghetti and her second glass of wine, her hand was firmly on his thigh, and he caressed it secretly under the table.

After a spumoni ice-cream dessert, they all cleared the table. Ronnie dried the dishes after Jen washed them, and Chris packed them carefully in the wicker basket that Jen had brought. Ronnie wanted to stay up and play with Jen, but Chris reminded her that it was a school night and it was way past her bedtime. The three of them together completed the nightly rituals of brushing teeth, reading a story, saying prayers, and turning out the light.

When Ronnie was tucked in, Chris gently kissed her cheek and Jen followed with a big bear hug and smooch. Ronnie looked up with sleepy eyes and said, "You know what I wish?"

"No, honey, what do you wish?"

"I wish that Jen could sleep over some night."

Chris sheepishly glanced at Jen, who looked away with a blush. "I wish that too, Ronnie. Maybe someday she will." With a final good night, the two adults quietly left the room.

Once they were clear of Ronnie's room, Jen grabbed Chris's arm and said, "You creep, propositioning me in your own daughter's bedroom. You ought to be ashamed of yourself."

But before she could say anything else, Chris grabbed her cheeks between his hands and passionately kissed her. Then he gasped, "I've been wanting to do that all night."

"Me too," Jen responded as she threw her arms around his neck and plunged her tongue into his mouth. They kissed with a mounting passion as their embrace grew in intensity. Despite his best efforts to keep himself in check, Chris couldn't stop his hands from grasping and stroking Jen's body. And Jen held nothing back as she ran her tongue up his neck and nipped at his ear.

Suddenly there was a sharp knock on the door. Chris and Jen stopped, frozen in each other's arms.

"Maybe it's Jeanine," Chris whispered. "She probably wants to make sure we're not doing what we were just doing."

Jen giggled and straightened her blouse. Chris opened the door and stood there stunned.

"Hi, Chris," said the petite, attractive woman in the hallway. "I'm sorry to drop in on you, but I guess you didn't get my text this afternoon." She added after a pause, "It's good to see you again."

The woman, dressed in a short black leather jacket with matching leather jeans, reached up and kissed Chris fully on the mouth. She motioned to a dark-haired man in the hallway who was also wearing head-to-toe leather.

"Chris, this is Jean-Luc. Jean-Luc, this is Chris." Chris shook hands with the man, who was very handsome in a European sort of way. A strong scent of musky cologne came through the doorway with him.

"Oh, I'm sorry, Chris, I didn't realize you had guests," the woman said as she noticed Jen, but there was something mocking in her tone that was irritating and insulting.

"Forgive me," said Chris, regaining his composure. "Jen, this is my … uh, Ronnie's mother, Mimi. Mimi, this is my good friend, Jen." He stepped over to Jen and clutched her hand as if he wanted to protect her.

Jen reacted quickly. "Oh, Mimi, I'm so pleased to meet you. I've heard so many nice things about you." She reached out and gave Mimi's chilly fingers a squeeze. Mimi could do little more than nod. "Won't you come in and have a glass of wine with us?" Jen added as if she had expected the two leather-clad creatures to arrive any minute.

Chris found two more wine glasses and poured out the contents of the bottle evenly between the four glasses. Taking a cue from Jen, he smiled and asked, "What brings the two of you all the way up to Ashton Falls?"

Mimi sipped her wine and answered, "Jean-Luc and I were riding his Harley up to his place in Montreal, and I asked him if he could find Ashton Falls. We've been working pretty hard on a production in Greenwich Village, and we both decided we really needed to get away from the city."

"How did you ever manage to find us?" Chris asked with a hint of irritation.

"We just pulled into a gas station off the highway. A cop was having a cup of coffee there. He knew exactly where you live," she explained.

Chris nodded.

Mimi drained her wine glass, took a deep breath, and leaned forward. "I was hoping I could see Ronnie."

"I'm sorry. She's asleep and it would probably upset her almost as much as the morning you walked out." Chris's voice could barely conceal his anger.

Mimi looked down at the floor. "I guess I deserved that. Please, Chris, please can I see her for just a few minutes? I promise I won't wake her."

Chris looked at Mimi's pleading eyes. Then he glanced at Jen and could read her soft, gentle look that said, "Go ahead, let her. Her heart must be breaking." Jean-Luc stared up at the ceiling as if he wanted to be somewhere else.

Chris rose from the table. "All right, but let me check to be sure that she's asleep."

As Chris left the dining room, Mimi looked at Jen with a forced smile. Noticing the roses on the table, she picked up the card nonchalantly and said, "I never liked roses very much, but these are very pretty, I guess." After reading the note on the card, she set it down with a scowl and peered intently at Jen with a look that barely hid her jealousy.

Chris came back into the dining room. "All right, Mimi. Just a few moments, and please don't wake her. I don't think she could take it again." His voice was soft and almost pleading.

Mimi tiptoed toward Ronnie's room. Jen cleared away the last of the dishes and began rinsing them in the kitchen sink, relieved to have a reason to escape from the dining room. Chris sat silently as Jean-Luc looked around the room, sipped his wine, and frequently glanced at his phone.

After a few minutes that seemed endless, Chris heard the click of Ronnie's bedroom door closing. Mimi slowly came back into the dining room, softly sniffling, holding a tissue to her eyes. Jean-Luc suddenly stood up and cradled her in his arms, tenderly whispering to her in French.

Mimi dried her eyes, forced a smile, and said, "Jean-Luc wants to get back on the highway. It was good to see you, Chris." She dried her eyes, cleared her throat, and said, "Can my lawyer reach you at this address? Can you give me a card or something with your office phone number on it? I promise, this divorce thing will be quick and painless."

Chris reached into his wallet and gave her his card. Jean-Luc formally shook his hand. Mimi softly touched his arm and said, "I guess this is good-bye." As she stepped out the door, she called, "Oh, good-bye, Janet, it was nice meeting you."

Jen called back from the kitchen, "Good to meet you too, Mimi."

Chris watched as Mimi left and called after her, "Please call before you stop by the next time, Mimi."

He heard her faint reply from the bottom of the stairs: "There won't be a next time." Chris closed the front door and locked it.

Jen stood in the kitchen doorway drying her hands on a flowered dish towel. She looked tired. "I think I should be heading home now."

"Please don't," Chris pleaded, "at least not yet. Come here and sit with me and let me explain."

She tossed the dish towel into the sink and hesitantly followed him into the living room. She sat next to him on the old secondhand couch. The living room was dimly lit by the light from the adjoining dining room, but she could see that Chris's eyes were moist with tears.

"I know this is messed up. I know this wasn't what you were looking for. I know that you deserve better." Chris took her hand and caressed it. "But I also know that my little girl needs a mother, and it isn't that woman who just walked down the stairs. I also know that, ever since I first saw you, I've known that I need you and not that woman in the leather jacket who almost ruined my life."

He stroked her cheek gently and looked into her eyes. "I also know that you've brought joy and meaning into my life, Jen." Then he gently kissed her lips.

She paused, looking into his eyes searchingly. Then she kissed him with a passion that came from deep within.

They clung to each other tightly as they kissed. Slowly the fire from earlier in the night returned, smoldering and flaring until it gradually reached its previous intensity. But this time it was different. It wasn't so much a lover's game; it was serious and almost as painful as it was sweet.

Chris looked intently into her eyes. Then he stood up, took her hand, and silently led her to his bedroom. Jen sat on the bed as he pushed the door shut. Her sense of reason told her to leave, but the flames inside her raged with desire. He gently eased her back onto the pillows and kissed her with a slow, burning heat that could no longer be contained.

Chris unbuttoned Jen's blouse, and she quickly shrugged it off her shoulders. He unfastened her bra until her soft, round breasts were uncovered so he could lovingly caress them. Her breathing became heavy as he slowly passed his hand down her flat stomach, unzipping her jeans and pushing them down to the floor. She lay back naked on the bed and beckoned to him silently with her outstretched arms. She had nothing to hide and nothing to hold back.

He stood and surveyed her luscious body. Her eyes begged him to hurry as he peeled off his pants and shirt. He climbed on top of her, kissing her neck, and shoulders, and soft white breasts, teasingly licking her taut nipples. He gently entered her with a groan of satisfaction that matched her sigh of pleasure. His hands swept all over the curves and valleys of her soft skin as he plunged deeper and quicker. They twisted and thrust until Chris was on his back and Jen rose up to the full length of her extended arms. He looked into her moist eyes. The intensity and desire he saw there almost made him weep. They thrust together faster and harder, not noticing the lamp that crashed to the floor as they neared their climax. Perhaps it was her cries or his loud gasps as they found that all-too-brief moment of perfect ecstasy that made them oblivious to the noise that echoed through the apartment.

The noise that woke a little girl who called out softly, "Daddy, where are you?" as she searched from room to room. She stopped suddenly in the darkened hallway where the unlatched door to her father's bedroom was ajar. Why were Jen and Daddy on the bed with no clothes on? Was Daddy trying to hurt Jen? She knew instinctively that what Daddy and Jen were doing was bad and secret, and something she wasn't supposed to see.

She tiptoed back to her room, climbed under the covers, and started to cry. She just wanted to tell Daddy that she had the nicest dream—Mommy came back and was kissing her so sweetly. Now who could she tell about her dream? Maybe Brother Adelard would know what to do.

Chapter 14

JEN AWOKE IN the early morning darkness. She turned around in Chris's arms and studied his face as he slept. She thought how contented and handsome he looked as she gently swept his unruly brown hair from his forehead. Quietly she gathered up her clothes and tiptoed down the hall to the bathroom. She splashed some water on her face, combed her hair a bit, and brushed her teeth with her index finger and some toothpaste to get the stale garlic taste out for now.

She looked in the mirror, tilted her head to disapprovingly examine some little crow's-feet by the corner of her eye, and thought, "What have you gotten yourself into now, girl?" Then she took a deep breath, turned off the light, and muttered, "Let's see what happens next."

The bedroom was bathed in the dim, gray light of a rainy dawn. Jen moved gently to the side of the bed, shook Chris softly, and whispered in his ear. "I have to go now or I'll be late for work. Please call me later on today," and she added silently, or I know I'll just die. Then she bent over and kissed him ever so lightly on his scratchy, stubbly cheek.

Suddenly she felt a strong hand grasp her wrist and pull her down to the bed. Chris looked up, his curly, brown hair almost hiding his eyes. "What's your hurry, little girl?" Then he sat up and kissed her passionately. Although his breath tasted like wine and garlic, she didn't mind at all. "I can think of a great way to start the day," he growled.

Jen pushed him away and whispered, "Get your hands off of me, you pig. You make me cook dinner for you then take advantage of me. Now I suppose you want breakfast. Well, not today." Then she gently slapped his face.

Chris looked up at her silently, his eyes scanning her face. Then he muttered, "God, you're amazing. Can you cook dinner again tonight and tomorrow night and the night after that?"

"What do you want, a lover or a domestic servant?" Jen giggled. "Seriously, I have to go. Call me or else there's no more spaghetti for you." She kissed him quickly and quietly headed out the front door.

Chris and Ronnie went through the steps of their typical week-day routine. As usual, little was said between them; neither one would ever be called a morning person. Even as they drove through the wet streets plastered with fallen leaves, Ronnie was quiet, staring out the car window most of the way to school. Chris was too preoccupied with thoughts of last night and Jen to notice that his little girl answered his questions with single words and looked like she was about to cry.

When Chris reached his office, Peggy took one look at him and remarked, "Wow, it looks like you had a great time last night. Is this a serious thing?"

Chris blushed and responded, "Is it that obvious?" which, of course, confirmed his secretary's fishing expedition. "And, yes, maybe it is a serious thing." Then he added as he turned toward his office, "Why don't you mind your own business?"

Chris called Jen twice that morning. No, she couldn't come over tonight because she had to go food shopping with her dad. But, yes, it would be fun to go to the movies on Saturday night. Maybe the three of them could take in a family movie and get ice cream afterwards. Chris really wanted to make plans for a more adult Saturday night, but, you never know, maybe he could work that in, too. After all, didn't Ronnie say that she wanted Jen to sleep over some night?

As the afternoon wore on, Chris found it difficult to get anything done. He looked out the window at Meeting House Hill and stared at the glowing orange leaves in the gloomy haze, like flames in a smoky forest fire. Maybe it was the drizzly weather. Maybe he didn't get enough sleep last night. Maybe it was just Friday, but suddenly he felt very, very tired. He decided to pick Ronnie up a little early today.

When he reached Holy Rosary School, the rain was coming down harder and he could hear it tapping on the fallen leaves. Joe waved his finger at him as Chris's wet shoes left marks on the front hallway floor. Chris apologized and Joe patted him on the arm, smiled, and said, "That's okay, my friend."

Chris passed a classroom where Ronnie and three other little girls were cutting out Halloween jack-o'-lanterns from orange construction paper under the careful supervision of an older teenage girl. Their chatter and laughter told Chris that

Ronnie was enjoying herself. Chris heard a rustle in the hallway and the soft clatter of rosary beads. The smell of starch mingled with fresh floor wax announced the arrival of Brother Adelard.

"Christopher, you are early today," Brother Adelard stated. "That is fortuitous because I wanted to have a word with you."

"As you wish, Brother. Is it something Ronnie has done?" Chris answered with a note of concern.

"Oh no, nothing like that," said the older man. "Can we talk in private?"

Brother Adelard motioned for Chris to follow him into a nearby classroom. He waved his white, spindly hand toward a chair just underneath the mournful figure of a crucified Jesus hanging high on the wall, then he turned and closed the door.

This isn't going to be good, Chris thought as he braced himself for the worst.

The brother paced back and forth, his rosary beads jingling with the swish of his cassock. Finally he stopped and looked down at Chris as he began. "Christopher, you know that Ronnie has a very special place in my heart. Most recently she has confided in me that she is very concerned about her mother. Can you tell me where her mother is now and how it is that she no longer is a part of your family?"

"Certainly, Brother." Chris told the story of Mimi's abandonment of Ronnie with just a touch of bitterness in his voice. Brother Adelard listened to Chris's story intently.

"Have you heard from this woman recently?" the older man asked.

At first Chris hesitated, but you can't lie to a holy man, who oddly seemed to know more than he should about Mimi's visit. "As a matter of fact, Brother, Ronnie's mother surprised us last night and came to our apartment with her new boyfriend. Thankfully Ronnie was asleep, and Mimi left quickly. If Ronnie had to watch her leave one more time, it would break her heart all over again."

"Yes, but picture your daughter's joy if her mother came back to stay," Brother Adelard urged with intensity.

"What are you saying, Brother?" Chris asked sharply.

Brother Adelard stood up. "I'm saying that it's your duty as a father and as a Catholic to do everything in your power to hold your family together. You owe it to that sweet, innocent little girl to at least attempt to bring her mother back to her."

He paced as he continued. "The family is our Lord's most sacred gift to us. The Blessed Mother's devotion to the child Jesus serves as a model for us and reminds us of the very special role, the sanctified role, that mothers serve in our lives. Indeed, one could say that mothers bridge the gap between human frailty and the divine love of God. It is a terrible thing for a child to grow up without the love and nurturance of his or her natural mother."

Brother Adelard stopped pacing and faced Chris directly. His voice grew louder. "You should be following the example of the ever-faithful Saint Joseph, who endured the uncertainty of his wife, the Blessed Virgin Mary, carrying a child that was not his own seed. Despite the questions he must have had, Joseph trusted in the good Lord's plan for him." He paused and waved a bony finger at Chris as his eyes narrowed. "Instead, you are keeping company with that divorced woman, that Mercier woman, in a rather shameless way, indulging your own selfish feelings of lust at the expense of your daughter's happiness."

The older man was now shaking his fist at Chris as saliva gathered at the corners of his mouth. "These are the sins of the flesh that drove the thorns into our Lord's brow and pounded the nails into his hands and feet. These are the sins that scourged his flesh and plunged the spear into his side. These are the sins that caused his agony and final anguish as he hung from the cross—"

Chris jumped up from the chair. "All right, I think I've heard enough! I don't care who you are. You have no right to judge me or tell me what I should or shouldn't do with my life. And if I find that you've filled my daughter's mind with this sanctimonious bullshit, you'll never see her again."

Brother Adelard lurched toward Chris and waved his fist inches from Chris's face. "Sanctimonious, you call it! You can't understand the truth when you hear it. Instead of listening to my counsel and taking your proper role as father to that dear child with Saint Joseph as your guide, you justify your sinful behavior and allow your thoughts to be guided by your loins as you lie with that divorced woman. Then you have the impertinence to raise your voice in anger and threaten me." The old priest's eyes narrowed as he snarled, "Mark my words, Christopher Murphy, you'll pay dearly for your transgressions."

Chris raised his fist to the old man and said, "So help me God, if you come near me or my daughter ever again, I don't care whether you're a priest or not, I'll break every bone in your body."

He turned and slammed the classroom door on his way out of the classroom. Chris quickly found Ronnie and hurried her out to the car.

Brother Adelard watched from the classroom window with fire in his eyes. Chris fastened Ronnie's seat belt in the Volvo, and rain dripped down from the heavens like tears.

Chapter 15

FRIDAY'S SOAKING RAIN continued into Saturday, and with the cold, wet weather, a gloom set in on Chris and Ronnie's home. Since Chris had grabbed Ronnie and stormed out of Holy Rosary School on Friday afternoon, she hadn't spoken more than a few words at a time to him. On the ride home from school on Friday afternoon, she had asked him, "Daddy, will you take me away from Brother Adelard and school forever?"

In his silent rage after the confrontation with the old man, he simply grumbled, "I don't know at this point, honey. I have to think it over." After that, it was like Ronnie had curled up into a shell where no one could reach her.

Saturday, usually the day that flew by filled with laughter and fun, now became pure drudgery. He read the paper and had an extra cup of coffee. He vacuumed the living room, and he hated to vacuum. Then he cleaned the bathroom and caught up on the laundry. He even sorted out his closet and matched up his loose socks. Chris noticed that he was oddly aware of the ticking clock in the living room. On any other Saturday, Ronnie would have been at his side, but now she sat in front of the television in the living room absorbed by whatever show she was watching.

When it came time for grocery shopping, Chris asked if Ronnie wanted to come along and pick out her favorite treats. Without looking away from the television, she asked if Grandmère could watch her so she could stay home. He called downstairs and Jeanine said she had nothing better to do, so of course she'd be happy to watch Ronnie.

Driving through the rainy, windswept streets everything seemed dark and ugly, from the puddled black roadway to the naked gray limbs of the trees stretching their thin, pleading fingers to the dismal sky. Chris thought he'd cheer himself up by calling Jen.

"I don't know what it is, Jen," he explained. "Ronnie seems like a different kid. She doesn't talk to me. Nothing seems to please her. It's like the life has gone out of her."

"Kids are funny, Chris," Jen replied. "She's been through a lot—moving out of the city, starting in a new school, not to mention having her mother abandon her."

"I know, I know. Sometimes I forget that we really have gone through a lot of changes in a pretty short time period," he said. "And the nicest change was the one that happened last Thursday."

"What was Thursday?" Jen asked teasingly. "Oh, do you mean my spaghetti? Is it a change in diet you're referring to?"

"I think you know what I mean, smart-ass," he responded. "When do you think we can find the time to arrange another serving?"

"Slow down, buddy," she said. "Right now we need to spend some time with a very needy little girl. Let's take Ronnie to her favorite restaurant tonight and spoil her a little. It sounds like she needs it." Then she added, "And if you're a very good boy, we can talk about another spaghetti dinner early next week."

Chris smiled. "You make the sun come out, even when the weather's shitty."

Jen whispered into the phone, "That's not all I can make come out. Wait and see what's on the menu for next week."

The memory of making love with Jen made Chris's heart beat faster. "Hey, knock it off or I'll come over there and wash your cell phone out with soap."

Jen just giggled. "See you around six thirty tonight? I gotta go. Love you."

"I love you too, darling." He was a little startled that the words just came out naturally. But, as he thought about it more, he had to admit that he was falling in love with Jen. The sky and wet trees and slick road all seemed a little brighter to Chris as he pulled into the supermarket parking lot.

Chris carried the bags of groceries into the apartment and found Jeanine and Ronnie sitting in front of the television. "How was our little girl this afternoon, Grand-mère?" he asked quietly as he put the cereal boxes in the cabinet.

"I don't know, Chris," the old woman responded as she helped him with the groceries. "She's very quiet today. Did something happen lately to upset her?"

Chris stopped and looked at Jeanine. "As a matter of fact, I had a pretty heated argument with Brother Adelard yesterday. He was trying to tell me that my relationship with Jen was inappropriate or sinful or immoral. I basically told him to mind his own business." Chris grabbed the flour bag and emptied it into a canister. "I know he's been good to Ronnie, but, to tell you the truth, Jeanine, I've been worried about his relationship with her. Something just isn't right." Chris stopped, his back to the old woman. "All morning long I've been trying to decide whether I should crawl over to that school and apologize for Ronnie's sake or if I should find another school for her far away from that judgmental old man."

He continued as he put the rest of the groceries away. "Sometimes I think you just need to listen to the voice inside you that tells you what's wrong and what's right. Right now that voice is telling me loud and clear that Jen is the best thing that ever happened to Ronnie and me and that pompous monk is hiding something."

"Bravo for you, Chris," Jeanine responded enthusiastically. She paused as if checking to ensure that no one else was listening and continued in a low, confiding voice. "My friends at church tell me that Brother Adelard is up to no good. There have been too many unexplained bad things going on since he came here. They say he holds secret prayer vigils at all hours of the night and keeps a mysterious room in the school basement locked up. No, sir, I don't like the look of him or what I see happening in this town." The old woman looked intently at Chris and made the sign of the cross as she said, "God forgive me for saying this, but there's evil in that man. Take your sweet daughter, my boy, and get her as far away from that brother as fast as you can." She added, almost as an afterthought, "And hold that Mercier girl as close as you can. She's a keeper." The old woman got up stiffly from her seat at the table and squeezed Chris's arm. "I'm going to the four-thirty mass this afternoon. I'll pray for you all."

Ronnie and Chris silently got ready to go out to dinner and the movies. As they got into the car, the little girl looked out the window at the trees shrouded in gray mist, diverting her attention only temporarily to hug her doll and whisper something that Chris couldn't hear. He watched her intently in the rearview mirror and thought, I hope Jen can help me get her out of this gloom.

Suddenly a flash of black feathers exploded in front of the windshield. Chris swerved to the left as two squawking black crows flew up over the Volvo, barely missing the grill. He slowed down and looked in the mirror long enough to see the pink and brown carcass of a dead squirrel in the middle of the road. Chris had spoiled the birds' ghoulish dinner.

"What was that, Daddy?" Ronnie asked in a flat, listless voice.

"Nothing, honey, nothing at all," Chris responded as his heart rate returned to normal. He saw an opening to draw her out. "What are you saying to your doll, sweetie?"

"Nothing, Daddy, nothing at all," was her barely audible reply as they pulled up in front of Jen's house.

Jen ran down the front steps and breathlessly climbed into the car. Knowing that Ronnie wasn't in the best of spirits, she didn't want to put the little girl through the awkwardness of meeting the Mercier family.

Jen gave Chris a friendly peck on the cheek and turned around to face Ronnie in the backseat. Her eyes met the glare of the little girl's hard, persistent brown eyes and she was temporarily unnerved. Recovering, she said with forced good cheer, "How's my little friend doing tonight? We're going to have a great time at the movies. What movie do you want to see, Ronnie?"

The little girl looked down at her doll and replied in a singsong voice, "I don't know, whatever movie you and Daddy want to see."

Jen shot Chris a look of concern and grasped his warm, strong hand. This was going to be a tougher evening than any of them had planned on.

Jen tried diligently to draw Ronnie out during their dinner at Friendly's restaurant, but Ronnie wouldn't respond to Jen with more than a word or two. Throughout dinner, the little girl looked around the restaurant listlessly and hardly touched her clown sundae, despite its whipped cream, colored sprinkles, and miniature candies. Her pale little face was a blank mask.

The three of them left the restaurant and drove silently to the movie theater. Chris decided that the Disney classic cartoon festival might be the best choice. They bought their tickets and popcorn and settled into their seats. The first cartoon was "The Sorcerer's Apprentice" from *Fantasia,* which Ronnie watched with some interest. Jen and Chris exchanged glances and Jen squeezed his hand. Maybe there was some hope that Ronnie would come out of her shell after all.

Just as the cartoon was ending, Jen began to rub her temples and quickly excused herself as she headed for the lobby. Chris looked after her with concern, but chose to stay with Ronnie, who was now engrossed in the next cartoon.

After five minutes or so, Jen returned to her seat, still clutching the side of her head.

"Are you okay?" Chris asked.

"As a matter of fact, I don't think I am," Jen replied with a look of concern on her face. "I've never had a migraine before, but I think that's what's happening now. I've got this intense pain across my forehead."

"Should I take you to the emergency room?" Chris responded with alarm.

Jen forced a smile. "It's just a headache. But I really do think I need to go home and lie down. I'm awfully sorry to ruin our evening."

"It's okay, honey, but now you'll have to go out on another date with me, because this one doesn't count." Chris noticed the look of pain on Jen's face and quickly explained to Ronnie that they had to leave because Jen wasn't feeling well.

They drove in silence through the darkness until they arrived at Jen's house. Chris walked her up the front stairs. Ronnie sat quietly in the blackness of the backseat. A strange smile slowly appeared on her face.

Chris and Ronnie went through their usual Sunday-morning routine as they got ready for the eight o'clock mass. Chris half-heartedly thought of keeping Ronnie home just to avoid any awkwardness with Brother Adelard. Perhaps it was the thought of seeing Jen, perhaps it was simple Catholic guilt about missing church on Sunday, or perhaps it was his faint hope that God would show him the way out of the mess he found himself in.

Whatever the reason, Chris decided that he and Ronnie would attend mass as usual.

The morning was overcast and dreary again, and the last of the brown leaves clung sadly to gray limbs here and there. Ronnie was a little more talkative this morning and reminded him that tonight was Halloween. Chris had entirely forgotten about Halloween - Ronnie didn't have a costume and they didn't buy any candy for the trick-or-treaters. Chris was lost in his own thoughts about Ronnie's school and Brother Adelard as he absentmindedly replied that he'd take care of what they needed for Halloween.

As they walked up the wet, shiny stone steps of the church, Chris and Ronnie came face to face with Brother Adelard in the entryway. The old man seemed particularly menacing in his long black cassock. He scowled and looked away from Chris, but when Ronnie smiled and waved to him, he made the sign of the cross over her head with his long, thin white fingers. Then Brother Adelard disappeared into the stairwell that led to the choir loft. As Chris made his way to their usual seat, he thought, God just sent me a sign. My child is not going back to any school that includes that nasty old man.

Chris didn't hear much of Father Scanlon's sermon or any of the last half of mass for that matter. He looked around the church for Jen, and, not seeing her, became increasingly worried that last night's headache was more serious than he thought. When the service was over, he headed straight for the car, pulled out his cell phone, and called Jen. Just as he feared, the call went to voice mail. Then he called her house and asked for her father. Her brother answered and said that Gus was up at Harrison Hospital. Jen had been admitted last night, but, other than that, he really didn't have much more information.

Chris raced home and, after a quick explanation, he dropped Ronnie off with Jeanine. When he reached the hospital waiting room, he found Gus Mercier pacing back and forth. His face was gaunt and unshaven, and he looked sadly pathetic in his wrinkled flannel shirt, gray sweatpants, and unlaced work boots. When Chris approached him, Gus grasped his hand and said, "Thank God you're here. She was asking for you last night before she lost consciousness. Maybe if she hears your voice …"

Chris reached out and grasped the older man's arm, the two of them united in fear and concern. "Do the doctors know what happened to her?" Chris asked quietly.

Gus shook his head. "One guy thought it was a seizure. Another thought it might have been a stroke. They don't know. I don't know." Then he added, "She means the world to me."

Chris nodded. "Me too. Can I see her now?"

Gus called the duty nurse and talked with her for a few moments, then motioned to Chris. The middle-aged nurse looked at Chris grimly and said, "We don't usually allow anyone into critical care who isn't immediate family, but I'll take a chance on this one. Just do exactly as I tell you."

The three of them stepped into the dim room that smelled of gauze and disinfectant. Jen looked small and frail in the hospital bed. Chris was aware of the faint beeping of an array of machines that monitored her weak vital signs. He stood over her for a moment. Her skin tone almost matched the color of the light-blue hospital johnny she wore. A breathing tube rested under her nostrils, and intravenous lines were taped onto her wrists. He took her left hand in his, but it was cold and lifeless. Then he leaned over her and gently kissed her forehead as he whispered, "Don't give up, Jen, I couldn't live without you. I love you." As he stepped back, he noticed a twitch, the slightest muscle quiver, in Jen's left eyelid. He quickly shot Gus a glance. The look on Jen's father's face told him that he too had seen Jen's reaction. The nurse quickly responded to the changing beep of a life-support machine and waved Gus and Chris out of the room.

"Did you see that, Gus?" Chris asked with faint hope.

"It's the most positive thing I've seen in ten hours," the old man responded.

"Maybe there's hope," Chris said as if he were trying to convince himself.

Gus rested his hand on Chris's shoulder. "I think all we can do now is pray."

"Maybe there's something else I can do," Chris replied mysteriously. "I'll be back in a few hours. Here's my cell phone number. Please call me if there's any change." Chris jotted down the number, handed it to Gus, and bolted for the parking lot.

He raced home and knocked on Jeanine's apartment door.

"Oh, Chris, I've been praying for Jennifer all morning. How is she?" the old woman asked with tears in her eyes. "It's a shame that something like this should happen to such a wonderful young lady."

"I just don't know, Jeanine." Chris shook his head. "I might be crazy, but I think that evil monk had something to do with this."

"I don't think you're crazy at all," Jeanine responded. "Someone needs to stop him or his next victim could be you or me or Ronnie."

Neither of the adults noticed that Ronnie was standing in the doorway, listening to their conversation. Now she spoke, barely holding back her tears. "Brother Adelard is a good and holy priest, and he's close to God. He says that Grand-mère is a good woman, but Daddy has sinned since he met Jen." The little girl's voice began to rise. "He says that Jen is bad because she makes Daddy turn away from God and because she made Mommy go away. And I know Brother Adelard is right but I didn't want Jen to get sick." Then Ronnie fell abruptly silent and began to sob.

Chris grabbed Ronnie by the shoulders. "What are you talking about? Mommy went away because she couldn't live with us anymore. She wanted to find a new life."

"No, she didn't. You're lying, just like Brother Adelard said you would. I saw her in our house and she kissed me and hugged me. And then I was in the hall and I looked in your bedroom and you and Jen were doing something bad." The little girl's tears streamed down her cheeks in fear, grief, and anger. "I even asked Brother Adelard, and he said it was a very bad sin what Jen was doing with you. He said that unless we said our special prayer, you were going to burn in the fires of hell forever. So we said our special prayer on Friday. And now Jen's sick and it's my fault."

"What special prayer? What did that monster make you do?" Chris's face was inches from Ronnie's.

"It's the prayer we always say together in Brother Adelard's secret place when he pricks my finger," Ronnie sobbed. "I don't want Jen to get sick, but I want Mommy back with us just like it used to be. Brother Adelard promised me if we said the special prayer Mommy would come back." Now the little girl was convulsed with tears. Jeanine gathered her up in her arms and took her to the bedroom. Chris just stood there, shocked, astonished, and filled with shame. Then rage boiled up into his throat.

Jeanine returned from the bedroom, looked intently at Chris, and asked, "What are you going to do now?"

Chris said through clenched teeth, "I'm going over to Holy Rosary and beat the hell out of that twisted bastard."

"I was afraid you'd say that. Sit down and listen to me," Jeanine commanded. "This evil monk has survived for many years by his wits. I'm sure he's ready for you right now and knows exactly how to fight you."

"Then I'll go to the police," Chris blurted out.

"And what would you tell them?" she asked. "That some demonic priest is casting spells on people? Do you really think they'd listen to you for more than a moment before they write you off as a fool?"

Chris nodded. "Then what do you think I should do?"

"Before you can defeat him, you need to know your enemy," Jeanine stated carefully and slowly. "They say that Father Costello was struck down because he knew too much. Father Costello is being treated in a nursing home for elderly priests

P. G. Smith

and nuns over by the coast. I'll give you the address in a few moments. Drive out there today and see what you can find out from the poor old man." She waved a finger in warning. "But before you act against Brother Adelard, be very, very careful. He holds the power of an evil force that you and I can never understand. He's a cunning and vicious enemy, Chris, but you must defeat him. Your life and the lives of those you love the most depend on it."

Chris grasped Jeanine's hand. "Where is Father Costello's nursing home?"

Jeanine wrote down the address and handed it to Chris. "Now go quickly before it's too late. I'll take care of little Ronnie. Whatever happens, I'll keep her safe. Get going and I will pray as hard as I can that God will guide you and give you strength."

Chris raced to his car, and the tires squealed on the wet, brown leaves as he headed for the coast.

242

Chapter 16

CHRIS COULD BARELY see beyond the next bend because of the milky gray fog that concealed the roadway up ahead. Soggy leaves scattered in the wake of the station wagon as Chris raced to the coast. He gripped the wheel with both hands until his knuckles were white, and he fixed his attention on the slick, twisting roadway. Chris knew that his only hope was to locate Father Costello and learn what the old priest knew about Brother Adelard. It was his best chance to find the evil monk's vulnerabilities and defeat him. Chris's mind was filled with rage that Brother Adelard had used his daughter, his angel, for his own diabolical purposes. But Chris had no idea, no plan, about what to do when he arrived at the nursing home.

Saint Jude's Home was just outside the center of Rock Harbor, a sleepy little fishing village on the coast. As Chris parked his car in the almost deserted parking lot, a half-baked plan came to mind. He forced himself to stride confidently across the parking lot, although inside he was trembling. What if I can't talk my way inside? he thought. What if I can't find Father Costello? Then I'm lost ... and we're all doomed.

He resolutely opened the front door and stepped into the dimly lit lobby. It smelled of coffee and air freshener. Benny

Goodman big-band music played softly on the sound system. Two residents played cards at a table in the corner. They looked up from their game and stared at Chris through their silver-rimmed glasses. He smiled at them and nodded politely. Then he approached the nun who was seated at the information desk.

"Good afternoon, Sister." He smiled confidently. "Can you tell me where I can find Father Michael Costello?"

The nun was probably about Chris's age. She was dressed in an immaculate white gown with a black veil on her head, and she was wearing rimless glasses. Chris thought, Why do all nuns wear wireless glasses? She automatically began to scan her computer monitor, then stopped and examined Chris carefully. "I'm sorry, sir, personal visits for patients in Father Costello's ward are only permitted for immediate family members. You're not an immediate family member, are you?" This statement was phrased more as a reproach than a question.

Chris was in a panic, but he thought quickly and used his desperation to his advantage. "No, Sister, I'm not immediate family, but I feel as if Father Costello is my spiritual father. From an early age, I considered him a role model and a mentor. It's very important that I see him one last time before, well, you know, no one knows how much time they have left. Only the good Lord knows for sure." He looked pleadingly into the nun's eyes.

The nun looked back at her computer. His story had worked, but not as well as he had hoped.

"Come with me," the nun said, rising from the reception desk. "I'll take you to Mrs. Davis, our assistant director.

Perhaps she'll be willing to make an exception to our rules for you." She added with a hint of apology, "It's beyond my authority to bend the rules." She allowed herself an apologetic smile, but it was a good sign.

Chris followed the nun down a short hallway. She motioned for him to wait in the dim corridor while she stepped inside the office. After she left, Chris noticed that he was standing next to a statue of Jesus with his arms outstretched. "Please help me, God. If this doesn't work, we're all screwed." He blessed himself with the sign of the cross as if to make up for his unconventional prayer. The nun spotted the last motions of the gesture and smiled. "Mrs. Davis will see you now."

Chris entered the office. It was decorated in shades of beige and, like everything in the nursing home, was dimly lit. A formidable middle-aged woman in a gray suit reached out her hand. "Hello, I'm Cynthia Davis, assistant director of Saint Jude's Home. What can I do for you?"

Chris summoned up all the false sincerity he could muster. "Pleased to meet you, Mrs. Davis. My name is Christopher Murphy. I'm here to see my old pastor and spiritual advisor, Father Michael Costello. However, the sister in the lobby tells me that only immediate family members are allowed to visit."

"That's correct, Mr. Murphy," the woman replied. "Residents in Father Costello's fragile condition can't easily tolerate the excitement of many visitors. We feel it's important for them to avoid anything that might cause trauma or stress to their delicate physical and mental well-being."

"But, Mrs. Davis, I've traveled thousands of miles to see Father Costello. Ever since I was a child, when he first taught me to serve the good Lord on the altar, he has been with me in my thoughts and with me as a role model." Chris realized that he was laying it on thick, but the woman seemed to be softening. "If I can't see him one last time before he crosses over to receive his reward in heaven, I'll never forgive myself."

The hospital administrator studied him carefully. Chris was confident that his act was working, but she said slowly, "Let me just ask you to consider if it wouldn't be kinder, wouldn't be better for both of you, to remember Father Costello as he was, full of life, and good humor, and sanctity. The man who lives with us here is not the same person that you recall. He may not remember you at all, or he may act in a way that you've never seen before or could imagine that he ever would act." Mrs. Davis paused for a moment, then looked directly at Chris. "Father is receiving treatment in a wing of our facility that serves the needs of those who suffer from significant mental illness.

Chris took one more shot. "I don't know if you've ever sinned, Mrs. Davis, but I have. I can't fly back to LA until I can confess to Father Costello. Even if he can't offer me absolution, if I can at least confess to him, my burden will be lifted."

Mrs. Davis looked at Chris's pleading face, thought for a moment, and pushed back from the desk. "Well, Mr. Murphy," the woman said with a sigh as she stood, "I hope your visit with Father Costello is fulfilling for you both, but don't say you weren't warned." She shook her head, reached into her desk, and took out a massive ring of keys. "Follow me."

She led him down a long, green corridor. On either side were doorways with frosted glass so no one could see out or see in. Chris was struck by the odor of stale urine and disinfectant. Attendants and nurses in white glided silently up and down the corridor. A sharp cry pierced the stillness, but nobody seemed to pay any attention. It made the skin on the back of Chris's neck tingle.

At last Mrs. Davis stopped in front of one of the doorways. "We have to keep the doors locked in this ward because the residents are likely to wander. Remember, Mr. Murphy, this is not the same Father Costello from your younger days." Opening the door, she looked inside and called in a loud voice, "Father, wake up, you have a visitor." Then she turned to Chris and pointed to a red button on the wall. "We have to lock the door behind us. If you need assistance, push the red button."

Chris stepped inside the room, and the lock clicked shut behind him. The green linoleum floor and faded white walls seemed to close in on him. The walls had stains all over them, and one looked like feces. The only furniture was a white iron bed, a white plastic chair, and a white chest of drawers. High up on the wall a tiny television was broadcasting a baseball game, but the sound was so low that you could barely hear it. Right next to the television hung a silver crucifix from which a tortured Jesus looked down on the frail old man in a wheelchair.

Father Costello sat slumped in his wheelchair. His black cassock was stained with what appeared to be clumps of oatmeal, and he wore a pair of orange terry-cloth slippers. Beneath his wispy, white hair his scalp was blistered and scaly. Chris's nostrils stung from the mingled scents of body odor and excrement.

Chris pulled up the chair and faced Father Costello. The old priest's chin was covered in white stubble, and his left eye was closed. He stared dully at the television with his right eye, which was the bloodshot and crusted. His thin white hands lay still on a plywood board that served as a wheelchair table.

Chris tried to look the old priest in his one open eye. "Father Costello ... Father Costello, it's Chris Murphy from Ashton Falls. We only met a few times, but I need your help desperately." The priest's eye blinked, but he stared away from Chris.

Chris looked at the priest and, in despair, realized that the old man hadn't heard him, or was too impaired to understand. He laid his hands on the priest's skeletal hands, lowered his forehead onto them, and groaned, "Oh God, what will I do now? I must stop that monster, but I don't know how. Please help me, God, please help me." Chris began to weep in anguish and despair.

Suddenly he felt a hand on his head. "Will you pick up your head and quit bawling," the voice croaked. "I was just watching the third game of the World Series and praying that those Yankees would get the snot kicked out of them." The voice gained strength, and Father Costello cleared his throat. He tried to sit up a little, and his one clear eye focused sharply on Chris. "I can't be too careful these days. The workers around here are a bunch of cutthroats and thieves. I needed to be sure of who you were before we could talk."

Chris stared at the old priest in amazement and grasped his feeble hand. He looked at the priest intently and said, "I know you probably don't remember me, Father—"

"Of course I know who you are," the priest replied. "You're the new guy in town with the young daughter." He straightened up as best he could in the wheelchair. "I'm also willing to guess that you came to see me because of that demon, Adelard. I've been waiting for someone with enough guts to finally take on that twisted bastard, if you'll forgive my French. You need my help, and I'm ready to give it."

Chris replied hopefully, "Just tell me what to do, Father. I'll do anything to stop that menace."

"First things first," said the old man with a sly look. "You don't happen to have a smoke on you, do you?"

Chris replied that he didn't smoke.

"Darn it!" Father Costello uttered. "I haven't had a cigarette since they locked me up in here, and I'm dying for one. I guess if this place does nothing else for me, at least they'll get me to quit smoking after six decades." He shifted his gaze onto Chris's face, and his tone suddenly became serious. "We don't have much time before they throw you out, and you need to know as much as possible before you choose to do battle with that fiend. And if you fail, you could end up like this. So listen carefully."

Chris leaned forward and stared into the old priest's face. "I'm just going to tell you the whole story from the beginning," said the old priest. "Listen carefully, and stop me if you don't get it. But we don't have a long time to chitchat." Father

Costello focused his one eye on Chris like a laser and began to speak slowly and clearly.

The old priest briefly summarized what he had read in Brother Siegfried's diary as succinctly as he could, explaining Adelard's history from his tragic boyhood in France, through his upbringing in Austria, and up to his discovery of the Prayers for the Damned.

"After what I learned in the diary," Father Costello's voice croaked, "I called the bishop's office in Portland to find out how Adelard came to be in Ashton Falls."

The old priest's voice trailed off, and he turned his head toward the door in response to the sound of approaching footsteps in the hallway.

Chapter 17

CHRIS HEARD THE heavy tread of someone approaching followed by pounding on the door. "Visit's over in there," the deep voice bellowed. "It's almost time for dinner and meds."

The old priest looked at Chris in desperation. Chris stepped over to the door. "Please, I've just begun to become reacquainted with my old friend. We have so much to tell each other and so little time together." He sensed that his attempt at winning the attendant's pity wasn't working, and he adjusted his tactics. Reaching into his wallet, he took out three twenty-dollar bills and slid them under the door. "Look, I really need another hour here. Will that do it?" Chris waited nervously for an answer.

"You just bought yourself another twenty minutes," the rough voice whispered back. "I can't give you more than that."

Chris smiled and decided to push his luck. "How much will a cigarette cost me?" he asked quietly.

He heard the keys in the door, and it slipped open a crack. A hairy hand reached in with a smoldering Marlboro. "That'll be another twenty bucks," the voice muttered. Chris slipped another twenty through the slim door opening as he took the cigarette. He heard the keys in the lock and the voice respond,

"I'll be back in twenty minutes, and that's it." Then the attendant added, "Pleasure doing business with you."

As the footsteps died away down the hall, Father Costello caressed the cigarette in his white fingers, inhaled deeply, and blew a smoke ring as he exhaled. "Ah, delicious." His eyes closed as he drank in the smoke. "And they said these things would kill me."

Chris waited as the old priest savored the cigarette, but he soon became aware that twenty minutes would pass quickly and he was far away from learning what he had to know. He gently nudged the old priest's arm. "Father, we don't have much time," he whispered.

"Of course, of course," Father Costello sputtered, carefully crushing out the half-smoked cigarette. "I need to save this for a special occasion anyway. Now where was I?"

"You were explaining how Brother Adelard came to Ashton Falls," Chris responded quickly.

"An old seminary colleague of mine works in the clergy assignment office at the archdiocese," the old priest continued. "He looked into Brother Adelard's file and told me as much as he could find about Adelard's journey to Maine. I also made a few discrete inquiries in Austria, France, and Canada to fill in some missing pieces.

"Apparently the citizens of Salzburg became concerned when mysterious accidents kept occurring to people who had earned Adelard's deadly attention. Things reached the point where the local people referred to the old monastery as 'the haunted place,' and the townspeople avoided it as if it contained the plague. Church leaders in Austria had no choice but to close the monastery and reassign the monks to parish churches or other monasteries throughout Europe."

Father Costello coughed and cleared his throat. "Let me make this quick—because of his French citizenship, Adelard was then assigned to the parish of Saint Pierre in the Montmartre section of Paris, which overlooks the infamous Pigalle neighborhood, Paris's red-light district. Needless to say, Adelard found an abundance of victims there and was eventually transferred to a small village church in Saint Sebastian, a quiet village near Montreal, because of his fluency in French and English. Unfortunately, Adelard soon occupied his time prowling St. Catherine Street in Montreal, a venue noted for pimps, prostitutes, and drug dealers. After several years of mysterious deaths, he was sent to Ashton Falls, probably because we have a large group of French speakers in our parish and someone believed he couldn't find as many victims here. I guess they were wrong."

Chris listened but finally interrupted impatiently. "Please, Father, tell me quickly how I can stop this madman and save my daughter."

Father Costello grasped Chris's hand with startling strength. "The ancient text, the Prayers for the Damned, is somewhere in Ashton Falls. Together with the relic from Jesus's Crown of Thorns, the book gives him the demonic power to punish those whom he believes have sinned. Apparently he is using your little girl to obtain the third important element for his curse—innocent blood."

P. G. Smith

"Oh my God, that explains the punctures in Ronnie's little finger." The blood rushed to Chris's face. "I'll kill that fucking bastard!"

"Now, watch your mouth, and listen carefully before you set off half-cocked," the old priest cautioned. "In the basement of the school, that demon has a secret room. I believe the book and the thorn are most likely hidden there. Get into that place somehow and destroy the tools of his evil work. Burn them, and make sure that they are totally destroyed. That's the only way to defeat him. After his power is gone—"

Father Costello stopped abruptly as he was interrupted by a heavy pounding on the door. "Hey, buddy, you need to get out of here. The head nurse is making her evening rounds, and I'll catch hell if they find you here. I'll show you the back way out. Come on, let's go."

The old priest was already muttering a blessing as he raised his right hand with two fingers extended. "God go with you, my son, and thanks for the butt."

The station wagon raced along the black, shiny roadways in the fading light of the late October afternoon. His hands clamped to the steering wheel, Chris was transfixed by one single thought, and he repeated out loud, "I must stop him, I must stop him." Thoughts of Ronnie and Jen half formed in his mind, but they quickly evaporated as snatches of Father Costello's raspy, desperate voice came back to him. He tried to pray, but the words wouldn't come.

Chris rounded a curve past an inlet of the sea and glanced at the gray-green churning water wreathed in white mist. Medieval

254

curses, Nazi legend hunters, ancient relics—I must be the crazy one, he thought. This can't be real. I must be losing my mind. But the gaunt, earnest features of Father Costello flashed in his mind only to be replaced by the drained, ashen face of Jen as she lay in the hospital bed, which was then transformed into the wide-eyed innocence of Ronnie. Finally they were all blotted out by the sharp, angular features and haughty sneer of Brother Adelard shaking his fist at Chris. He gripped the wheel even tighter and pressed down more firmly on the gas pedal.

When he reached the center of Ashton Falls, darkness had already fallen. Here and there groups of children were trick-or-treating in their costumes. Pale angels held hands with crimson devils as dainty ballerinas in pink skipped ahead with blood-thirsty pirates. They scampered and stumbled from house to house, their flashlights shooting out cones of light against the shadows. As Chris jolted to a stop at an intersection, a tiny skeleton with greenish-white reflective bones passed in front of his headlights holding the hand of a little witch in a black gossamer gown and a tall pointed hat. An older teenage vampire stared at Chris as he crossed the street behind the two little ones, scarlet theater blood dripping from his plastic fangs. The sight of dripping blood turned Chris's thoughts to Ronnie, and rage boiled up within him. He knew where he needed to turn for help.

The Volvo's tires squealed on the damp pavement as the car roared into the driveway next to Holy Rosary rectory, where the priests lived. Bounding up the front steps, Chris hammered on the door with his fists. Father Scanlon came to the door in an old Notre Dame T-shirt, wiping the last crumbs of his dinner from his lips with a napkin.

"Father, thank God you're here. I really need your help," Chris blurted out as he stepped into the hallway.

"Certainly, Chris, whatever you need," the priest responded, his eyes carefully studying Chris's face. "Please come in. Let's sit in the study."

Chris didn't wait until they reached the study. "It's Brother Adelard, Father. He's using some kind of curse against Father Costello, Jen, and God knows who else. I have to stop him. I need your help." Chris's words tumbled out in a steady stream as Father Scanlon gently took his arm and steered him toward a couch.

The priest closed the door to the study and pulled a chair up next to Chris. Father Scanlon leaned forward and said, "You seem terribly upset tonight, Chris. Why don't you take a deep breath? Start at the beginning and tell me the whole story."

Chris told him everything from the gruesome madness of the dogs, to the death of Big Bill, to the old veteran's accident, to Jen's strange illness, and finally his visit to Father Costello in the nursing home. Throughout Chris's story, Father Scanlon looked away from him, his hands folded in front of his face. The priest encouraged him from time to time by saying, "Go on, what happened next?" As Chris reached the end of the story, he became more and more agitated.

"That's it, Father," Chris said, clenching his fists in his lap. "We have to stop him. Maybe we can't save Father Costello, but we have to save Ronnie and Jennifer." Then he added in a whisper, "We have to save them or I think I'll die," as he looked away from the priest and wiped his eyes.

Father Scanlon gently placed his hand on Chris's shoulder, pulled his chair closer, and looked intently into Chris's face. "Okay, Chris, here's what I think is the best way to deal with this situation. You've been under a great deal of stress lately. Your life has changed dramatically in only a few months. Think about it—your wife abandoned you and your daughter, you moved to a new state, and you took on a stressful work assignment. You even began a new, and somewhat complicated, relationship. That's enough stress to test any man's limits. Before you do anything that you might regret later, I really think you should talk to a professional."

The priest stood up and rummaged through the top drawer of a desk. "I have a good friend's card over here. People tell me he's one of the best therapists in Maine. I can make a phone call and get you in to see him first thing tomorrow morning. I'm sure you'll like him," the priest continued in a soothing voice.

Chris sprang up from the couch. "You think I'm crazy, don't you?" he shouted. "You're going to let this demon continue to practice evil in this parish while people die? What's the matter with you? What kind of a priest, what kind of a man of God are you?"

"Look, Chris, you came in here and interrupted my dinner with some fantastic tale of Nazis and medieval curses and haunted books," the priest snapped back. "What do you want me to do? Why don't I get Adelard down here right now and ask him straight up if he's the boogeyman? Do you want me to ask him if he'd please tell us about his demonic rituals? Is that what you want?" Father Scanlon's face took on a look of regret as Chris clenched his fists, anger shrouding his face.

"You need to pray, Father," Chris growled. "Pray that Adelard doesn't reach out and strike someone close to you. Pray that you're not this bastard's next victim. Pray that I get him before he can work his evil again." Then he bolted for the front door.

"Chris, please come back," the priest pleaded as he followed him out the door. "I'm sorry. Please take this therapist's number and call him. I beg you, don't do something foolish."

Chris turned and shook his head when he reached the bottom of the front steps. "God help you, Father." With that, he disappeared into the misty darkness of the night.

Chapter 18

CHRIS STUMBLED THROUGH the dark. He nearly fell over a pile of leaves and fallen tree branches on the lawn as he made his way behind the rectory to the back door of the school building. He had no idea what he planned to do next, but the rage and desperation that surged inside him dictated that he must find the relic and the ancient text and destroy them.

As his eyes slowly adjusted to the blackness of the night, he made out the form of a rusty steel door at the back of the school. Grasping the handle, he tugged with all his might, but the door wouldn't budge. Chris slumped down against the door in despair and raised his eyes to the sky. Please, please, help me, he silently pleaded.

Suddenly he heard a strange sound from the other side of the door. It sounded like a low, rhythmic growling, and it grew louder and louder as Chris pressed his ear to the door. He pounded his fists against the steel in desperation, hoping that whatever made the sound would hear him. He grabbed a rock from the ground, prepared to strike if the source of the growling was some part of Brother Adelard's diabolical ritual.

The sound stopped. Chris gripped the rock tighter as the door opened a crack, letting a ray of dim light out into the darkness. His heart pounded. Chris seized the door handle with his free hand and threw it open with the rock poised to strike in his other hand. Just inside the doorway stood Joe the janitor with his iPod in his hand.

"Hey, it's Ronnie's dad," Joe said as a wide grin lit up his face. But his smile faded as he watched Chris surge into the hallway and tug the door shut behind him. He stared at Chris with a frightened expression.

Chris grasped Joe by both shoulders and looked intently into his eyes. "Joe, I'm going to tell you something very serious, and I need your help. Brother Adelard is a wicked, wicked man. He has done terrible things to hurt innocent people, like Father Costello, and he's hurting my little girl."

The janitor nodded his head and returned Chris's serious look.

"Somewhere in this building is a secret place where he does evil things," Chris continued breathlessly. "I need you to help me find it. I need you to help me stop Brother Adelard."

Joe looked surprised. No one had ever trusted him to help with anything serious before. His eyes brightened as he appeared to remember something. "I know where. It's downstairs in the basement. Come."

The two men raced down the dimly lit iron stairway until they reached the bottom floor. The damp brick and cement cellar was cold and musty. Joe pointed to a solid oak door back against the far wall of the cellar. "This is where Brother prays with Ronnie."

As Joe stepped over to the light switch, Chris stopped him. "Don't turn on the lights, Joe. I don't want to alert Brother Adelard."

Chris rushed through the darkness to the door and tugged on the handle, but it was locked tight with a sturdy hasp and a high-security padlock. "Joe, do you have a key to this door?"

"Brother never lets anybody have a key to that door," Joe replied.

"Do you have any tools—maybe an ax or a sledgehammer? Can you find a flashlight?" Chris's voice came quickly, and he panted with exhaustion and anxiety.

Joe nodded his head and raced up the stairs. Chris stood in the gloom, every muscle tensed, knowing that he couldn't afford to fail or everything that was dear to him was lost.

Moments later, Joe returned with a flashlight and an old, rusty ax. Chris grabbed the ax and began to hack at the sturdy oak door as Joe shined the light on the lock. Wood splinters flew, and within moments Chris was able to tug the thick door open. He grabbed the flashlight from Joe as they stepped through the doorway.

The air inside the room was chilly, and it stunk of mold and decay. To Chris's surprise, there were three or four candles burning within red glass holders, casting a flickering red glow across the room. As their eyes adjusted, Chris and Joe gasped in horror at what they saw.

Around the room were life-size statues of martyrs depicted in the final throes of their tortured lives. Saint Denis in his white robes stood erect, holding his severed head under his right arm. The eyes, sunk deep in gray sockets, looked to heaven as if beseeching "Why?" The bearded, bedraggled figure of Father Isaac Joques raised up the stumps of his fingers chopped off by the Mohawks. The glistening blood ran down his arms. Saint Sebastian stood tied to a tree with a dozen arrows protruding from his naked body and his face contorted in agony. Joan of Arc writhed in the midst of flames that consumed her mortal life, her singed and blistered skin visible through the remnants of her charred gown. The images seemed to be alive in one moment and then frozen in another moment as the candlelight flickered. Chris fought back the urge to retch at the macabre images, then spotted something at the far end of the room.

He raised the flashlight and shined it on a small wooden altar. In front of it was an ornate carved oak kneeler with a much smaller, much simpler, kneeler beside it. Over the altar was a carefully painted sign that read "The Chapel of the Holy Innocents." The altar was covered with a perfectly pressed snow-white cloth with simple red crosses embroidered on each end. In the center of the altar was an elaborately carved wooden box.

"This must be it," Chris uttered aloud, although his mouth was as dry as dust. He raced to the altar, grabbed the old box, and carefully examined it. He studied it for a moment, noting the intricately carved figures of saints and angels. Remembering the urgency of his mission, he tugged at the cover of the box. Although there was no visible lock, the cover wouldn't budge.

"Joe, get the ax," he barked, almost fearing that if he left the altar or put down the box, it would disappear. He grabbed the ax from the janitor, placed the box on the altar, and raised the ax high over his head. He brought it down with all his might, and the solid box split in two with a rush of air as if a coffin had been pried open. The powerful odor of sulfur suddenly filled the chapel.

Chris threw the ax to the floor and reached among the splintered remnants of the box. There he found a medieval illuminated book bound in the finest leather. The gold edges of the pages were bright and shiny in the flickering candlelight, and the pages were radiant with the red, blue, and purple inks painstakingly applied by monastic scribes so many centuries ago. The leather cover was as supple as if it had been polished the day before, and etched into it were the bright gold letters that formed *Precis Intemporaliter Damnare.*

Lying amongst the splinters was a small red velvet bag. Chris opened it and found a long, sharp twig, curved like the talon of a hawk. The sharp end was stained a deep crimson red. He quickly grabbed the book and the red velvet bag and gripped them tightly.

"Joe, is there a fireplace in the school or a place where you burn trash?"

Joe nodded and motioned for Chris to follow. They traveled farther into the basement until they came to another dark room. Chris shined the flashlight into the room and saw an old furnace. The rest of the room was empty expect for some discarded yard tools and a few chipped statues. Joe grabbed the handle of a small steel door at one end of the furnace, and the leaping flames from within lit the darkened room.

It looks like the depths of hell, Chris thought, which is where this book belongs. But before he could toss the book into the flames, he felt razor-like claws dig into his neck and a powerful force threw him to the concrete floor. He looked up, and although his vision was clouded from the impact of his fall, he could clearly make out the dark form of Brother Adelard in the flickering light. Spittle formed in the corners of the old monk's mouth as he sneered at Chris, and his eyes seemed to glow red in fury.

Brother Adelard pounced on Chris and grabbed him by the throat. Despite the old man's age, Chris needed his full strength to keep the monk from strangling him. Chris spotted Brother Adelard's rosary beads dangling by his waist. Seizing the black beads, he reached up, wrapped them around the old man's neck, and twisted them with all his might.

He could feel Brother Adelard's strength fading. Just as the monk's grasp was loosening, the string of beads broke, and his grip on Chris's throat regained its strength. Chris fought back with the last of his waning strength, but the monk succeeded in banging his head against the floor. In desperation, Chris clawed at Brother Adelard's face, but the monk slammed his head against the concrete again. Chris could taste the blood in his mouth, and his vision became hazier as the monk squeezed his throat tighter and tighter in a viselike grip.

Chris's consciousness was quickly slipping away when suddenly he heard a loud crack. He felt the monk stiffen as the deadly grip went slack. Brother Adelard's eyes rolled back in his head, his face contorted in pain and shock. Then he pitched forward, face-first, on top of Chris. Chris could feel a warm liquid oozing over his neck and chest. He regained his breath and shoved the monk's body off to the side. Chris turned to his left and saw the head of the old, rusty ax protruding from the back of Brother Adelard's skull. Looking up, he saw Joe standing at his feet, shaking, with tears running down his cheeks.

Struggling to his feet, Chris scooped up the ancient book and the small red bag. Grasping them firmly, he hurled them into the flames of the furnace. There was a loud hiss and a flash of light, almost like fireworks, as they were engulfed in fire. Chris slammed the steel door shut and secured the handle.

Joe stood sobbing, motionless in the center of the room. Chris took him in his arms and wiped away his tears. "You saved my life, buddy," he said as he hugged him as tight as he could.

After a few moments, Chris became aware of the spreading pool of blood on the floor surrounding the lifeless black figure of the old monk. He patted Joe on the back and whispered, "You better get home now, my friend. You need to be as far away from here as you can." Joe nodded, slowly turned, and headed for the stairway as if he was in a trance.

Chris looked down at the bloody form on the ground. He found Brother Adelard's cold, damp left wrist, felt for a pulse, and confirmed that the old man was dead. He pondered what he had to do next, and with a deep sigh realized that what lay ahead would be the toughest challenge of all.

Chapter 19

THE RAIN STOPPED, and the fog lifted. Chris drove through the silent streets of Ashton Falls more slowly than he had since he first came to this place. Shattered pumpkins lay in the street where mischievous teenagers had smashed them. Here and there a jack-o'-lantern still faintly glowed on a house porch that had escaped teenage treachery.

The tiny ghosts had already counted out their pieces of candy, the junior pirates were brushing their teeth in their pajamas, and the little witches were snuggling under their covers. Mothers and fathers, under the pretext of checking for any dangerous items, shuffled through little goblins' trick-or-treat bags, sneaking a Charleston Chew or a Snickers bar.

There was a touch of frost on the piles of maple leaves in the silver light of a clear crescent moon. Chris drove past the dark and silent Holy Rosary Church, past the empty bank, through the deserted center of town until he arrived at Harrison Hospital. The parking-lot lights cast a soft orange veil over the cars as if Halloween was being celebrated here at the hospital.

Chris turned off the key in the ignition, and his head slumped over the steering wheel. He raised his eyes to the night sky in a silent prayer, or actually more of a plea, and realized that he was more exhausted and more frightened than he had ever been in his life.

Summoning his last bit of strength, he made his way into the silent hospital. He stepped into a public restroom to splash water on his face and scrub the blood off his clothing as best as he could. When he looked in the mirror, he was surprised to find that there were no traces of blood on his clothes or his skin. He wondered if he had just imagined Brother Adelard's blood running down his neck and chest as he lay dying on top of him. Chris swept back his hair, straightened his clothing, and headed for the intensive care unit.

When the elevator door opened to take him to the ICU, he gasped as he saw a nun, in her white habit, already inside the elevator. Oh God, is she going up to pray for the dead? he thought. But the cheerful woman just smiled at him and said, "Good evening, young man. Which floor?"

Chris stepped out of the elevator and made his way down the long corridor of beeping machines and blue-clad nurses gliding in and out of rooms until he came to the empty ICU waiting room. He went to the nurse at the counter and asked frantically, "Is Gus Mercier here?"

The middle-aged woman replied without looking up from her computer screen. "He's been living here round the clock. If he's not in the waiting room, then he must be in with his daughter."

Chris took a deep breath. If Gus was with Jen, then … he couldn't bear the thought. "Can you tell him Chris Murphy is here?"

"When I get to it," the nurse said with some annoyance. "There are a few other things that are little bit more important. Have a seat in the waiting room."

Chris went to the waiting room, but sitting was beyond him. He paced back and forth as his thoughts raced. What if Adelard's curses were permanent? What if the burning of the book sealed the fate of its victims? What if he really was crazy and this was all some kind of hallucination?

Gus burst into the waiting room and wrapped Chris in a bear hug. There were tears streaming down the old man's face. "It's the damnedest thing, Chris," he blurted out, wiping away the tears. "Jen just sat up in bed about an hour ago and asked for something to drink." Gus's words came in spurts between chuckles and sobs. "We've been talking since then. She keeps asking for you. Come on, I know she wants to see you."

The old man took Chris by the arm and led him to Jen's room. The night nurse followed in protest, but gave up once they were in the room. Chris could barely see Jen in the dim light, but he clearly saw her right arm raised as she beckoned to him. There were dark gray circles around her eyes, and her face looked pale and drawn, but her smile was clear and it grew stronger as he leaned over and gently kissed her cheek.

"You can't get rid of me that easily, Murphy." Her voice was little more than a whisper. "I'm back and I'm here to stay."

He gently caressed her right hand, the only one free of tubes and wires. "I was so frightened, Jen. If I ever lost you, I don't know what I'd do." He was surprised to feel tears rolling down his own cheeks. Moments later, he was aware of Gus's hand resting on his shoulder.

Chris stayed with Jen for nearly a half hour, sometimes making small talk, but the two spent most of the time just looking into each other's eyes. The attending nurse, now accompanied by a young doctor, bustled into the room. "Okay, boys, the party's over," she said quietly but firmly. "We need to be sure your angel here gets her strength back, so I'll kindly ask you to get back to the waiting room and let us do our job."

Gus kissed Jen on the forehead and did as he was told. Chris lingered after Gus left the room. He kissed Jen's lips tenderly and whispered, "Whatever happens from here on in, always remember that I love you." Then he followed Gus to the waiting room.

"The doctor had no explanation," Gus exclaimed when they reached the waiting room. "He said the way Jen came out of the coma made no medical sense."

The old man's expression changed and he looked directly into Chris's eyes. "But I know what brought Jen back to us," he slowly said. "I've never been much of a believer, but I think it was because of our prayers. It was a miracle."

Chris returned the old man's intense gaze. "You may be right, Gus, but I'm afraid even miracles have their cost. I have to go now," he continued. "Please remember, whatever you hear, or whatever people say, or whatever you read in the newspapers, I did what I did because I love your daughter."

Chris headed toward the parking lot as he pondered what would come next. He sat behind the wheel of the Volvo for a long time and looked up at the clear night sky as he carefully thought out the consequences of each possible option.

The simple fact was that he was guilty of killing an old man, or more correctly, guilty of helping to kill an old man. After they found Adelard's body, the police would question Father Scanlon, which would lead them directly to Chris. He could go home and wait for the police to arrest him, but that would just delay the inevitable. He could pick up Ronnie and drive as far west as possible, but life without Jen would hardly be worth it and the police would catch up with him in the end. He actually considered driving straight into the Micmac River and ending it all, but he couldn't bring that much pain and sorrow to the people he loved.

With a deep sigh, he turned the key in the ignition and headed the Volvo for his apartment. He knew what he had to do. Chris dragged himself up the front stairs of the two-family house that had become home to him and his little girl. He had never been so weary in all his life, and he had all he could do to turn the key in the lock.

Once he was inside, Jeanine limped stiffly over to him, took his arm, and put her finger to her lips. Somehow he knew she'd be there with Ronnie.

"We had a grand Halloween, Chris." The old lady's eyes sparkled as she whispered. "I found a few things, and I made Ronnie a little costume. I hobbled along with her as we trick-or-treated at every house up and down the street. Oh, we had such fun. It was just like the old days when my boys were little."

Chris smiled sadly.

"She ate a few pieces of candy, not too much, mind you, and then she drifted off to sleep." Jeanine grasped Chris's hand and whispered, "Come look at her."

They tiptoed to Ronnie's room where she lay on her bed still dressed in her costume. A white sheet was wrapped around her with two small cardboard wings sprouting out of the back of the sheet. Her silver tinsel halo had fallen off and lay next to her golden hair on the pillow. "Isn't she the perfect little angel?" Jeanine glowed like she really was Ronnie's grandmother.

Chris and Jeanine made their way to the kitchen. They both wearily slumped into the chairs. Jeanine was worn out from the fun of trick-or-treating, while Chris was exhausted from the tensions and terrors of the longest day of his life.

Jeanine broke the silence. "Chris, did you get over to see Father Costello?"

Chris nodded.

"Well, what did he say?" she asked.

"It's all over," Chris replied flatly.

"What's all over?" the old woman persisted. "What did you do?"

"I killed Brother Adelard. I burned the evil book," Chris replied in a barely audible voice as if he wasn't really sure of what he had done.

The old woman sat quietly for a few moments, too shocked to speak. "What will you do now?" she asked with tears in her eyes.

"I guess I'll call the police and go back to the school," he replied with resignation. "I have to face what comes next."

Jeanine reached across the table and grasped his hand tightly in her two soft, wrinkled hands. "Oh, my dear, dear boy, you've done a brave thing for all of us. Surely if you explain, if you tell them the whole story, the police will understand."

Chris chuckled in a sad, bitter way. "The police will think I'm crazy, just like Father Scanlon did when I went to him for help. I killed an elderly man tonight, an old priest, and the best I can hope for is a few years in prison if I can convince them it was temporary insanity or self-defense."

The old woman persisted, "You killed a devil tonight. You prevented a demon from terrorizing our town, and you saved countless innocent lives. Surely the law will consider that."

Chris just shook his head. "I don't know, Jeanine, I don't know. Whatever happens to me, please take care of Ronnie. You're all she has in the world."

Jeanine motioned for him to come close. She hugged him as the tears rolled down her cheeks. Releasing her grasp around Chris's neck, she reached in her pocket and pulled out a set of old, worn rosary beads. "I'll care for your little girl as long as I live, Chris Murphy, and I'll pray my heart out that the truth will win out in the end."

"Thank you, Grand-mère, thank you." Chris smiled faintly as he turned toward Ronnie's room. He leaned over her bed and listened to her soft breathing. Then he stooped down, ran his hands gently over her hair, and ever so softly kissed her cheek. The little girl twitched slightly and murmured in her sleep. Chris straightened up and whispered, "Goodbye, my angel." He turned away as the lump rose in his throat. He quickly brushed away his tears.

Once he was outside again, Chris could think more clearly. The cold night air, the sinking sliver of a moon, and the pinpoint stars brought him back to reality. He dialed 911 on his cell phone and stated flatly, "I need to report an accident at Holy Rosary School. I think a man has been killed. My name is Christopher Murphy."

Ten minutes later he stood in the darkness outside the door that led to the basement of Holy Rosary School. A police cruiser jerked to a halt on the street, the red and gold leaves now aglow in the kaleidoscope of whirling blue lights. He could hear the crackle of a radio as a pinpoint beam of white light shone in his eyes and blinded him.

"Are you Murphy?" the booming voice of the police officer came from behind the light.

"Yes, that's me," Chris replied flatly.

"Take me to the accident scene," the officer directed. "You know, you never should have left the injured person alone," he added with a note of disgust.

Chris started to respond, but thought better of it.

The two men descended the old iron stairs in silence. Chris could smell a sweet odor like burning incense as they made their way through the dark hallway. Chris shuddered as they passed Brother Adelard's chapel. The policeman pointed his flashlight at the shattered door, glanced into the chapel, grunted, and moved on.

Chris took a deep breath as he pushed the door of the furnace room open. "The accident was in here, officer, and the body is on the floor." The policeman stepped in first. Chris waited outside the door as the beam of light flashed around the furnace room.

"Okay, wise guy, what accident happened in here?" the officer's voice bellowed in irritation.

Chris stepped through the door and was shocked at what he saw. The steel furnace door was wide open, and the flickering flames lit the room. A clean ax leaned against the wall with a perfectly intact set of black rosary beads carefully wound around the handle. There was no blood on the floor. There was no body.

The police officer broke the silence as he radioed the dispatcher to redirect the ambulance that was speeding toward the school. He was clearly annoyed. "I guess your funny little prank is over now, smart-ass. I've got a good mind to drag you into the station for wasting my time. Now, if your fun is over, I've got another call over on Maple Street. It seems some guy with Down Syndrome says he murdered somebody, too. Who knows what other calls we'll get tonight—maybe UFOs have landed or Bigfoot is smashing pumpkins."

Chris was in a state of shock and disbelief, but the realization that he wasn't going to jail—that he was free to go home to Ronnie and Jen—was beginning to sink in. He followed the angry policeman up the stairs and out into the frosty, clear night.

As the policeman reached his cruiser, he turned to Chris and shouted, "Hey, asshole, Happy Halloween!"

Chapter 20

... from the *Portland Daily Mail* :

WEDDINGS

⇥▬◉ ◉▬⇤

Jennifer Mercier
Christopher Murphy

⇥▬◉ ◉▬⇤

Jennifer Marie Mercier and Christopher Edward Murphy were married on June 14th in Wilson Memorial Chapel at Ocean Point, Maine. Father Michael Costello officiated at the ceremony, with the assistance of Father John Scanlon.

Mrs. Murphy, 36, is a loan officer with Seacoast Federal Credit Union in Ashton Falls, Maine. She graduated from Boston University and holds an MBA from Harvard University. She is the daughter of Augustus

Mercier and the late Nancy Mercier of Ashton Falls. The bride's father is a retired Foreman with the Bath Iron Works shipyard.

Mr. Murphy, 35, is a Power Plant Manager with Northeast Power Utilities in Ashton Falls. He graduated from the University of Massachusetts at Amherst with a degree in civil engineering. He is the son of the late Patrick and Eileen Murphy of South Boston, Massachusetts.

The bride was attended by Matron of Honor, Mrs. Cynthia Sullivan, as well as bridesmaids, Mrs. Donna Watson and Ms. Jane LeBlanc, all of Ashton Falls. Ms. Veronique Murphy, the bride's stepdaughter, attended as Flower Girl.

Groomsmen were Best Man, Mr. Joseph Wilson of Ashton Falls, and Ushers, Mr. Thomas Gilligan, of New York City and Mr. Bruce Mercier, of Ashton Falls.

Following a honeymoon trip to Martha's Vineyard, Mr. and Mrs. Murphy will reside in Ashton Falls.

About the Author....

P.G. Smith

P.G. Smith has written for *Country Living, Career World, Military History, GX, Canada's History, the Boston Globe, and the Worcester Telegram & Gazette.* He is a former special education teacher, mental health counselor, school administrator, and U.S. Army officer. He divides his time between Ashburnham, Massachusetts and Boothbay Harbor, Maine.

Visit him online at www.paulgregorysmith.com